THUNDER AND
WHITE LIGHTNING

Thank you!

THUNDER AND WHITE LIGHTNING

A 1940's family story of moonshiners,
whiskey trippers, dirt tracks, soldiers,
stock cars and the untamed characters
who made NASCAR possible.

Grace Hawthorne

Published by BookLocker.com, Inc., St. Petersburg, Florida.

Printed on acid-free paper.

This is a work of historical fiction, based on actual persons and events. The author has taken creative liberty with some details to enhance the reader's experience.

BookLocker.com, Inc.
2018

First Edition

To Freeman

Foreword

Thunder and White Lightning's setting in Dawsonville, Georgia is fitting given that it is the Birthplace of Stock Car Racing. Moonshine and bootlegging—a large part of our heritage—gave rise to racing through back woods and ultimately to NASCAR.

~Bill Elliott

In Praise of *Thunder and White Lightning*

Thunder and White Lightning is a feast of dialogue, events, characters, humor and stories so real you'll taste the moonshine, hear the roar of engines and smell the gasoline of the racing cars.

Betty Hanacek

There's nothing more fun than getting the inside story on who did what to whom. *Thunder and White Lightning* is the Downton Abbey of North Georgia in the 1940s.

S. I. Nichols

My husband grew up in the 40s and he and his friends idolized Roy Hall and the other drivers. *Thunder and White Lightning* rang true to his teenage memories.

Fontaine Draper

Grace Hawthorne's books are a piece of the tapestry of Americana, part of the strong tradition of storytellers. *Thunder and White Lightning* is no exception.

Nanette Trainor

Grace Hawthorne has written an engaging tale of two families living in the hills of north Georgia who were caught up in a world that is being remade.

Frank McComb

Another great story by Ms. Hawthorne. As always, her story line is tight and many of her characters seem to be people I know. But what I enjoy most, is that I always learn something new.

Jim Reeves

Also by Grace Hawthorne

Shorter's Way
Waterproof Justice
Crossing the Moss Line

The Real Characters

Some of the characters in this book were/are real people with real histories. Their stories were fascinating and there's no way I could have made them up.

Harold Brassington defied minnow ponds and Mother Nature to build Darlington, the first paved track in the South.

Red Byron bolted his war-damaged leg to the clutch and become a driving legend. *Georgia Racing Hall of Fame, 2002, NASCAR Hall of Fame 2018*

Glenn Dunnaway won and was then disqualified from NASCAR's first official race.

The Flock Brothers had more wild adventures than a barrel of moneys. **Bob,** *Georgia Automobile Racing Hall of Fame Association in 2003.* **Fonty,** *Georgia Automobile Racing Hall of Fame Association in 2004.* **Tim** *NASCAR Hall of Fame 2014.*

Jocko Flocko was the monkey that rode with Tim.

Big Bill France organized and incorporated NASCAR. *NASCAR Hall of Fame 2010*

Gordon Pirkle is the founder of the Georgia Racing Hall of Fame. He is also the current owner of the Dawsonville Pool Room and appears as Mr. Gordon in this book.

Roy Hall, known as hell-on-wheels, drove cars owned by his cousin Raymond Parks with engines that were built by master mechanic, Red Vogt. They were an unbeatable trio. *Georgia Racing Hall of Fame 2002*

Johnny "Madman" Mantz won the first Southern 500 in Darlington driving a second-hand Plymouth. As of 2010, the speedway presents the Johnny Mantz trophy to the winner of the Southern 500.

Sam Nunis was a big-time promoter at the Lakewood Speedway in Atlanta. He and Bill France were long-time rivals.

Raymond Parks left home at 14, worked hard, saved money, bought cars and formed the first racing team. *Georgia Racing Hall of Fame, 2002, NASCAR Hall of Fame, 2017*

Lee Petty rolled a borrowed car four times in his first race, lived to tell the tale and fathered a racing dynasty. *NASCAR Hall of Fame, 2011*

Lloyd Seay drove fast, died young and left a beautiful memory. *Georgia Racing Hall of Fame, 2002*

Curtis Turner loved to outrun revenuers—he was never caught—as much as he loved to race and party. *NASCAR Hall of Fame 2016*

Red Vogt was the master mechanic who customized whiskey cars and got more out of a flathead Ford engine than anybody. He named NASCAR. *Georgia Racing Hall of Fame 2002, TRW/NASCAR Mechanics Hall of Fame, 1987*

The Georgia Racing Hall of Fame opened in 2002 in Dawsonville, GA

The NASCAR Hall of Fame opened in 2010 in Charlotte, NC

The Georgia Automobile Racing Hall of Fame Association began in 1997 in Kennesaw, GA

True Confessions

I have made every effort to be accurate, with the following intentional exceptions.

Gordon Pirkle's famous siren actually sounded every time Bill Elliott—awesome Bill from Dawsonville—scored a victory during the 1980s. I attributed that honor to Lloyd Seay in the 1940s.

Jocko Flocko did not ride with Tim Flock until 1953.

First, second and third place winners in the inaugural Southern 500 were Johnny Mantz, Fireball Roberts and Red Byron.

IN THE BEGINNING, THERE WAS MOONSHINE

(1940 – 1941)

"Too much of anything is bad, but too much good moonshine whiskey is barely enough."
Mark Twain

CHAPTER ONE

"Freeze!"

Duncan McLagan stopped dead still. Other than the black locust wood crackling under the cooker and the bees buzzing in the mountain laurel, there was no other sound for miles through the quiet Georgia hills. The voice didn't have a threat in it, but the gun pointed at his chest told a different story.

Duncan glanced down at the cracked bowl on the ground between his knees. He'd been mixing up a paste to seal steam leaks because losing steam meant losing money. For a second he considered flinging the bowl in the face of his tormentor and making a run for it. But, considering the circumstances, he stood up and wiped his hands on his overalls instead.

The tall man slowly put the gun back in his holster. "You're Duncan McLagan, that right? I'm Homer Webster. I'm a federal agent."

"I know who you are, Homer. Glad you put your gun away. Was you plannin' to shoot me?"

"Naw, the gun's mostly for show. We're just gonna bust up your still and then we're gonna take you to jail."

That was about what Duncan expected from what he knew about Homer. However, he was relieved not to have a gun pointed at him. He walked over to wash his hands in the creek and took his time rolling a cigarette from the tin of Prince Albert tobacco he kept in his overall pocket. This gave him a little time to think. He knew he'd been caught red-handed, but

Homer sounded friendly enough, so Duncan decided to follow his lead. "Homer, if I'd known you were comin', I wouldn't have wasted my time patchin' up leaks. But you know, since you're causin' me all this trouble, you oughta let me keep at least one jar. Lord knows, I deserve a drink."

Homer just laughed and nodded to his men.

Duncan managed a sad smile and sat down on a nearby rock to watch as the revenuers took an ax and a sledgehammer and destroyed his still. It broke his heart to see it go. His father had helped him build the still shortly after his son Gus was born. That was 15 years ago now. Duncan had laid every slab of rock, plastered every handful of mud around the furnace, connected every pipe, sealed every joint, carried countless pounds of corn and sugar, tended the still in all kinds of weather and hauled out thousands of gallons of the best moonshine in North Georgia. He and that still were old friends. They knew each other's weaknesses and strengths.

He closed his eyes and tried to ignore the destroying-noise all around him. As Homer's men carried water from the creek to put out the fire, they crushed the red horsemint along the banks and its scent mingled with the smell of whiskey and smoke. Duncan remembered his pa saying, "You need to find a good place, a creek that's got horsemint and you'll find soft water, that's what you need to make the best whiskey."

And it *had* been a good place, but now it was just a pile of rocks, smoldering wood and useless pieces of copper and tin. Duncan saw one of Homer's men throw the coil into the woods and he made a note of where it landed. No need to buy a new copper worm if he didn't have to.

By the time it was all over, the sun was beginning to set and it always got dark on the backside of the mountain first. Homer sized up the situation and looked at Duncan. "It's gettin' late and there's no sense in takin' you to jail now. You go on home tonight, but be at the courthouse by 9:00 sharp tomorrow. You know where the courthouse is, don't you?"

Homer couldn't resist having a little fun at Duncan's expense. Like many small southern towns, Dawsonville had grown up around a courthouse. Doc Fletcher's office was on the north side of the square between the drug store and the beauty parlor. Junky Brown's Garage and Filling Station covered most of the south side. Kelly's Grocery—which eventually became the Piggly Wiggly—was on the east side next door to the Pool Room. Key's Quality Furniture Store and Showroom took up most of the west side.

"I reckon I can find it," Duncan said.

"Good. I don't wanna have to come get you."

"I'll be there. Then what's gonna happen?"

"I'm gonna take your picture and get your fingerprints and then there'll be a hearing. After that you and the commissioner can settle on your bond. The bondsman's office is in the basement of the courthouse."

Duncan nodded. He'd been making shine more than 30 years and in all that time, he'd never been caught. However, he had a general idea of what Homer was talking about.

"Once you pay the bond, you can be released until the trial." The revenuers picked up their tools and all the men walked down the mountain together. When they got to the gravel road, the lawmen got in their Ford sedan and Duncan turned to walk home.

He was sentimental about losing his still, but he wasn't too upset about the rest of it. Almost every moonshiner he knew was sent to "build days in Atlanta" sooner or later. It was just part of doing business. Besides it was his first offense, so maybe he'd get off easy.

Before he went into his own house, Duncan stopped next door to get some advice from Sean Calhoun. The two men had been friends all their lives. So had their wives, Mattie and Emma. Both couples married young and started having babies right away. In ten years Mattie and Duncan had five boys and Emma and Sean had five girls. The women assumed their baby-making days were over, but Old Mother Nature had a different idea. Mattie gave birth to Gus when she was 42. At the same time, Emma, who was 41, had twins, Finn and Skye.

From the time they were able to crawl, the three children were inseparable. Wherever you found one of them, you found the other two. Folks in town never bothered to distinguish between them, they just referred to them collectively as "the kids."

The name on Emma's new son's birth certificate was Patrick Seamus Calhoun, but Sean insisted the boy be called Finn after Finn MacCool, the grandest of all Irish heroes. "I'm havin' no son of mine called *Paddy* and that's a fact!"

When it came to naming the other twin, Emma took one look at the clear blue eyes of her new daughter and named her Skye. Sean started to point out that was typically a Scottish name, but on second thought, he held his tongue. He'd had his say about Finn, better not push his luck with Emma.

Duncan drained the last of the moonshine Sean had poured for him and headed home to talk to Mattie. He knew she would be upset, but she had helped other women when their husbands "went away" so she would know what to do. Mattie always knew what to do.

Early the next morning, Duncan and Gus loaded up their wagon with a lot of hay and a dozen or so Mason jars of shine. Finn and Skye came out to help. When the shine was secure, the teenagers piled into the wagon and they all headed to Dawsonville.

While Duncan went inside the courthouse to take care of business, the kids got busy. In no time they had sold their supply of shine. When Duncan came back outside, they gave him the money and he went back to pay the bondsman. Once that was done, they started the journey home.

Court week was always a source of entertainment and drama in Dawsonville. Mattie usually stayed home, but not this time. She shared Duncan's hope that the judge would let him off with a warning, but no matter what happened, she was going to be there.

She knew everybody would turn out for the trial because Duncan McLagan not just an ordinary moonshiner. He was a pillar of the community. Contrary to popular belief, not all Scots are tightfisted; they just know the value of a dollar. It was Duncan—along with Sean Calhoun—who gave money to add a room to the old schoolhouse and build the new Baptist church even though Mattie was a Methodist.

Duncan was well respected around town. He stood nearly a head taller than most of the men in Dawson County. He attributed that and his straight nose, high cheekbones and dark eyes to a most fortunate encounter between his great, great grandfather and a Cherokee maiden. They fell in love, married and had 12 children.

The Cherokees and the Scots found they had a lot in common. Both of the tribes were loyal, honest, hard-working, spiritual and somewhat reserved. The only serious difference was whiskey. It did not agree with the Cherokees, but it was mother's milk to the Scots.

Finally, Federal Judge Edwin Dunbar got things underway and they got around to the case the audience had been waiting for. Homer Webster presented his evidence. Then the judge called on Duncan, who unfolded his six-foot-three frame and faced the judge. "Mr. McLagan, this is the first time I've seen you here in my court. Now *I* know, that *you* know, that moonshining is illegal. You're known to be an intelligent man, so why do you persist in this activity? It has taken us a while, but you knew eventually you'd get caught."

Duncan straightened his suit coat—which had clearly seen better days—and took a deep breath. Mattie knew that Duncan wasn't accustomed to making long speeches unless it was absolutely necessary. Like everybody else, she wondered what he was going to do.

"Well, Judge, it's like this. My family came over here from Scotland back in the 1800s. We're Lowland Scots, just like St. Patrick. He wasn't Irish you know. No Sir, he was a Scot just like me. Born at Dumbarton and lived there until the Irish Celts kidnapped him.

"Anyway, like I was sayin', folks around here know that King James the First gave the world the King James Bible, but my people remember him for stickin' his nose into Ulster business where it didn't belong. No need to go into all the details, but that started a long history of anger, mistrust and hostility toward the gov'ment."

The judge started to interrupt, but he decided to just let Duncan ramble on a bit farther to see where this history lesson was going.

"Judge, when my kin came over to these mountains, they packed up those feelings—along with their knowledge of whiskey-making—and brought them all to the New World. I have to admit we're a cantankerous lot and we don't suffer fools gladly. My early kin was known to believe that anyone associated with the gov'ment was, by definition, a fool," he smiled slightly. "Of course we don't believe that so much anymore.

"Now, as I was sayin', my people left the poverty and persecution of the Old Country and come here full of hope and the promise of land. And they found land. Lots of it right here in Georgia was free just for the hard, back-breakin' work it took to tame it and 'improve the property.' When more land came up for sale, we bought it, a little at a time as soon as we were able to scrape together a few dollars.

"You've got to understand, Judge, that none of us will ever deal with rented land again. We learned that lesson the hard way. The landowner could raise the rent on a whim and demand payment on the spot. Landlords didn't care if there was no food on the table or if a sick child needed care. In this country, land means freedom and it has to be protected at all costs."

The judge tapped his gavel to get Duncan's attention. "Mr. McLagan, I appreciate this little stroll through ancient history, but what—if anything—does this have to do with making illegal whiskey?"

"I'm about to get to that part, Judge. See the only problem with Georgia red clay is it won't grow but two things: cotton and corn. Cotton is a good crop, but you gotta have a lot of open, flat fields and lots of hands to plant and pick it. But you can grow corn in small plots and one family can pretty much take care of it.

"Like most folks around here, my family has a garden and a patch or two of corn, some chickens, maybe a pig or two. That's plenty to provide for us, you know, tradin' back and forth for stuff we need. We don't hardly ever need foldin' money.

"But..." Duncan took another deep breath. Mattie was in a mild state of shock. She couldn't remember Duncan using that many words at one time in her whole life.

"But," Duncan continued, "when it comes to payin' our property taxes, then the gov'ment says we gotta have *cash* money. That's where moonshine comes in. I can grow about 50 bushels of corn per acre, but gettin' it to a mill and then gettin' the meal to market is most nearly impossible.

"Back when we were haulin' everything by mule, he could carry four bushels of dry corn, but that same mule could easily carry 24 bushels of *liquid* corn. Whiskey-farming just made sense and we all lived happily ever after, tax-free until the Civil War. Don't worry, I'm gonna skip that part."

The judge sat forward and raised his hand as if he intended to get on with the trial, but Duncan was not done, not by a long shot. Mattie soon realized the audience was enjoying themselves. It was not often they got a chance to hear their history told publically or in such an interesting way. And they were also wondering what all that had to do with Duncan going to jail.

Duncan started up again, "It was needin' money to pay for The War that gave the gov'ment the idea to tax whiskey and that's when moonshine became illegal. I just want to make it clear right now, that I might be what you call a tax evader, but I am *not* a criminal. I bought the land, I bought the stuff to build the still, I bought everything I needed to make the shine and I worked long hours up in those woods. I never stole nothin' and as far as I can see, I'm not guilty of nothin'.

"If you make me stop farming' whiskey, I won't have cash money to pay my property taxes and the gov'ment will take my land away and my family won't have a place to live.

"Now, Judge, you may not know this, but I got six boys and I keep them busy moonshining'. If I can't do that, they'll get bored with nothin' constructive to do and who knows what kind of devilment they might get up to. The long and the short of it is, I feel it's my civic duty to continue to make shine for the peace and prosperity of Dawsonville and this entire county. I thank you."

Duncan bowed and sat down. The audience laughed, rose to their feet and gave him a hardy round of applause. The judge banged his gavel, but it took some time to restore order.

Once the room got quiet again, the judge looked at Duncan and shook his head slowly. "Mr. McLagan, just what is your occupation?"

Duncan was clearly confused by the question. "Well, Sir, I would say I'm a farmer."

"I would say we're all lucky you didn't decide to be a preacher or a politician. Do you always talk that much?"

"No, Sir, only when somebody's tryin' to send me to jail."

"Ah yes, that's what we're here for, I almost forgot. Since this is your first offense, or at least the first time you've been caught, I'm inclined to be lenient. If I let you off with a caution, do you think you could refrain from making illegal whiskey?"

Duncan stood and faced the judge once more. Mattie, Gus, Sean, Emma, Skye, Finn, and everybody else in the court room, waited anxiously to see if Duncan had actually talked the judge out of sending him to jail. Now that would surely be a story worth repeating.

Duncan knew what he *should* say, but the momentum of his speech and the sweet sound of the applause temporarily robbed him of all reason. In his most sincere voice he said, "Judge, I could promise to do my best, but to tell you the honest-to-God truth, I just don't think I can manage to give up moonshinin'. I'd feel too guilty."

The courtroom broke into laughter again. And so it was, that in the Year of Our Lord 1940, Duncan McLagan was sentenced to a year and a day to be served in the Federal Penitentiary in Atlanta.

CHAPTER TWO

When their men were sent down to Atlanta, some mountain women considered that a blessing or at the very least a vacation. Not Mattie. She never thought of sex as a duty. To her, what she and Duncan shared was a gift.

Although they never talked about sex out loud, Mattie was pretty sure Emma felt the same way. Whenever there was music and dancing, Emma's long red hair and skirts would be flying. But at the end of the evening, it was always Sean she went to find. And the smile on Sean's face at being found, told their story loud and clear.

It was customary for women in that community to wear their hair long and most of them were prideful about it. However, when she started having children, Mattie took her sewing scissors and cut her hair short all over her head. The soft curls offset her sharp features, especially her dark eyes.

The night before he left, Duncan lay very still beside Mattie. Since their first night, they had never been apart. Mattie still hadn't talked to him about what happened in court or the judge's decision. Making a big fuss wasn't her way, but Duncan knew she was worried.

Without a word, Duncan ran his hands through Mattie's hair. When she turned to him, he traced her face and her body with his fingers, like a blind man trying to remember every curve. The made love slowly, with a touch of sorrow, but as was almost always the case, it ended in soft laughter, like a child's happiness at getting exactly what they wanted for Christmas. "I'm sorry about what happened in court," Duncan whispered. "I need to know you're not mad."

"I'm not mad," she said. She wrapped herself in his arms and fell asleep.

Next door, Gus heard them. For years he had wondered about the laughter because it wasn't funny-joke laughing. It was different. If he had been forced to describe it, he would have said it was a joyful noise. However, he didn't think that was what the preacher had in mind when he used those words. All Gus knew was the sound made him feel happy and he wanted to share that sound with someone someday. No, he wanted to share that sound with Skye.

Little did the adults—or anyone else for that matter—know that from the first time Gus looked deep into Skye's blue eyes, he was smitten. That was long before he knew the meaning of the word and years before he had even a vague idea of what to do about it. It wasn't anything he felt a need to talk about, certainly not to Finn, who would have thought the whole thing was a fine joke. Gus's love for Skye was just a fact. Like air.

When Duncan woke at 6:00 the next morning, he heard Mattie in the kitchen and smelled coffee and bacon. The sky was overcast with dark gray rain clouds hanging low over the mountains. Reluctantly Duncan got dressed. He wore the same suit he'd worn for his day in court. At least if he was going to jail, he'd go looking his best.

Mattie served breakfast and they sat down to eat. She had wanted to go into town with him, but Duncan firmly said no. "I don't know exactly what's gonna happen and I don't want none of y'all to see them take me away."

There wasn't much to say at breakfast. Talking about what was going to happen later didn't seem right since Duncan wouldn't be there. Gus wondered how his father was feeling. Was he angry? Or scared?

In fact what Duncan was feeling was disappointed. Although he never mentioned it, his favorite time of year was spring. He knew city folks liked to drive up to the mountains to see the fall colors, but as far as Duncan was concerned, fall just meant winter was on its way. The trees would be bare, there would be rain and cold and occasionally snow and stills had to be tended in all kinds of weather.

Spring was a different story. The trees started out naked and then they began to get dressed a layer at a time. First soft green undergarments, then soft, lightweight leafy dresses and finally thick green leaves and flowers for decoration. The warm air lifted everyone's spirits with the promise of better things to come. No sir, give him spring and summer any day. He was more than a little perturbed that he was going to be locked up and miss most of it that year.

There was one bright spot. The week before, he had found an early blooming wild azalea back in the woods. The bright orange flowers were different from the common pink and purple azaleas that grew in almost every yard in Dawson County. Duncan carefully broke off several sprigs, brought them home and transplanted the shoots near the front porch.

"Mattie, come here a minute." He showed her the tiny plant. "Maybe it'll take root while I'm gone, what do you think?"

"Maybe," she said.

Duncan realized he couldn't put off leaving any longer. It was a long walk into Dawsonville. He gently kissed Mattie good-bye, hugged Gus and headed down the dirt road to town. He walked with his back straight and his head held high, at least until he was out of sight of the house.

More than once he thought about disappearing into the woods. He knew he could hide there, but what was the use? Eventually he'd have to give himself up, so he kept walking. When he got to town, he presented himself at the courthouse and was met by two uniformed U.S. Marshals.

"Where's Homer?" Duncan asked. Homer was a fed, but Duncan felt comfortable with him. He knew he had nothing to fear from Homer and just assumed he would be the one to take him to jail. Duncan had almost been looking forward to the trip.

"You ain't Homer's problem no more. From here on out, you deal with us. Put out your hands." The marshal's voice was sharp, angry. Duncan did as he was told and the lawman clamped handcuffs on his wrists.

"You don't need to do that. I'm not gonna give you no trouble," Duncan said.

"Be glad I didn't cuff 'em behind your back. We ain't takin' no chances. It's for your own protection, 'cause if you was to try to escape, we'd have to shoot you. Ain't that right Charlie?" The two men laughed.

With Homer, that would have been a joke, but now Duncan wasn't so sure. Obediently he got into the back seat of their car and they headed south on Highway 9, the dirt road leading to Atlanta. Until that moment, Duncan had never thought much about his freedom to come and go as he pleased. Now with a sudden chill he realized he had lost that. For the next six months—assuming he got out early for good behavior—he was no longer his own man.

One of the marshals shuffled through some papers and spoke to Duncan without looking at him. "Listen...ah McLagan, when you get there, keep your head down and for God's sake keep your mouth shut. Don't make waves and you might just survive." Although the marshals continued to talk to each other, for the rest of the trip they totally ignored Duncan.

That gave him a lot of time to think. Once again Duncan went back over what had happened in court. He hadn't meant to sound like a wiseass, the words had just come pouring out so fast he couldn't stop them. Well, it was water under the bridge and nothing could change it now.

Duncan didn't often drink shine, but he suddenly realized he would give anything for a swallow at that moment. Dawsonville was the moonshine capital of the United States, but curiously, within the population of 3,500 in Dawson County, there was not a single moonshiner to be found anywhere on the official rolls.

Occupations included several common-school teachers, a few mechanics, four merchants, two preachers, one doctor, one mail carrier, one brick mason and all the rest were farmers. Whiskey-farmer was not an official category, but everyone knew there was hardly a creek anywhere in the hills that didn't have a still or two on it somewhere.

As the marshals drove along at 30 miles an hour, Duncan had a chance to get a good look at Highway 9. It was a two-lane, dirt road with lots of twists and turns. He had sent many loads of shine down it to Atlanta. Now he imagined Gus and Finn trying to outrun the revenuers by driving as fast as their souped up Ford V-8s would go on that dark road with no headlights. It was a frightening prospect whether you were being chased by revenuers or not.

When they got to downtown Atlanta, Duncan was shocked. Five Points was a mish-mash of tall buildings—some 15 stories high—with automobiles whizzing by in all directions, trolley cars crisscrossing the intersection every-which-way and people casually weaving in and out of the traffic, heedless of the danger.

Even with its grim destination, the trip was an eye-opening experience. Duncan massaged his wrists where the handcuffs were beginning to chafe. That brought him quickly back to reality. He sensed they were getting close to the end of the journey because the neighborhood—if it could be called that—changed. There were no more grand houses like on Peachtree Street, no gardens, no trolley cars, in fact, no other cars at all. The few houses they did pass were rundown, sad looking places, almost like they were ashamed to be so close to a prison, a place no one ever wanted to visit.

Until that moment, Duncan hadn't spent much time worrying about the particulars of where he was going. He assumed the Atlanta Federal Penitentiary would be like the red brick Dawsonville jail just off the square—only bigger. The county sheriff and his family lived downstairs and the six cells with bars on the windows were upstairs. The building was surrounded by grass and flowers and trees. In fact, if you didn't notice the upstairs windows, it just looked like any other two-story house in town.

Duncan couldn't have been more wrong.

CHAPTER THREE

Duncan was shocked when he looked out the window at the 50-foot high, solid concrete walls and the numerous guard towers that surrounded the United States Penitentiary in Atlanta. The driver stopped and his buddy turned to Duncan with a smirk. "Hey, what'd you think of your new home, McLagan? Pretty nice, huh? Built in 1902, but I reckon you'll be stayin' in the new section. They say it'll hold 3,500 scumbags like you. Sit back, we're gonna drive real slow along the front 'cause we wanna make sure you see the *whole thing*." They laughed.

As the car started to move forward, Duncan watched out his window. The wall on the west side of the property came to a right angle at the near end of the main building which rose another 50 feet. The gray stone matched the dirty gray clouds hanging over the area and seemed to suck up all the light and all the sound. There was no color anywhere, just parched grass in all directions. Duncan continued to watch as they drove slowly along McDonough Street. The building was over a block long. He had never seen anything so massive or so frightening.

The front was dominated by a series of tall narrow windows stretching from side to side. They were covered, not just with bars, but with a steel grid. There was no light coming through the windows and Duncan was sure very little light or air got through to the cells inside. He felt the bile rise in his throat, so he closed his eyes and swallowed hard a couple of times. He was not going to allow himself to throw up.

Finally they reached the main entrance crammed between watchtowers where several men with rifles guarded the prison grounds in all four directions. The gate guards were armed with pistols. The marshals showed their identification and the guards waved them through. Duncan was used to guns, everybody in Dawson County hunted. But it was clear these guards did not use their guns to hunt, at least not in the usual sense. Duncan was reasonably sure they were under orders to shoot to kill.

In no time, the marshals turned Duncan over to the prison staff who told him to strip and gave him a black and white prison-stripe uniform, which made him indistinguishable from several thousand other inmates. Paperwork changed hands and he was taken to a cell. His heart was pounding and he was covered in a cold sweat. He could hardly breathe.

A guard opened the door to a cell and pushed him in. The sound of the heavy metal door slamming shut caused another wave of nausea. Duncan sat down on the bottom bunk. For several hours he sat perfectly still, somehow afraid if he moved he might set off an alarm somewhere. Finally another guard opened the door and an old man shuffled in. He and Duncan looked at each other in silence. The man was shorter than Duncan. His arms were hard, his ropey muscles covered with tattoos. Duncan stood up and held out his hand, "I'm Duncan McLagan."

At first the old man didn't respond. When he spoke his voice was raspy, like dry leaves, probably from cigarettes or shine or both. "Don't nobody use their right name in here." He looked Duncan up and down as if measuring him for a suit. Eventually he nodded his head and the two men shook hands.

"Everybody calls me Mississippi. Reckon I'll just call you Mac."

The old man's movements were relaxed, fluid. He sat down on the bunk Duncan had just vacated and offered Duncan a cigarette, a Chesterfield out of an open pack in his pocket. They shared the ritual of lighting up and drawing the first smoke deep into their lungs. Duncan relaxed a little. Finally the old man nodded toward the other end of the bunk and began to talk.

Several days later, Mattie got her first letter from Duncan. He told her about Mississippi. "Originally he got a one-year sentence like me, but they tacked on another year because he tried to escape. He warned me not to do anything stupid like that. His advice is to just nod, pay attention, do exactly what the guards tell you to and keep moving. He's down to his last six months so me and him may get out about the same time.

"Boy do I miss your cooking. We don't have plates, just tin trays and the inmates serving the food just plop it down any old way. Sometimes I have to force myself to eat, but I know better than to complain. We got no knives or forks, just spoons. No talking and no eye contact." Mattie finished the letter, folded it carefully and put it in a shoebox under their bed.

Gus only wrote one letter. "Dear Pa, I am doing OK. I drove three loads of shine down to Atlanta for Mr. Curtis Slone and he paid me."

"Damn kid," Duncan said before he read the next line. "You do not have to worry about me getting caught because I have figured out a new system. I will tell you all about it when you get home.

"Me and Skye and Finn have been real busy. I'll tell you about that when you get home too. We went down to the Pool Room and had a Bully Burger. Wish I could send you one."

Duncan slowly realized that life did not stop when he left Dawsonville. Who knew what might be going on by the time he got back.

After lights-out at night, Duncan got a crash course in how to survive his time in prison. The most important thing was to understand the guards Mississippi explained. "The best ones are those who consider themselves professionals. Their job is to keep the peace and make sure everybody does their time and leaves alive and well. Sometimes you can ask them for small favors or to report abuse if it borders on life or death.

"Then there are the guards who do everything by the book. In their case, you better know the rules. They've got the power to put you in the hole, a tiny, dark cell with food passed through the door and only one hour of exercise a day, alone in the yard. The secret to working with them is to do exactly what they order."

It was the third group that frightened Duncan the most. They were the ones who enjoyed their power and were always looking for an excuse to give an inmate a beating or send him to the hole. In all three cases, the best way to get by was to keep your head down and not draw attention to yourself in any way. In other words, become invisible. Armed with that bit of advice, Duncan did his best to disappear.

Mattie's letters were short and to the point, but she wrote faithfully every week. "Sean is helping the kids take care of our small stills. It is good practice for them because someday they will have to take over. We have enough shine stashed away to keep our regular customers satisfied. They are not real happy, but they understand."

Each letter ended with, "I miss you. I love you. Please be careful. Mattie."

Duncan knew Mattie loved him, but seeing the words written out that way made him smile. He carefully put the letter back in the envelope and put it on his end of the shelf above the sink.

His next letter started, "I love you too." He hoped that made her smile. "Food's not bad, just bland. Breakfast's the best. Pancakes, oatmeal, cereal, eggs, biscuits and gravy. What we get for dinner and supper never changes. You get the same thing on a five-day turn-around. Nobody pays attention to weekends in here.

"My cell has two bunks with one blanket each, one sink, one toilet, one shelf, one table bolted to the wall and one window. According to Mississippi, spring is the best time to start doing time because the cells got real cold in winter. I'm like him, I can handle the heat, but I sure do hate being cold. I'm doing my best to be invisible and with any luck me and Mississippi will both be out of here before next winter."

CHAPTER FOUR

It didn't take long to figure out that well over half of the 2,200 inmates serving time were there on liquor charges of one kind or another. Duncan took some comfort in that. Mississippi cautioned against trying to find people he knew. Just looking too hard at somebody could get you in trouble.

As the letters piled up, Mattie learned more about prison life. "I've been assigned to a road crew. The warden says moonshiners behave better working outside. He says we get fractious being inside all the time. I reckon he's right. I like working outside a whole lot more than being locked up in here. Sometimes when we're working outside, I can almost forget where I am."

Duncan didn't tell her that the last time he worked on the road crew one poor guy decided to escape and the guard shot him as he was running across a field. They threw his body into the back of a truck and drove him back inside the walls. Duncan wondered if the dead man's body would be turned over to his family or buried on the grounds. If that happened, he'd have to spend all eternity locked up.

There was one period of the day most prisoners looked forward to. After supper they filed into a common area next to the chow hall where they were allowed to listen to the radio, play cards, smoke or just talk. Everyone was on his best behavior because if one person caused trouble, everyone lost his privileges and the guilty party would be "disciplined" by the rest of the inmates.

Stories about how-I-got-caught were a favorite topic of conversation. Everybody had a story and they listened even if they'd heard the tale a hundred times. The stories came rapid-fire, one after the other.

"Revenuer caught me at one of my stills and I took off runnin'. I knew I could outrun that tub of lard 'cause he was too fat to get far. 'Bout the time I figured I was safe, this other guy stepped out with a gun and I knew right then the jig was up."

"I made the mistake of runnin' by a tree I couldn't see around. Damn revenuer just stuck out his arm and knocked me flat."

"I had this ole dog that could smell revenuers a mile away. He'd start in to barkin' and that'd give me plenty of time to skedaddle. Well, this one time he goes off into the woods and the next thing I know, I'm surrounded by feds. They marched me out of the woods and on the way I seen that ole dog gobblin' up a mess of store-bought dog food. Sold out by a damn dog."

The most unusual inmate was a college professor from Tennessee who had set up a still in his chemistry lab and got caught selling shine to the fraternity houses. He had the best stories.

"Are any of you gentlemen familiar with the Italian artist Leonardo da Vinci? Painted 'The Last Supper...' Well, he did a lot of his paintings on wooden panels. Now he might not have *made* whiskey, but he discovered if he soaked those panels in spirits, it not only killed any bugs living there, it made the wood impervious to insects for all time. That, my friends, is a true fact and you can easily check it out the next time you visit Italy, because his paintings are still there for everyone to see and admire."

Card players often set up their tables close enough to listen, but if they weren't in the whiskey business, it wasn't smart to get too close. One night Duncan asked Mississippi about a group of men who always sat off to themselves.

"Them's the money men," he explained. "You know, they're in here 'cause they robbed a bank or stole money, you know, embezzled it. See that one feller over there? His name's Carlo Ponzi. From what I hear, he concocted this scheme to get folks to give him money to invest. Told 'em he could turn a little bit of money into a whole lot more in no time. Seems like he was robbin' Peter to pay Paul and in about a year the whole scheme fell apart. I'm not exactly sure how it worked, but no matter. He got caught just like the rest of us."

"I'm glad they caught him," Duncan said. "Here we are workin' hard to provide our customers with a quality product that cures their ills and makes them happy and they throw us in jail with real criminals like that low-down scoundrel who cheated his fellow man. It's a dirty rotten shame, that's what it is."

Duncan and his fellow moonshiners might have felt better about Ponzi if they had known that as soon as he was released from the Atlanta Federal Pen, he was arrested in his home state of Massachusetts. He sued. In his defense, he explained that he had pled guilty to the federal charges in return for getting any other charges against him dropped. He claimed double jeopardy. The Supreme Court disagreed. The feds had charged him with *mail fraud*. The state of Massachusetts was charging him with *larceny*. No double jeopardy. So he served nine more years as a "common and notorious thief."

Sometimes the inmates talked about Prohibition. "Hell, Georgia was a dry state way before the feds got involved," Duncan said. "We always vote dry, but we drink wet."

"Down home we say Alabama will stay dry as long as we can stagger to the polls to vote."

The professor added, "W.C. Fields said Prohibition had once forced him to live for days on nothing but food and water." He always waited a moment for his listeners to catch the joke.

Whether it was called it moonshine, white lightning, firewater, corn squeezings, blockade whiskey, scorpion juice or panther piss, any moonshiner worth the name knew the proper was to determine the proof of the whiskey. It was common knowledge and every moonshiner knew it just like every Catholic child knew catechism.

"How do we proof the whiskey by the bead?"

"We proof the whiskey by the bead by filling a fruit jar half full of shine and shaking it hard several times."

"What does that tell us?

"That tells us the proof. Big beads or bubbles that float half in and half out of the liquor tell us it is 115 to 120 proof. The longer the bead stays there, the higher the proof."

"Is there another way to state this fact?"

"Yes, there is another way to state this fact. The proof figure is twice the amount of the alcohol content. In other words, 100 proof is 50 percent alcohol."

Time passed. Mattie carefully marked the days off the calendar. Duncan wrote, "I'm due to get out early. One month to go and Mississippi and me are counting the days. Some of the old guys say that's bad luck, but we do it anyway."

CHAPTER FIVE

"Doc, come quick, it's Finn!"

Doc Fletcher looked up from the paperwork on his desk. Finn was leaning on the back of a chair, pale and sweating profusely. "My God, has he been shot?"

"Lord no, Doc. We were on our way...we were back in the woods..."

Doc knew better than to press for details at the moment. Working back in woods meant tending a still and no one ever gave up the location of a still, no matter what.

Gus continued, "Finn stepped over a log where this old snake was just wakin' up and he sorta stepped on the snake and the snake sorta bit him."

"Well, come on over here, Finn and let's have a look. What did this snake that sorta bit you look like?"

Finn saw the opportunity to spin a tall tale. "It was awful, Doc. He was all red and black..." That got Doc's attention. He jerked his head up in surprise.

Skye waved him off. "Oh, don't worry, Doc, it wasn't a coral snake, I know the difference. 'Red touches yeller, kills a feller. Red touches black, friend of Jack.' It was just an old king snake. I washed the bite out real good with branch water and Gus poured some shine on it just to be on the safe side."

Doc nearly burst out laughing. He knew of shine being used for everything from croup to childbirth, but moonshine for snakebite was a new one to him. Although, since the snake wasn't poisonous, it was probably as good a treatment as anything else.

Finn looked out from under the tousled red hair hanging in his eyes. "I guess I shoulda been more careful. My leg still hurts, but it wasn't nothin' like when Gus poured that shine over it. I'm tellin' you that burned like a son-of-a gun."

"Yeah, but you didn't die, did you?" Skye shot back.

Gus was surprised and secretly pleased that Skye defended his action.

Death was nothing to joke about, they knew that. People died, there was no getting around it. The old people died, sometimes babies died. Some folks died because they did something foolish, some for no good reason at all. The loss always seemed to hit the women the hardest. The religious ones chalked it up to God's will, the rest of them cursed their bad luck and figured out a way to survive and carry on.

Doc examined the area around the snakebite. There was no swelling, no change in skin color. "I'm not gonna put a bandage on this. It would just make a warm place for infection to set in and grow."

"Good, Doc. Bandages are for sissies." Finn was already forming a story to impress the girls.

Doc gave the boy a couple of aspirin and pronounced him cured. Finn tested his leg and found it more or less reliable. "Thanks, Doc. Listen, I'll drop off some of my pa's shine tomorrow, you know, to pay you for savin' my life."

"It's more likely that Gus and Skye saved your life, but I've never turned down your dad's shine. Much obliged." Moonshine was legal tender in Dawson County and Doc clearly preferred that to a mess of greens or a sack of potatoes.

Unaware of the drama playing out at Doc's office, Mattie opened her latest letter from Duncan. "Last week there was a fight in the chow hall. One inmate grabbed the guy serving food, pulled him across the food table and nearly broke his arm. Mississippi grabbed me and we headed toward our cell block. Then the whole prison went on lock-down. For two days we sat in our cell, quiet as church mice. The guys who started the trouble ended up in solitaire.

"Me and Mississippi are holding our breath. Less than a week to go. We're almost there."

***

Before they left Doc's, Gus said, "Doc, if you don't mind me askin', why did you think Finn might have been shot?"

Doc hadn't told anyone the story yet, because he knew once it was out there, the news would spread like grease in a hot skillet. "Couple of nights ago, this family from way up in Gilmer County brought one of their boys in. They don't have a local doctor and I was the closest one they knew about. The kid was about 14 and he had been driving shine on one of the back roads. He saw the feds behind him and thought he could outrun them, but they shot out his tires. He'd been driving long enough to know what to do, so he left the car and took off running through the woods."

"Is that when they shot him?" Finn asked, already getting caught up in what promised to be an exciting story.

"Fact is, they didn't shoot him at all. There were four of them and they ran him down, beat him up real bad. One of them broke his arm and then laughed and said, 'Let's see you drive with that.' And another one said, 'Be sure you show that to all those other white-trash trippers.' They left him in the woods to die then went back, dumped his shine, torched his car."

"That's awful. Dumpin' shine is bad enough, but beatin' the kid up was just downright mean!" Skye said. "I never heard of the feds doin' anything like that around here."

"That's not all," Doc continued. "The family thought their son was lucky. It seems a couple of trippers up in that area *have* been shot in the back running from the revenuers. Seems the government is sending in feds from out of state, agents used to dealing with hard-core criminals in places like New York and Chicago.

"I might not have found out about it if that family hadn't come to me for help. So far, I don't know of anything like that going on here in Dawson County, at least not yet. Anyway, y'all be careful out there. I don't want to be patching you up 'cause some fed decided to use you for a punching bag. Or decided to shoot you in the back."

After they left, Doc lit his pipe and pulled a nearly empty jar of shine out of his bottom desk drawer. It was all that was left from his last payment of Calhoun shine. He took a swallow, smacked his lips and reflected on what he'd just heard. Doc had a soft spot in his heart for those kids, after all he'd delivered all three of them.

Doc was pretty sure neither Mattie nor Emma had planned on getting pregnant after 40. As it happened, they gave birth on the same day and at the same time. Doc spent half the night running back and forth between the two houses trying to tend to them both. Planned or not, as soon as the babies were born, the mothers wrapped them in love and the relatives began pouring in to greet the newest members of the families.

As they left Doc's office, the kids were unusually quiet, thinking about the boy with the broken arm and the two who got killed. Revenuers had always chased moonshiners, but in the past, it had always been like a game of cat and mouse. Most of the time, the moonshiners in their fast cars outran the feds. Sometimes they got caught, but nobody ever got hurt and they sure enough didn't get killed. Of course, nothing like that could happen in Dawson County, but still…

The news about what was going on in Gilmer County and the excitement of the great-snake-bite-adventure had left the kids hungry, so they trooped into the McLagan's kitchen to see what was left over from supper. "Ma!" Gus called out. There was no answer. "I guess she's out makin' a delivery."

Mattie *was* making a delivery, but not to a customer. Twice a week she drove to a poor farm about five miles out of town. The front yard was always swept clean and there was a small, well-tended garden beside the house. The kids playing in the yard paid her no mind and there was no one else around. She walked up the porch steps and left a jar of moonshine by the door. She picked up the empty one and walked back to her car. The father of that family was dying of cancer. She knew the shine couldn't cure the disease, but it could knock the pain down a notch or two. Mattie did what she could.

The boys looked around the kitchen. They knew better than to ask Skye to fix them something. Her response was always the same, "God gave you hands, feed yourselves." They found some biscuits, ham and milk and sat down at the oilcloth-covered kitchen table.

"Are y'all goin' down to the creek to watch the trippers race after church on Sunday?" Gus asked.

"We might meet y'all over there," Skye said, "but Pa says we're not going back to church 'till they get rid of that new preacher."

"What's wrong with him?"

"Last Sunday he called moonshiners lazy and you know how that gets Pa riled up. It was a wonder him and the preacher didn't come to fisticuffs after church."

Sean's feelings about the life of a moonshiner were well known. "Anybody calls moonshiners lazy, is a damn fool. I'd like to see one of them sissies bend their backs and walk five miles carrying what-all it takes to build a still. And that don't take into account bushels of corn and sugar going in and gallons of shine coming out. You gotta be tough as a mule and just about as stubborn to make shine and I'll bust up any man says different."

The kids knew it was true. Like all their friends, they had been still-hands since they were old enough to help out. They learned the art of distilling whiskey hands-on and from the ground up. That was their real education.

By the time they were twelve, mountain kids quit going to school. Book learning was important up to a point and that point was when they could read, write and do simple arithmetic. History went back only as far as family stories could take it. What happened before that wasn't any of their business. The knowledge of herbs and healing was a gift, not science. Literature and music came from folktales and folksongs. Family alliances were far more important than ancient politics, which all smacked of government interference and was therefore not to be trusted.

Gus finished his last bite and wiped his mouth. "I think I found a good place for a new still. We were almost there this morning when Finn decided to upset that snake. It's in the middle of a batch of mountain laurel. That's good 'cause the roots trip up the revenuers and the top leaves keep off the rain and filter the smoke. There's plenty of loblolly pines and prickly holly bushes too."

Finn was still eating and only half listening. "What's the big deal about the trees and bushes?"

"Evergreens. You gotta have 'em all around your still or come fall you'll be sittin' out there high and dry, naked as a jay-bird."

"How do you know all that stuff?" Finn demanded.

"I pay attention."

The kids would all turn 16 in January. Gus had grown two inches since his dad had been gone. Pretty soon he'd be as tall as Duncan. Like his father, the blueprint for handsomeness was already visible in his intense dark eyes, high cheekbones and straight nose. Finn had grown some too. He was no longer a skinny little kid, he was becoming as sturdy as a mountain oak.

Skye was an entirely different story. As far as Finn was concerned, she was just his sister. Gus wasn't sure Finn even knew she was a girl. But Gus knew. He was also reasonably sure Skye was the prettiest girl in the county and that made him feel proud, although he wasn't exactly sure what gave him the right to feel that way.

They finished eating, washed up the dishes—they knew better than to leave them for Mattie to find—and headed to Junky Brown's Garage and Filling Station to see if any of the trippers were working on their cars. Gus knew Finn would be on the lookout for someone to listen to his how-I-got-bit-by-a-huge-snake story. Sure enough, as soon as they saw Sara Beth Doherty on her way to the grocery store, Finn began to limp.

"What's the matter with your leg?" she asked.

Finn smiled, and then remembered to look wounded. "We were way back up in the woods and I guess I wasn't payin' attention, 'cause the next thing you know I saw this big old timber rattler. He musta been six feet long, with a dozen rattles, a real mean one. He looked me right in the eye and then he crawled straight over and bit me. I wasn't even messin' with him. It hurt real bad, but I didn't cry or nothin'." He lifted his pants leg so Sara Beth could get a better view of the snake bite.

She hardly glanced at his wound. "Finn Calhoun, you're lyin' through your teeth. Everybody knows rattlers only strike when they're coiled up. No way you got bit by a rattler."

"Well, it *coulda* been a rattler or a coral snake and I *did* get bit and it hurt real bad and I had to walk..." Finn, like every good Irishman, knew the cardinal rule of storytelling: never let the facts get in the way of a good story. "You tell her, Gus."

"It was a king snake," Gus said.

Sara Beth just shook her head and walked away without giving Finn so much as a backward glance. Skye went along with her.

"What's the matter with that girl, anyway?" Finn was clearly disappointed. "She didn't even give me a chance to tell her the whole story. And what's the matter with *you*? You coulda backed me up, you know."

"Forget about it," Gus said. "Come on. I only got a nickel, but I'll split a Coke with you if you promise to stop talkin' about your stupid snakebite." Finn gladly agreed.

In the weeks that followed, they made regular visits to the new still site. Gus and Finn—with Skye supervising—laid the rock foundation for the copper pot. They got a supply of corn, soaked it, sprouted it and dried it. Then they loaded it into the back of Duncan's car and drove it to the nearest mill to have it ground into malt.

They were counting down the days until Duncan was due to be released. Their idea was to have everything in place and be ready when he came home. They even hiked back to Duncan's ruined still and rescued the copper coil from where the revenuers had discarded it in the woods. Once all that was done, they waited for Duncan to come home. As they saw it, all that was needed now was someone willing to front them the money so they could go into business for themselves.

When Duncan's release day came, he realized he had not only survived, he had actually made a friend or two, learned a few tricks of the trade and lined up some new customers.

He and Mississippi turned in their prison stripes and picked up their civilian clothes. They walked out the gate together, shook hands and headed home. One went west, one went north.

CHAPTER SIX

From the time he was a kid, Junky Brown had been taking things apart. When his mother complained that her electric washing machine bounced around so much it left puddles on the floor, Junky removed the wringers then took the motor apart and laid the pieces out on the kitchen table. He made some minor adjustments, put the machine back together and it ran smoothly from then on. He had a few parts left over and he carefully cleaned those and put them on a shelf in his father's blacksmith shop out back.

Sometime later, Junky tried a similar experiment with his dad's ham radio. He was sure he could make it sound better. However, the radio took offense at having its insides poked with a screwdriver and gave Junky a shock that knocked him on his backside. That dampened his curiosity for electricity and from then on, he stuck to mechanical devices.

Junky had grown up working with his father at his livery stable and blacksmith shop. Big Jim, as he was known, had a reputation for being able to fix almost anything that got broken. On top of that, he built moonshine stills. After his father passed on, Junky took over the business.

When cars replaced horses, Junky closed the livery stable and started to work on Model Ts.

Junky soon realized he needed a Model T to take apart and study. A fair number of cars came through the garage but no one was willing to let Junky dismantle one of their cars just to satisfy his curiosity. Nevertheless, Junky was patient. He believed where there was a will, there was a way.

Like everyone else in Dawsonville, Junky and his family went to church on Sunday. Baptist or Methodist, take your pick. He stood outside under the trees, smoking and talking with the other men and on occasion even went inside where he did his best to stay awake during the sermon.

After church, folks went home for Sunday dinner and then they congregated down along Flat Creek to watch the trippers race. Model Ts and Model As made up one group. The owners of V-8s rightly considered their cars far superior to the early model Fords. They raced separately.

Half the fun was listening to the noise the jacked-up whiskey cars made. The cars lined up at the starting point and raced along the creek to the finish line. Winners got to claim bragging rights for having the fastest car. Junky bided his time. Sooner or later he knew a car would get damaged enough so he could buy it for a song.

In the meantime, it was moonshine that made up the real money-making portion of his business. For as far back as anyone could remember, almost every copper pot still in Dawson County had its beginning in his father's blacksmith shop and now in Junky's workshop.

Folks said Big Jim used to send six-year-old Junky down inside the pots to hold things together while he put in the rivets. True or not, Junky's family was known to make top-notch stills. Following the family tradition, Junky made stills as large as 135 gallons, but 35 to 50 gallons was the usual order.

Customers were charged a dollar a gallon and they had to furnish the copper and the rivets. Half a sheet of 16-ounce copper ran about $25. Add in the cost of the rivets and Junky's fee, and setting up a still represented quite an investment.

Junky took pride in his work, but in truth it wasn't copper stills that captured his imagination, it was cars. And finally his patience paid off. One Sunday afternoon a young tripper crashed his Model T and broke his arm. Junky wasted no time in offering the boy $5 for what he said was only useful now as spare parts. The young man took the money, which he paid to Doc Fletcher to set his arm, and gave up driving for a while.

Heaven has been described in many different ways by different people, but it is probably safe to say no one else had ever seen heaven in a busted up Model T like the one Junky hauled back to the garage.

Before he made any attempt to disassemble it, Junky studied the car from the starting crank to the rear axle. There were hundreds of parts and he intended to learn exactly how each one of them worked. Clearly he needed something bigger than his mama's kitchen table, so he parked the car in the middle of an old barn on the back of his property.

Everybody knew that Mr. Henry Ford assembled his cars piece by piece as they were pulled along an assembly line. The parts had to go together in a certain order, so it only made sense that they should come off in the same way.

In no time at all, news of the Great Dismemberment spread throughout Dawsonville and Junky found himself with a revolving audience. In Biblical terms, the Model T was being rent asunder and everyone wanted to watch and incidentally to listen to Junky cuss. He was known far and wide to have an extensive vocabulary of foul language and a practiced knack for stringing curses together that was just shy of poetry. At least that was the opinion of some folks.

Of all the people who came to witness the Great Dismemberment, the kids were front and center. As soon as she heard what Junky was doing, Skye insisted that they go.

Gus and Finn warned her about Junky's colorful language, so she promised not to listen.

Every day they showed up at the barn. Once the motor was free of its mounts, Junky and several men carefully lifted out the engine and the transmission and put them on Junky's work table.

Junky stood back and marveled at the simple beauty and complexity of the machine. Henry Ford wasn't just a genius for inventing the assembly line. He was a genius for knowing his creation so well he could break it down into a thousand tiny steps. The process was meticulous. Each worker had a part, each part had a place, each action had a time from the beginning until the finished product rolled off the line. Everything fit perfectly, one piece at a time.

With infinite care, Junky continued working with the Great Dismemberment. He started removing each part, studying the way it was made, what it was designed to do and how it fit into the grand scheme of things. Then he cleaned it and stacked it neatly nearby. The folks who originally gathered to watch gradually lost interest. All except Skye.

Without being asked, she took to sweeping up, cleaning parts, picking up tools and putting them back where they belonged. Junky appreciated that because he insisted on a clean workshop where everything was carefully laid out like instruments in an operating room.

Occasionally Skye came over to watch Junky work and when there was nobody around, he explained what he was doing. Much to Junky's surprise, she caught on quickly and her small hands fit into tight places Junky couldn't reach. He kept expecting her to lose interest, but that never happened. Eventually Junky offered to pay her to make small repairs on older cars that came into the shop.

Things were fine until Junky's wife, Leeann, realized who his new employee was. Leeann normally left the garage strictly up to Junky, but this situation demanded her attention. "Junky, you can't go on cussin' like you normally do. Not in front of *Skye Calhoun*. I know her mama from church and I tell you *it will not do!*

"Well, what the hell do you want me to do, Woman?"

"Learn some new words."

From then on, Junky made a sincere effort to curb his tongue, but swallowing that many words nearly choked him to death. He finally settled on "that GDSOB," but that didn't give him nearly the satisfaction of the real thing. In desperation he finally decided to more or less stop talking all together. The garage got a lot quieter and to Junky's surprise, the work got done anyway.

Skye had the makings of a good mechanic, but she presented a problem of another sort. Junky realized something had to be done about her looks. She was a girl and men would not take kindly to some female kid working on their cars. But the real problem was she *looked* like a girl and Junky knew *that* problem was only going to get worse as she got older.

A large pair of coveralls and a cap to hide her red hair solved things temporarily. Skye never hesitated. She rolled up her sleeves and pitched right in. Junky had offered her a job and she knew he held the keys to a fascinating new world.

Never in her wildest dreams had Skye considered being a mechanic. In fact, she'd never thought of herself as anyone other than part of the kids. What she was learning with Junky made her different. It set her apart from Finn and Gus, not to mention the rest of the teenage girls in town. For the first time in her life she was doing something on her own. She missed the boys, but not as much as she thought she would.

Skye was full of questions and since Junky was just feeling his way through the Model T's innards, he couldn't always come up with an answer. However, between the two of them, things slowly started to make sense.

Skye was a natural. She came in early and worked steadily to get all the assigned repairs finished so she could watch Junky as the Great Dismemberment proceeded. They studied the starting crank, clutch fingers, reverse and slow speed bands, drive shaft, differential gear, driving pinion, and the rear brake housing. Once they completed the front-to-back route, they moved on to the engine to study the pistons, connecting rods, crank shaft, valves, push rods, magneto, commutator, spark and throttle lever rods and the high, low and reverse pedals.

As the parts came off, Skye carefully cleaned them and laid them out side by side. They finally finished taking the car apart, sat back to admire their work and then started putting the car back together again.

***

The Sunday races down by the creek continued through the summer and Junky occasionally saw Gus and Finn lined up to race their family cars. The way things were set up, all the drivers could do was race from a starting point along the creek to the finish line. The races were over too quickly. Slowly, a plan began to take shape in the back of Junky's mind.

He owned a large open field that he wasn't using and he decided to borrow a tractor and lay out an oval racetrack. That way the length of race could be determined by how many times the cars had to go around the track.

The way Junky saw it, with a fair number of cars bunched up together driving fast, there were bound to be accidents and accidents meant car repairs and—better yet—the occasional wreck which could be salvaged for spare parts which were hard to come by otherwise.

The track proved to be a big success. The trippers loved it and so did the spectators. For the South, which had no other form of public entertainment, it was a godsend. Junky sprayed the track with water to keep the dust down. It helped a little, but the real advantage was that it turned the red Georgia clay into a slippery-slidey mess. Cars frequently ran off the track or crashed into each other which just added to the excitement. Races started in mid-afternoon, after church and Sunday dinner, and lasted until dark.

With an eye to bigger and better things, Junky built bleachers and put up some chicken wire to protect the spectators from flying parts, flying tires and—God forbid— the occasional flying car. As he had hoped, folks were more than happy to pay a dime to sit in the bleachers.

During the week, the trippers came to Junky's Garage and Filling Station to get their engines tuned up. The Ford V-8 soon took over as the best—and fastest—whiskey car. When Junky realized just how good Skye was, he let her join him when he worked on the V-8s. Unbeknownst to the drivers, Skye and Junky now worked side by side to figure out ways to make the cars go faster. And since moonshiners paid better than revenuers, it was clear where their best efforts should go. Simply put, more speed meant more money in Junky's pocket.

Since Ford V-8s all looked alike, drivers started painting numbers on their doors using white shoe polish that easily washed off after the race. At Skye's suggestion, Junky added "Built by Junky Brown" on the cars that came through the garage.

In the beginning, races were just for fun. But eventually someone got an idea to pass the hat and collect nickels and dimes from the spectators. The winner went home with a smile and a couple of extra dollars in his pocket. The big winners, though, were the ones who won money betting on the fastest car.

As word of the Dawsonville track spread, Junky watched with keen interest as young men like Lloyd Seay and Roy Hall in their jacked-up Ford V-8s went roaring around his track.

Henry Ford had designed his cars to be practical, reliable and affordable. They had not been designed for speed, but thanks to the Great Dismemberment, Junky and Skye were discovering numerous ways to take care of that.

One hot August afternoon Junky stood listening to the bone-rattling noise of 20 drivers revving their engines and feeling the power vibrate in his chest. He looked through the exhaust smoke and the clouds of red clay dust and caught a glimpse of the future.

CHAPTER SEVEN

As he looked out of the bus window on his way home, Duncan felt soothed by the warm colors of fall. He had missed spring and summer in the mountains, but he was so glad to be home it hardly mattered. The station was just off the square and as soon as Duncan stepped down from the bus, he was immediately surrounded by Mattie, Gus, Sean, Emma, Finn, Skye and a host of other friends and relatives. He filled his lungs with the smells of home and tried to hug everyone at once.

As was the custom with any celebration, several jars of McLagan moonshine were passed around. Duncan took a big swallow of shine and thanked his lucky stars to be back again. His suit hung loosely on him because he had lost so much weight, but otherwise he was in good health. The first thing he noticed when he got to the house was the little azalea bush by the porch steps. "It made it." Duncan smiled.

"Yeah," Mattie said. "I've been waterin' it and I think it's gonna be fine." She took Duncan by the hand, "I think we're all gonna be fine now."

Mattie fixed Duncan's favorite supper of fried pork chops, mashed potatoes, sweet potatoes, corn on the cob, fresh garden tomatoes and apple pie. Gus cleaned up the kitchen and let the grownups have a chance to talk. Mattie and Duncan turned in early. There was a lot of joyful noise in the McLagan house that night.

The next morning Duncan woke up with a smile on his face. As usual, Mattie was already up. Duncan found his overalls washed and folded on the end of the bed. The simple act of putting them on after all those months of prison stripes made him happy. For a moment he wondered what Mississippi was doing. Strange that they had spent so much time in such close quarters, watched each other's backs, shared stories, occasionally found something to laugh about and now they would probably never see each other again.

Duncan washed his face, shaved and wandered into the kitchen led by the aroma of strong coffee and bacon. When he sat down at the table, he saw his family had grown by the power of two. Finn and Skye sat next to Gus across the table from him, not eating, just watching and waiting. After six months in prison, all that attention and scrutiny made Duncan a little uncomfortable. "Y'all got something on your minds?" he asked as he buttered two of Mattie's fresh baked biscuits.

"Yessir," Gus said, "but you go ahead and finish your breakfast. We can wait."

Duncan smiled. He'd never seen anybody expend so much energy trying to sit still. Exercising his right as the head of the house, he took time to enjoy his first breakfast at home. After two extra cups of coffee, he finally pushed back from the table and rolled a cigarette. "OK, what's goin' on?"

"We got something we want you to see," Gus said.

"Do I need to crank up the car?" Duncan asked.

He was met with a chorus of Nos. "We don't wanna leave any trails," Skye said. And so they walked around the back of the house, across a field, along a dirt path, out to the gravel road and finally across a deep ditch and into the dense woods. Gus led the way, then Duncan, followed by Skye and Finn. A mile or so farther on, they stopped. Gus stepped back and proudly presented the new still site to his father.

Duncan took his time looking it over. He smelled the horsemint and heard the creek before he saw it. He stepped over and around the mountain laurel roots and finally he noticed the carefully built rock foundation. He nodded at the flat clearing and his practiced eye detected at least six escape routes through the woods. Always pays to be prepared. A little early planning had saved many a moonshiner from getting caught by revenuers. Duncan found a tree stump and sat down. The kids looked around for a place to sit and finally settled on the ground.

"Y'all did this?"

Three heads nodded in unison. "That's not all. We got the malt and sugar all ready to go."

Duncan wondered if Mattie knew about all this and if perhaps she had helped finance the adventure. As it turned out, Gus had bought all the materials and until that moment Skye and Finn had not thought to ask how he had managed it.

"How'd you pay for all this, Son?"

"Remember I wrote you about drivin' shine for Mr. Curtis Slone? And I told you I'd worked out a new system. Since you were, well, since you weren't here I didn't want to take any chances with the revenuers, so I thought the whole thing through first. Like everybody else, I'd been drivin' hell-bent-for-leather down gravel roads in the dark, but now I got a better way."

Finn and Skye looked at each other. This was the first they had heard about any "better way."

"What I did was to leave about five in the morning, you know, just after daylight. I drove real slow 'cause I didn't want to draw attention. When I got close to Atlanta, I pulled off the road by a creek and I cleaned all the red dust off the car. Then I put on one of your old coats and a hat I found in the back of the closet and I just blended in with all the other men going to work."

Duncan looked closely at his son and realized he didn't look like a kid anymore. With a hat pulled down at an angle, he could pass for a man without much trouble. Gus was obviously proud of the way he had worked things out and Duncan couldn't help but be impressed. "Well damnation! I got to hand it to you, Son. That's a hell of a plan." He crushed out his cigarette.

"Yessir. Nobody took notice of me at all. Anyway, I made my delivery and got paid. Then I stopped by The Varsity Drive-in on North Avenue and had myself a hot dog and a Dr. Pepper."

"All y'all in on this?" Duncan indicated the still site. Finn and Skye hesitated slightly, then they smiled and nodded. "Something else you wanna tell me?"

Gus swallowed hard and took a deep breath. "Well, Pa, it's like this. I got $5.45 left after buyin' all the stuff we needed and Junky Brown said he'd build us a 50 gallon still for $35. That's a real good discount 'cause he usually charges by the gallon." Gus realized his father already knew that so he rushed on afraid he'd lose his nerve if he stopped.

"We rescued the worm from your old still, so we don't need to pay for a new one. And we know that half a sheet of copper's gonna cost about $25 and then there's the rivets and we were hopin' ah…we were hopin'…" That's when he ran out of steam.

Finn would normally have butted in to finish the story, but he and Skye knew it wasn't their place to get in on what amounted to a family negotiation, so they waited.

Duncan scratched his head and wiped his brow. "So, lemme see if I understand this. You want me to loan you the money to hire Junky to build you a still. Is that right?"

"Sorta," Gus said. "We just need half of it from you 'cause if you say yes, then we plan to ask Uncle Sean for the other half." Again they all waited.

"Who's gonna run this still?"

"We are."

"So you wanna go into business for yourselves, is that it?"

Cautiously they nodded again. This wasn't Duncan's first experience with horse-trading and he smelled a rat. "There's more to this, ain't there?"

Skye decided now it was time to lend Gus some support. "Uncle Duncan, while you've been gone, there's some things that have been goin' on you might not know about."

At first Gus and Finn thought she was going to tell Duncan about the Gilmer County troubles. Instead she said, "I guess you haven't heard anything about Junky Brown's Great Dismemberment, have you?"

Before Duncan could get the wrong idea, Skye explained about the Model T in Junky's barn. "I helped him take the Model T apart and he's been teachin' me how to fix cars."

Now it was time for all three men to be surprised. Duncan had a hard time believing Skye was learning how to be a mechanic. The boys were vaguely aware that Skye had been spending time at the garage, but they thought she was just sweeping up. This was the first they had heard anything about Skye working with Junky.

"He's been payin' me to do some simple repairs on the old cars and I got nearly $12 saved up to add to what Gus has got."

Now that was the real shocker. The boys looked at each other again. Not only was Skye learning how to fix cars, but Junky had hired her and was paying her real cash money to fix cars that belonged to actual grown-up men. They couldn't quite get their minds around all this new information. Duncan felt the same way. Thank goodness he hadn't been gone more than six months. He already felt like Rip Van Winkle.

Gus spoke up, "That's not all. Aunt Emma's been teachin' me bookkeeping, you know, how to keep track of everything like she does for their shine business. She says it's a little early to tell, but I might have a real head for business."

"Now that's one for the books," Duncan thought.

"Ma says Gus is doin' good," Skye added. "Everybody knows that if she didn't keep track of our family money, we wouldn't have nothing 'cause Pa can't be bothered to do anything but spend it."

There are few secrets in a small town and Skye was right, it was common knowledge that Sean had a free hand with whatever money he happened to have in his pockets.

Finn was sitting by himself trying to work out how Skye could have gotten a job without his knowing about it. And when had his ma found time to teach Gus to keep books? But then he realized he'd been racing a lot on Sundays and he wasn't sure how much anybody knew about that. Seems like everybody had secrets, so he decided to drop a bombshell of his own.

"Uncle Duncan, last Sunday I won at the track and I've got that money to add to the pot too," Finn said.

"Track? What track?"

The kids realized they needed to bring Duncan up to speed on some of the other things that had been going on in the six months he'd been away. By turns Skye explained how she came to be working on the Model T in Junky's barn. And the boys told him nobody raced along the creek anymore because Junky had built an oval track in his back pasture.

Duncan was trying to picture that. "So you put all those cars in there together and just drive around in a circle? Is that it? How do you know when you've won? Don't y'all run into one another? It don't sound very safe to me."

"We do tend to knock into each other from time to time, but nobody gets hurt...much." Finn said. "I mean, we wear football helmets and..." slowly he realized he was not exactly helping their cause. He tried again. "It's pretty safe, you know, what with the chicken wire and all. That keeps the parts from flying into the bleachers."

Tracks, football helmets, flying parts and bleachers, the more he heard, the less Duncan understood. A race from start to finish made sense. A race going around in a circle didn't.

"Somebody decides ahead of time how many miles to race, you know, how many laps around the track. The fastest car wins. Sometimes they pass the hat to the spectators and give whatever they collect to the winner."

Duncan shook his head trying to take it all in. "Alright, let's say I understand all this—which I don't—what has that got to do with this still?

Silence.

"You've got a plan, I know you do. So let's hear it."

Silence

Duncan stood up. "Do you want my help or not?" He was losing his patience.

"We wanna buy a car," Gus said.

"A Ford V-8," Skye added.

"To race," Finn said hopefully.

Duncan sat down abruptly. Now he was the one who was at a loss for words. He used his usual stalling tactic of rolling a cigarette and slowly putting the tin of tobacco away. He lit the cigarette and crushed out the match on the bottom of his shoe.

He wasn't entirely surprised that the kids wanted to branch out on their own. But racing?! That was something totally new and as far as he could see, totally useless. How could anybody make a living driving around in a circle?

Duncan pondered the situation. Through experience he'd learned sometimes the answer was in the question. Right now they were asking for help to buy the equipment to setup a still. Then they wanted to buy a car. However, before they could even consider buying a car, they had to make a success of moonshining and he knew it was a big step to go from being a still-hand, to handling the whole shootin' match on their own. Part of making good shine came from trial and error, to say nothing of all the work involved.

As a means of giving himself some additional room in case he wanted to get out of the situation later he said, "Gus, have you talked to Ma about this?"

"Nosir. We figured we better talk to you first."

"I don't think we ought to mention the car to her just yet," Duncan said. "You don't need to be gettin' the cart before the horse. First you gotta get the still goin' and prove you can make shine folks are willin' to pay money for. You understand that?"

"Yessir," they answered in unison.

"And you know you're gonna need a lot of help and advice from me and Sean, assumin' he's willin' to get involved with this harebrained idea?"

"Yessir."

"Well, if he's willin' *and* if your mamas sign off on it, then I guess I will too."

Now it was Duncan's turn to wait. It took a minute for his words to sink in and then the kids all started laughing and jumping up and down and slapping each other on the back.

"Lord God, what have I got myself into now?" Duncan muttered as he looked around for the nearest escape route.

CHAPTER EIGHT

"If you're gonna make shine, you gotta do it right or don't do it at all," Duncan said. Gus, Finn and Skye sat at the kitchen table looking at the half-filled jars in front of them.

"That's right," Sean broke in. "Mother Nature's gonna do her part, but it's up to you to know what to keep and what to throw away."

Before he could take a breath, Duncan jumped in. "The first vapors to boil off is fore shots. It won't be very much, but you wanna throw that out."

From then on the conversation went back and forth like a ping pong ball.

"Next you're gonna get the heads. You don't wanna keep that neither."

"You can taste it. It'll be bitter, so spit it out."

"I can't see why nobody'd wanna *drink* that stuff. It might not make you blind, but it'll sure give you one hellava bad hangover.

"Sean's right. You gotta wait for the hearts. When that starts to run, the shine'll have a real good taste, no bitterness."

Sean picked up a jar, unscrewed the lid and passed the jar around. "Taste that. It's kinda smooth and a little bit sweet. That's good whiskey and that's what you keep."

"Yeah, but you gotta keep an eye on it 'cause you also gotta know when the hearts end."

"When that happens, it'll start to taste kinda flat and bitter with no sweetness left. Here taste this." Duncan opened a second jar.

"If you got any doubt," Sean said, "just look at it. It'll look kinda oily on the top, sorta like gasoline floatin' on water."

"You can feel it with your fingers too. Throw that out! Don't keep nothin' but the hearts and you'll do fine."

It took them the better part of a year, but the kids finally mastered the fine art of making drinkable moonshine. They saved their money until they could afford a brand-new Ford V-8. At 17, they weren't just kids anymore, they were in business and they were looking to the future.

In Junky Brown's case, he had more or less plowed his way into the future. The South had nothing to offer in the way of public sporting contests until Junky's racetrack started a trend. Pretty soon it seemed like every vacant pasture within a hundred miles of the Dawsonville track had undergone a transformation.

Once again the mountain folks had found a way to eke a living out of Georgia's hard-packed land. North Georgia red clay proved to be the ideal surface for outrunning revenuers and dirt-track racing. Two great sports and anybody could play.

Contestants could buy a car off the local dealer's lot and drive it right onto the track. But in order to win, they needed the talents of a master mechanic to "improve" it. If they couldn't afford a mechanic, they visited the nearest junk yard and swapped out parts and engines on their own.

It wasn't too unusual for a racer to drive a Ford with a 1934 front end, a transmission from 1936 and an engine from 1939. Anything was possible. There was no organization, no rules, no limits, just speed, noise, danger and excitement. Paint a number in white shoe polish on the car, show up at the track, drive as fast as the car would go and the driver who won walked away with bragging rights until the next race.

Track owners started working with promotors who got the word out and gathered a crowd for every race. Sometimes they shared part of the proceeds with the winners and some lucky whiskey tripper might go home with as much as $50 in his pocket. A veritable fortune.

Sometimes the promoters just made promises which vanished as quickly as they could jump in their cars and hotfoot it out of town. Nevertheless, the drivers and the fans kept showing up and the crowds got bigger and bigger.

But that was just on the weekends. During the week, it was business as usual. Stills had to be tended, moonshine had to be delivered, revenuers had to be avoided and the best way to do that was to outrun them, which brings us back to Junky Brown's Garage which had undergone a change too.

If anyone had told Junky six months earlier that the best move he would ever make was to hire a teenage girl to train as a mechanic, he would have laughed them out of the shop. But it was true. Skye was a natural-born, honest-to-God genius when it came to engines. She could just listen to a motor and know how to make it run better. Her specialty was Ford V-8s, but she got along equally well with Chevys, Oldsmobiles, Buicks, Caddies, Lincolns, Hudsons and Packards.

She and Junky worked well together except when he had to go outside to get rid of all the cuss words building up. They had been his safety valve and giving them up had been an extreme sacrifice, but it was worth it. Skye had such a light touch that when drivers inspected her work, they frequently swore she hadn't done anything. When they complained, Skye just smiled—which was disarming enough—and said, "Just try it out."

Sure enough, come Monday morning the drivers came back to eat their words. Again, Skye just smiled. She absorbed their quiet praise and little by little learned to trust her instincts. Like Junky had done, she looked past the tiny garage and caught a glimpse of what her future might hold.

It took months before Gus and Finn realized their world had shifted slightly too. Skye continued to put in her time at the still, but she was different. For one thing, the three of them were not joined at the hip any more. Skye was spending most of her time working for Junky and she was meeting a lot of out-of-town drivers. They were making a name for themselves on the racing circuit and Skye was building a reputation at the same time. Gus paid attention and he was not sure he liked what he saw. Finn, on the other hand, loved bragging to drivers about his sister Skye. He stopped by the garage a lot hoping to meet some of the famous trippers.

The kids had originally agreed to split any winnings three ways and that Gus and Finn would alternate driving on weekends. Skye's talents were best used off the track and she tried out her ideas on their V-8 first.

The boys' driving styles were entirely different. Finn hit the track with his foot on the gas pedal and never let up. He took full advantage of the improvements Skye made on the Ford. With the grace of a bird flying through a forest, Finn picked his way through the other drivers like they weren't even there. Sometimes he won or managed to stay in the top five and came home with money in his pocket. When Skye asked him about the money, Finn casually said he had won it.

"You won the race?!"

"Well, not always. That's not the only way to win, you know. Sometimes I make a side bet. Just like Gus, I pay attention. When I hear some guy braggin' on his car—and I know I can beat him—then I start braggin' on mine. When he challenges me, I back off. He thinks he's got the upper hand, so I let him push me into a bet. In the beginning, it's just the two of us, head to head. It's even better if his buddies want to get in on the action. "

"But where do you get the money to bet with?"

"From some of my friends. I just tell 'em I need to borrow $5 or $10 'till the end of the day. Sheriff Hamilton holds the money and when the race is over, I collect my winnings. I pay my friends back and walk away richer than I was before."

"What if you had lost?"

Finn laughed. "Sister Skye, with you workin' on my car, there was no way I can lose."

It's been said that racing and betting started when the second car rolled off the assembly line and it logically follows that as the cars got faster, the bets got bigger.

Gus left the gambling to Finn, while he concentrated on racing. Rather than driving flat out, he held back and analyzed the other drivers. Once he spotted their weaknesses, he took advantage and frequently ended up in the money. Any way they won it, Finn and Gus agreed to save their racing money to buy another car. Eventually they wanted to own several cars and hire drivers just like Raymond Parks and his team of race drivers.

Sean and Duncan just sat back and watched. They had expected the kids to take over the moonshine business eventually and they were proud that they all seemed to take their work seriously.

Outrunning revenuers was one thing. It was dangerous, but it was necessary, just part of the business and there was only one car following behind trying to catch you. Filling up a racetrack with 20 or 30 cars all roaring around at top speed and running into one another, didn't make any sense. They were worried the boys were just wasting their time.

It was *Skye,* Emma and Mattie were worried about. They understood homes and husbands and children. They also understood some women worked as nurses or teachers, but they had absolutely no idea about all that mechanical stuff. They had always just assumed Skye and Gus would get married. For totally different reasons, they agreed with Duncan and Sean that all this car-racing nonsense was exactly that, nonsense. So they made a plan.

The next Sunday as the McLagans were finishing after-church dinner, Mattie said, "Gus, how's Skye gettin' along at her new job with Junky Brown? Emma says there are drivers from all over the county comin' in to the shop to get her to work on their cars. I sure hope she doesn't take a notion to go off to work in Atlanta or someplace like that." She turned an innocent face to Gus and waited for a reply.

"Atlanta! Is she thinkin' about going to Atlanta?"

"Oh, I don't know that she is, I just was wonderin'."

"Well, she's got a good job right here, why would she be goin' to Atlanta? And I don't know nothin' about all those other drivers." Gus abruptly left the table.

"What's got into him?" Duncan asked.

"I have no idea," Mattie said and hid her smile behind her coffee cup.

A similar scene was taking place next door. While Skye and her mother washed the dishes, Emma asked casually, "Did you notice those trashy girls throwin' themselves at Gus after the race last week? Nice girls didn't act that way when I was growin' up. I'm tellin' you, they were downright shameless. I didn't recognize most of them, I reckon they're not from Dawsonville."

"I didn't notice," Skye said and in truth, she hadn't noticed, but she would certainly be paying attention from now on. When she thought about it, she realized the girls at church

73

had started hanging around Gus lately, but for heaven's sake, he'd known them all his life. He wouldn't be interested in any of them, would he? The whole idea was just silly. As far as Skye was concerned, Gus was just like her brother Finn—only taller—and better looking—and kinda sexy. Maybe she was missing something, or *missing out* on something.

Emma and Mattie dropped the subject, but the seeds had been planted.

CHAPTER NINE

Because Gus's nearest brother was ten years older than he was, he had more or less grown up surrounded by adults. He was a serious kid who always thought things through. By the time Gus weighed all the angles, most of the neighborhood children had moved on to other things. Mattie and Emma were determined not to let that happen where *Skye* was concerned.

Maybe because toys were scarce in the mountains, Skye brought home discarded things and then happily went about trying to fix them. If she couldn't fix something, taking it apart just to see how it worked was almost as much fun. She spent time with Gus and her twin, but she didn't seem to mind being by herself. Emma and Mattie were determined not to let that happen where *Gus* was concerned.

Finn on the other hand, was a universe all by himself. He was always thinking, but no idea ever lingered more than a second or two in his mind before he turned it into action. When he was a kid he brought home every stray or wounded animal in the county. His cousins banned him from going hunting with them because he intentionally made so much noise he scared all the game away.

At the present moment, Finn was concentrating on driving. Skye had juiced up their Ford V-8 and he swore the faster he drove, the better the little car handled. He truly loved that car because he knew the two of them together made one hell of a team. Twin carburetors and stronger suspension meant he could take the winding roads in the dark at 100 miles an hour as easy as driving to church on Sunday.

He had pretty much given up his old childhood habit of bringing home stray animals, until one bright night he saw what he thought was a bundle of old clothes in the middle of the road. As he got closer, he realized it was a dog and he slowed down enough to open his door and sweep the startled animal into the passenger seat.

About the time Finn got back up to speed, he saw distant headlights in his rearview mirror. Revenuers! "Hang on, pal, we're going for a ride." The animal's fur was matted, he was scared and hungry, but he had enough sense to hunker down in the seat. "Atta boy," Finn said laughing out loud.

He took the next two turns so fast he almost stood the car up on two wheels. "Let's see you guys match that!" Finn was in his element. The engine was roaring and trees were going by so fast they were nothing but a blur. He knew he could outrun the feds without a problem. It was all a big game and Finn was having the time of his life.

He slid through another series of curves creating a storm cloud of red dust behind him. Every once in a while he reached over and patted the dog. Even one-handed Finn knew he could outdrive most trippers and he could certainly outdrive the feds. Just to mess with them, he slowed down to let them catch up a little. Staying too far ahead was no fun.

Then in an instant his whole world changed. He heard the unmistakable sound of a gunshot. The car started to drag on one side and Finn fought to gain control. "Goddamn fools shot out my rear tire!" Instantly he thought about Doc's story and a shock of fear went through him. He patted the steering wheel, "Come on, Baby, don't fail me now."

Up ahead Finn made a sharp turn into the woods. The car was already leaning in that direction and he took the turn with all the speed the little car could deliver. He was driving without lights and he prayed the deep pine needles would hide any telltale dust for the feds to follow.

Once under the protection of the trees, he cut the engine and kicked the passenger door open. "Run, dog!" Finn rolled out his door and hit the ground hard. For a second he hesitated with his hand on the side of the car. "Sorry I gotta leave you," he said, "but I got no choice." He knew the rules: leave the car, leave the shine, save yourself. And so he ran.

By this time his eyes were well adjusted to the darkness and the moon provided enough light for him to pick his way through the trees. He was running as fast as he could, but it felt like he wasn't moving at all. He stopped for a moment to lean over and suck air into his burning lungs. That's when he heard the revenuers crashing through the undergrowth behind him.

He had never been so scared in all his life. He couldn't breathe. He couldn't think. He couldn't move. Suddenly he remembered there was an abandoned logging road up ahead. If he could lure the feds to that, maybe they would follow it assuming he'd take it as the easiest way out of danger.

He ran 100 feet down the road, stirring up as much dust as possible. Then he dived headfirst into the woods, picked himself up and started running again, trying not to make any noise. Low hanging limbs, brittle bushes and thorns snatched at his face and tore his clothes, but he didn't stop. He ran until his lungs felt like they might burst.

Up ahead he saw a huge old mountain laurel. With his last bit of strength, he forced his way into the middle of its thick foliage and its tangled roots, fell to the ground and curled up in a ball. His heart was racing and he was breathing so hard he had to clamp his hand over his mouth to muffle the sound. Then he waited.

For a minute, he thought he had outwitted them, then he heard the revenuers' voices. They were getting closer. He was caught. There was no way out, nowhere to go.

"I got him boys. There's a piece of his shirt on this bush."

"Take it easy, Skinner. We're not down here to shoot up the whole county."

Finn heard the rough voices and then the hammers click on a double-barrel shotgun. He tensed his muscles and prepared to die. The gun fired, then the voice shouted, "Ah shit, that ain't him. It's just some raggedy-ass dog."

"Skinner, what the hell are you doing?" One of the feds grabbed for the gun, but Skinner was too fast for him. He reloaded and fired two more shots into the laurel bush. Leaves and branches rained down on Finn, but he didn't move.

"Damn stupid dog. No need to waste time here. That shit-head is probably long gone by now. Come on," Skinner said.

"Listen, you crazy bastard, I've had about enough of your hot-headed crap. Bein' a fed don't give you the right to go nuts. You keep this up and you're gonna get us all busted." The men stomped their way back out to the road.

As much as Finn wanted to know what happened to the dog, he didn't move. The guy they called Skinner might have stayed behind. Twenty minutes passed and still Finn didn't move. When the woods returned to normal night sounds, he heard an owl. Coo-coo-coo-coo, who-cooks-for-you?

He crawled toward an opening and looked out, but he couldn't see anything. About that time, he felt something cold on his neck. Every muscle in his body tightened. He was literally paralyzed with fear. He wanted to turn his head, but he couldn't. He wanted to duck, but he couldn't do that either.

Finally he forced himself to slowly look over his shoulder and came face to face with the dog. Finn realized he had wet himself, but he didn't care. He laughed so hard he couldn't stand up. The dog just sat there with his tongue hanging out laughing too.

"Come on, let's go home."

"Home? Did he say home? It sounded like home. I hope it was home." Dog got up and followed Finn down the road. It had been a long time since anyone had mentioned home to him.

It took them over an hour to walk home. They found their way back to Highway 9, but they stayed off the road and just inside the woods to be on the safe side. Finn dreaded having to tell Skye and Gus that he had abandoned their car. He wouldn't allow himself to think about what he knew the feds might have done to the V-8. It wasn't the first time one of Finn's grand ideas had gone wrong, but at least this one wasn't his fault... exactly.

As he walked up the road toward the house, Finn made out the shape of his father coming toward him and wondered what he was doing still up at 3:30 in the morning. When Finn got closer, Sean took one look at his only son and figured out something was terribly wrong. "Been waitin' up 'cause I had a feelin' something might have happened." Sean reached out to hug his son. Finn didn't realize just how scared he had been until he felt the safety of his father's arms. He did his best not to cry, but there was just no holding back the sobs. Sean let him cry.

"You're alright now, Son. I got you." Finally he held Finn at arm's length. "Damn, Boy, you look like you been in a fight, and lost." They both managed a weak laugh. "You get caught?"

"Yeah." Finn wiped his eyes. "Pa, they shot out my tire. I ain't never been so scared in my life. I thought we were goners for sure."

"We?"

Finn pointed to the sad, muddy dog sitting at his feet. The dog's hair was matted and he looked like a bag of bones. "That dog saved my life. After they run me off the road, I hid in this big old laurel bush. The feds were right on top of me and I thought they were gonna kill me. They did shoot into the laurel bush, but they missed me. Then this dog walked out and they shot at *him*. Missed him too, I'm glad to say. The guy with the shotgun was so mad he fired into every laurel bush in sight.

"I finally heard 'em leave, but I waited a long time to be sure. No doubt about it, Pa, this little ole dog saved my life. I think we oughta keep him. That OK with you?"

"I reckon, but Finn, that ain't no little dog. Just look at his feet. He don't have his full growth yet, not by a long shot." Sean saw the distressed look on Finn's face, "But, since he saved your life, I guess he can stay. So, they got the car and the shine?"

"Yessir. I didn't have a choice, I had to leave it. I'm real sorry. Skye's gonna kill me. She put a lot of work into that car."

"She'll probably let you live this time, but I wouldn't try this stunt again if I was you."

CHAPTER TEN

By the time they got close to the house, Finn saw Skye and his mother standing in their nightclothes in the light on the front porch. "Finn?" they called as they ran down the steps.

"I'm OK. Just scratched up a little." He was a pitiful sight. Bruises were already beginning to show and he was bleeding from scratches all over his face and arms. His shirt was torn, his pants were wet and covered with red dirt. He tried to avoid the women, but they hugged him anyway.

He stepped away to give them some breathing room. "Skye, I'm real sorry about the car." Finn was close to tears. "There was nothin' I could do. They shot out one of my back tires. I had to leave it."

"I know," she said quietly. "I'm glad you're OK, and by the way, you stink." He tried to laugh because he knew that was Skye's way of saying she forgave him. They turned to walk into the house and that's when Skye noticed the dog. "Where'd he come from?"

"Saved my life, I'll tell you all about it later."

Dogs were not generally allowed in the house and they were definitely not allowed into Emma's kitchen, but that's exactly where this dog headed. He was probably following the scent of food, but when he got there, he sat down directly in front of Emma and looked up at her with his big dark eyes.

"Oh Lord, Ma's gonna throw him out for sure," Skye said. Finn knew the rules and he was just about to grab the animal and hustle him outside when Sean said, "Wait! Y'all leave him alone. I believe that dog's got more sense than any of us."

When Emma finally noticed him, he tilted his head slightly and waited. Emma hesitated. Finally she put her hands on her hips and said, "Alright, you can stay, but no barkin' in the house and no chewin'. As soon as it gets light, y'all take him outside and clean him up. Finn, you go clean yourself up now. I'm not feedin' anybody who smells as bad as you do. Skye, sometime tomorrow will you get that old blanket and make a bed for that animal."

When Finn was cleaned up, Emma dabbed some shine on his cuts. "I reckon we ought to name this dog, seein' as how he saved your life," Emma said glancing at the disheveled creature smiling at her.

"He's already got a name. I call him Dog, with a capital D," Finn said.

Emma nodded. "Come here, Dog. It's time for breakfast." The family watched as the animal slowly walked across the room and sat down politely at Emma's feet. "Well, I guess that settles it," Sean said. "Emma's always been a pushover for good manners."

Emma shook her head as she put a plate of food in front of Dog. He waited. "Well, go on. You don't need an invitation."

Dog happily gobbled everything on the plate and waited. Emma had raised enough boys to know to always hold something back for a second helping. She added the extra portion and finally sat down at the table.

With everyone taken care of, Finn told his story from start to finish. For once in his life, he cut things short. He was feeling so bad about losing the car he couldn't bring himself to admit that if he hadn't slowed down to rescue the dog, he probably wouldn't have gotten caught. On the other hand, if it hadn't been for Dog, he might be dead. It would just have to be their secret. "I was really scared 'specially after what Doc told us about what's happenin' up in Gilmer County."

"What about Gilmer County?" Emma demanded.

"Damn, I didn't mean to say that out loud. It just kinda came out," Finn thought. He knew this was no time to be flip and certainly no time to try to talk his way around his mother.

"The feds shot out the tires on this tripper's car and then they beat him up real bad. Broke his arm. He was just a kid, younger than me and they left him out there to die." He turned to his dad, "Why would anybody do something that mean?"

"I don't know. I've been hearin' rumors too," Sean said. "Seems like the feds are sendin' a whole new wave of agents down here. Far as I can tell, they're hell-bent on shuttin' us down for good, one way or the other. Also heard one of them was actin' crazy."

Early the next morning, Finn grabbed a bar of Ivory soap and took Dog out in the yard. With Skye's help, he rinsed off all the mud, then he lathered Dog with soap, twice. When they finally washed that off, they discovered Dog wasn't a short-haired mutt at all. He was a silver and white fluffy aristocrat. Finn looked at him in amazement. "You ain't no country dog, so how did you end up lost in the woods?"

Dog hung his head and looked ashamed. Then he rolled around in the leaves and the dirt to make himself more presentable. Finn laughed. "Oh don't worry. I guess we can stand a little class around here." When Sean and Finn walked next door to tell the McLagans what had happened the night before, Dog went along.

There was no doubt that once the story got out, it would spread through the county quicker than feathers in the wind. Sean wanted to make sure Duncan and his family got the facts first and heard them directly from Finn.

Finn told the story once again. He apologized to Gus for leaving the car and his friend's reaction was about what he expected. "Wasn't nothin' else you could do," he said sadly.

Apparently Gus had decided not to tell his parents about the incident in Gilmer County either, so that part of the story was news to them. "Did you know about all that?" Duncan asked his son.

"Sorta. Doc Fletcher told us when we took Finn in to see about his snakebite. Didn't have nothin' to do with us. That's why I didn't say anything' about it."

"That boy's a tripper just like y'all, so I reckon it does have something to do with all of us. And now, with what's happened to Finn, it sure don't look good for what might be comin' our way in the future. Seems like the whole world is going crazy."

The nightly news proved that point. Duncan and Mattie listened to Douglas Edwards on WSB and tried to keep up with what was going on outside of Dawsonville. Even though they were half a world away, they didn't much like what they heard about Hitler and Mussolini. Duncan was getting the same sense of dread as he listened to what had happened not only in the county next door, but to young Finn.

Duncan decided not to say anything out loud, but he had a premonition of bad things to come in Dawsonville. His mother had sometimes had what she called "visions." Duncan never put much stock in that kind of thing, even though some of her predictions actually did come true. Now he wondered if perhaps he should have paid more attention.

Finn sat quietly in a corner and listened to his father and Uncle Duncan talk. He felt sorry for the boy with the broken arm. Although he hadn't broken any bones, he had done a pretty good job of beating himself up. As soon as he could, he asked to be excused and hobbled home. Dog followed.

Gus nodded to Finn as he went out the door and then he left the house too while the adults continued to talk. Clearly there were forces at work which demanded a plan of action.

The men decided to walk over to Sheriff Hamilton's office. They asked if he had heard anything about the trouble up in Gilmer County and he admitted he'd heard some rumors and there was talk about one of the feds who'd gone off the tracks, but nothing concrete. Finn's situation was news to him.

Sheriff Hamilton shook his head, "I'm sorry fellas, but from where I sit, we don't have much to go on. First of all, I ain't got no jurisdiction over the feds. Second, they mighta shot out the tires and chased him through the woods, but hell, that's pretty much standard procedure."

"What about the fed who shot up the laurel bush where he thought Finn was hidin'. He coulda killed him, the fact is, I reckon that's exactly what he was plannin' on," Sean insisted.

"That might be true, but he coulda just been tryin' to scare him. I mean he didn't hit him or nothing. Sean, you got to remember we ain't dealin' with our local agents no more. Not like Homer and his boys."

The discussion continued, but it all boiled down to the fact that the sheriff's hands were tied. The feds were just on a tear and he figured they'd calm down soon enough. Until then, his advice was to lay low.

Duncan and Sean walked home together. They could understand the sheriff's position, but neither one of them thought things were just going to blow over. Blow up was more like it.

When Finn hobbled home, Emma was reading the *Atlanta Journal*. She didn't just look at the paper every day, she studied it. She subscribed to *Life* and *Look* magazines and made notes about what was going on in the world.

"Ma, we got any aspirin?" Finn asked.

Without looking up, Emma pointed toward the bathroom. "Try the medicine cabinet."

Finn took three pills and went to lie down.

CHAPTER ELEVEN

Skye was feeling bad too. She didn't think aspirin would help, but she wasn't sure what would. For want of something better to do, she walked out the back door. She knew Finn wasn't to blame for what happened, but she just couldn't get past losing the V-8. Finn told her not to go looking for the car because he was afraid of what she would find. Skye ignored him and talked Junky into driving out Highway 9. They found the side road and walked back into the woods until they found the car. She should have listened to her brother. What she saw turned her stomach.

Gus was trying to clear his head too. When he left his house earlier that morning, he had walked back into the woods. He usually walked with his head up, paying attention to his surroundings both for the love of the land and because he was always on the lookout for revenuers. Today he walked with his head down, his hands crammed into his pockets.

Without thinking, he had gone back to the abandoned site of his dad's old still. It was all grown over with vines and weeds. Mostly folks avoided stills that had been destroyed by the feds. Kinda like the places were haunted. Gus squatted down by the creek and scooped up the cold water to wash his face. He was glad for the solitude.

He was normally able to analyze his way out of a problem, but the present situation left him worn out and depressed. He sat down on a log and leaned over with his hands dangling between his knees. He had no idea how long he had been sitting there when he felt a presence and turned around to see Skye.

"Hi."

"Hey."

Skye sat down beside him and waited. Finally she said, "Wanna talk about it?" She really hadn't expected Gus to open up, but once he started talking it was as if the words kept pushing themselves out faster and faster.

"I know it wasn't Finn's fault and I'm glad he's OK, but damn it, now everything is ruined. It was gonna be a surprise. I had some really big plans. Your ma has taught me a lot and I've been keepin' a sharp eye on our money. With this last run, we'd have had enough to buy a second car. Someday maybe we could be like Mr. Raymond Parks. We'd own the cars and hire the best drivers. And when that happened, then we'd be able to stop runnin' shine. We could move on to something better. I even thought we could set you up in your own garage, like Mr. Park's Hemphill gas station. That way you wouldn't have to fix old cars, you could just make the new ones run better, and faster."

Skye couldn't believe what she was hearing. Gus had bigger dreams for her than she had ever dared to have for herself.

"I've been payin' attention, not only to our money, but to the crowds at the races every weekend and they're gettin' bigger every time. There are some good promotors out there and they're makin' money and they're collectin' enough from the spectators so that even the drivers are makin' some money. I was thinkin' we might get some of the local businesses to sponsor a car or something, you know, to help pay expenses.

"I reckon this racing thing might turn out to be something big. A way for all three of us to be something more important than just a bunch of moonshiners racin' on weekends. Now it's all gone. Not only did we lose the money from the shine, but now we don't even have a car so we have to start over from scratch."

Skye reached over and took his hand. "I know what you mean. When I'm feelin' bad I always talk to Finn and he'll say something stupid and make me laugh. But this time, I can't talk to him, 'cause he's the problem. I'm like you, I know it wasn't his fault and I know he feels awful about the car... but Gus, I loved that little car, I really did.

"Finn told me not to go back there, but I went anyway. I got Junky to take me and I wish I had listened to Finn. I knew they'd dump the shine, but it was what they did to the car. Gus, they busted out the windows and slashed the inside." She was crying now, *"And then they burned it!!* They didn't have to do that, they didn't have to hurt it. Gus, it just looked so sad and alone. Why did they do that?"

She gave way to sobs. Gus put his arms around her and held her until she quieted down. Finally she looked up at him with tears still in her eyes and suddenly they were kissing. The first kiss might have been described as a "sorta" kiss, but there was nothing sorta about the second one.

When Skye and her friends went to the picture show in Dahlonega, they all watched with interest as actors kissed. It looked like they just put their mouths together, but there was no indication as to what else might be going on. Skye asked Sara Beth and the other girls and they just laughed.

"They can't show French kissin', because it's way too sexy. See they both open their mouths a little and then they touch tongues and it's heavenly. You gotta try it."

Skye was willing, but working inside car engines didn't afford any opportunity to try it out. That is, until now. This was the perfect opportunity. She started out with just the tip of her tongue exploring Gus's lips. He quickly got the idea and pretty soon they were exploring everything, kissing and touching and…well, almost everything. When they parted, they looked at each other in stunned silence. Then they both said, "Wow!" and started to laugh. There it was! A joyful noise!

Skye reached up and kissed him again. Things were going fine, but every once in a while, Gus would pull away. "Is something wrong?"

"No, I just gotta breathe."

Skye smiled. "You don't have to hold your breath, Gus."

"Oh." He tried it again and it was much better.

At one point, Skye put Gus's hand on her chest. She could feel the heat and she was waiting for him to put his hand inside her dress, but he didn't move. Odd.

Eventually they separated long enough to sit comfortably side by side holding hands. Gus wanted to tell the whole world what was going on, but instead he asked Skye what she thought.

"Let's just keep it our secret for a while, OK?"

Gus would have agreed to absolutely anything she suggested at that point. Keeping things a secret however turned out to be more difficult than they thought. The idea of privacy was something totally new. They both lived with their families. Everywhere they went, they were surrounded by people. They didn't even have the V-8 anymore.

Not having a place to be alone was frustrating, but in a way Gus was relieved. He was afraid Skye was going to ask him what was wrong again and he had no idea how to tell her. For well over a month he worried about it. Finally he decided to face the problem head-on and go see Doc Fletcher.

CHAPTER TWELVE

"Doc, can I talk to you?"

"Sure, Son, come on in." Doc went into his office and settled himself comfortably behind his battered wooden desk. Gus followed. Instead of his usual stride, the boy shuffled along like an old man, then sat stiffly in the chair opposite Doc.

Silence.

"You wanted to talk to me?"

"Yeah, Doc, I got a problem."

Doc wondered how many times in his life he had heard that phrase. They came, they sat, but they didn't talk. He waited.

"You see, Doc, I've got this girl…"

Doc almost smiled. He thought, "Well it's about time."

"See, I've been in love with her my whole life, but she didn't know that. Nobody knew. And I didn't know if she liked me, I mean like I liked her. Then after Finn got hurt and the feds tore up the V-8—you know the one Skye had worked on so hard—well she was real upset…"

Doc had a feeling Gus hadn't meant to identify the girl, but the boy was just no good at lying.

"I was upset too. Losing that car set us back a good bit. Anyway, this girl was cryin' and I sorta put my arms around her and then we sorta kissed and it was real nice and we've been seein' each other a lot and now I don't know what to do."

"Seeing her? Where exactly?" Doc knew there were not many places in Dawsonville where young people could meet without the whole town knowing something was going on. And when that "something" was between Gus McLagan and Skye Calhoun, well that would set tongues wagging for sure.

"We've got this place back in the woods where my pa's old still used to be. Don't nobody go back there, so it's pretty safe. Anyway it's a place we can...talk, you know without everybody in town stickin' their noses in our business."

"And how long have you been 'talking?"

"About two months and now Doc, I don't know what to do?"

Doc decided to save himself some time and get right to the point. "Gus have you gotten that girl in trouble. Is she pregnant?"

"Holy Cow! No. It's nothin' like that. Well, it's something like that, but it's not *that*. It's just that I like her a lot and I'm sorta scared and I just don't know what to do."

Doc was puzzled. "Could you be a little more specific about the problem, Gus?"

"I told you, I don't know what to do."

"About what?"

To his amazement, Doc realized Gus was blushing, not just a polite blush, but a real, full-on, ears-red blush. Seldom had Doc seen a more miserable human being. And then very slowly, the light began to dawn. He decided to take a chance.

"I think I understand. It's not that you don't know what to *do*, it's that you don't know *what* to do. Is that it?"

Gus breathed a huge sigh of relief. "Yes Sir, that's it exactly. I know what I *want* to do, but I don't know exactly how to go about it. I mean, we might not decide to go all the way—I know enough from Pa to let the girl be the one to say no—but Doc what do I do if she says yes?! This is the most important thing I'll ever do and I've got to get it right the first time."

"Oh God, was I ever that young and innocent?" Doc wondered. It took a great effort, but he put on his best poker face. "I'm glad you came to me, but I think what you need is a woman..."

"No. I got one already."

"Not a girl, Gus. You need to talk to an older woman, someone with experience to guide you...on your journey."

"I don't know any older women 'cept my ma or Finn's ma and I sure can't talk to them. There's the church ladies, but there's no way I could talk to any of them, besides I don't think they'd be much help anyway. Do you know any older women Doc?"

A face, a name and a body immediately sprang to Doc's mind, Rita Moretti. "I might be able to help you. I want to make an appointment for you in Atlanta after one of your trips, OK?"

Gus nodded hesitantly. "It'll be real late, after midnight."

"I don't think that will be a problem. Trippers aren't the only folks who work nights, you know." Doc wrote something on a prescription pad. "Here. Be there next Thursday."

Gus looked at the prescription. "789 Ponce de Leon Avenue, Apartment 4-F." The following week, Gus took a quick shower and put on clean clothes before he left for Atlanta. After he unloaded his shine, he drove slowly along Ponce until he saw number 789 on a five-story red brick apartment building. It was in an elegant neighborhood and he recognized the area because it wasn't far from the Ford Assembly Plant. He slicked down his hair and dusted his shoes on the back of his trousers when he got out of the car.

He walked into the lobby, not knowing exactly what to expect. To his left stood a man in a gray suit behind a wide counter. Behind *him* was a wall lined with numbered mail boxes with keys and other stuff crammed into cubbyholes. "Can I help you, young man?"

Gus checked the prescription. "I'm lookin' for apartment 4-F."

The manager smiled. "That would be Miss Rita, fourth floor, at the end of the hall. There's an elevator over there, but unfortunately the operator goes off duty at midnight. You'll have to use the stairs." He smiled and gestured toward the fancy Art Deco staircase in the middle of the lobby.

"Go right on up, she's expecting you."

That came as a surprise to Gus, but then he realized Doc would have called her. To calm his nerves, Gus counted the steps from the lobby to the apartment door. "Seventy-nine, 80, 81, 82." He took a deep breath and knocked politely.

The door opened and Gus got his first glimpse of life in the fast lane. Rita was nearly as tall as he was, her dark hair was swept up and held in place with two long silver ornaments. Her skin had a golden glow, her eyes were green and her voice was soft. But it was her body—which he could make out clearly through the satin gown she wore—that took his breath away. High breasts, small waist, firm hips, long legs. The dress covered everything, but it didn't hide anything.

Rita smiled. She knew the effect her body had on men. She looked Gus up and down. This was going to be fun. She particularly liked first-timers. They were always so sweet and polite. "Come in. You must be Gus. Doc told me about you."

She took him by the hand and led him into the living room. Pools of yellow light splashed off polished wood and rich crimson rugs. Rita walked to a table and poured him a drink. "If you know moonshine, then you will appreciate that this is the best bourbon to come out of the Georgia hills. I have a private source," she said sweetly.

Gus took a swallow. It went down easy and it didn't burn like the moonshine he was used to.

"Now tell me about yourself, who are you?"

Nobody had ever asked Gus that specific question before. Everyone knew all about him, in fact the old folks probably knew more about him than he did about himself. Nevertheless, he had to say something. He took another swallow of bourbon.

"Well, I'm the youngest boy in my family. We're six brothers all together. We're all moonshiners workin' with Pa. Here lately I've been drivin' in the dirt track races goin' on up in Dawson County. Do you know anything about that?"

"I've had occasion to meet some of the race drivers," Rita smiled. "Now because I know you've come a long way tonight and I don't want to waste your time, please tell me how I can help you."

Gus took a pencil and a small notebook out of his coat pocket. "I thought I might need to take notes."

"Now, that's a new approach," Rita thought.

"See there's this girl and I've been in love with her since we were kids. And we've just sorta gotten…together a little bit and that's been great, but things might get more serious and if that happens, I wanna make sure I do everything right."

"Ahhh. Well, tell me a little about your girlfriend. What's her name? What color are her eyes? How does she wear her hair? Is it long or short? What about her clothes?"

That caught Gus off guard. "Let's see. Her name is Skye, 'cause her eyes are so blue, real dark blue. Her hair is long and red and she usually ties it back with a ribbon or something. She doesn't wear anything special, just cotton dresses, nothing fancy. She wears overalls at work, she's a mechanic."

"A mechanic? How interesting. Now you just wait right here. I'll be back shortly." In about five minutes Rita called to him from the bedroom. "Gus, bring your drink and come in here."

He did as he was told and there, sitting on the bed, was Rita. Her hair was tied with a ribbon at the nape of her neck and she was wearing a simple white blouse and a cotton skirt. She smiled. Gus stood in the doorway waiting for further instructions.

"Come on in and don't be shy, we're going to do this together. Now, I'm going to tell you something most men do not know. The first thing you should do is to take off your shoes and socks."

Gus hesitated.

"You may think this is strange, but you realize you can't wear your shoes to bed and seeing a man wearing nothing but his underwear and a pair of socks is *not* conducive to romance. In your case, this is all about romance."

Gus made a note and followed orders.

"Now come sit here by me. Have you told Skye how you feel about her?"

"Yes, Ma'am. I told her I love her and I meant it too."

"Very good. Love is not something you ever want to toss around lightly."

Gus already knew that, so he didn't bother to make a note. The satin gown had been sexy, but Gus couldn't take his eyes off the buttons down the front of Rita's blouse. The top two were undone, a clear invitation to undo the rest of them. His eyes followed the curve of her breast underneath.

"Now the next thing you want to do is look deep into my eyes and reach around to untie my hair." She noticed the hesitation as he reluctantly shifted his gaze and followed her instructions.

"That's fine. Now run your fingers through my hair and fluff it up a little. Take your time, that's very important. You both want to enjoy this so there's no need to rush." Her hair was soft and warm and curled around his fingers. Gus made a hurried note with one hand.

"All right. Let's get you out of that coat. I appreciate that you put on a tie for the occasion, but let's get rid of that too." Gus was more than ready to take off the coat and tie, but he made himself go slowly.

"And now the shirt." With practiced fingers, Rita undid the buttons...slowly. Then she ran her hands over his chest and slipped his shirt off.

"Now take my blouse off."

This was the part he had been waiting for. In his haste, he fumbled with the buttons. "I know I'm not doin' this very good. I guess I'm a little nervous."

Rita leaned back to give him better access. "Nervousness is fine. It just builds the anticipation and that's half the fun. If the young lady is impatient, she'll help you."

"She will!?" Gus knew he would remember that, no need to make a note.

"Next take my slip straps down, one at a time. Then you can touch me. Don't be afraid."

Gus closed his eyes and ran his hands over her body. Slowly Rita moved on to the next step in the lesson. She stood up, slipped out of her skirt and let her slip fall to the floor. She wasn't wearing anything underneath. When she reached to undo Gus's belt, he threw the notebook over his shoulder and just followed his instincts. Going slow was out of the question, but Rita showed him how to refine his technique the second time. Finally they lay back, happily exhausted and Gus began to laugh.

"Gus?"

"Oh it's nothin' 'cept I've never felt this good before." Then he told her about hearing his parents making a joyful noise. Rita laughed too and then gave him a gentle, sweet kiss. "I think you're ready. And I envy Miss Skye. I'm sure her first time will be one to remember."

They said good-bye and Rita closed the door behind him. She smiled and poured herself a touch more bourbon. Gus left Number 789 Ponce de Leon Avenue, Apartment 4-F with a smile on his face and a notebook full of priceless information.

CHAPTER THIRTEEN

Skye was sitting by herself in the shadows on the front porch thinking about Gus. She had been doing that a lot lately. She knew Gus was in love with her and he seemed to like kissing well enough, but so far he hadn't tried to do anything else. Sometimes she thought that was nice, that he was respecting her, but other times she wanted him to be bold! She knew she was supposed to be the one to say no and to stop before things got out of control, but the problem was, he hadn't tried anything to say no to.

"I don't understand it..." she whirled around thinking maybe she was talking out loud and then she realized it was Finn. He walked up the steps and sat down next to her. Dog sat down next to Finn. "Why is Gus so mad at me? It's not like I'm the first guy to ever lose a load of shine or a car. I know *you're* mad at me about the car, but Gus..." Finn got up and started to pace back and forth across the front porch. Dog's head followed his movements from side to side.

"Skye, he's my best friend and now he won't hardly even speak to me."

Skye looked at her twin brother. His usual open, happy face was drawn into a tight frown. She wanted to stay mad at him, but he was just too pitiful. "He's not mad because you lost the whiskey or the car, he's mad because he thinks you lost our future."

"What's that mean?"

"Gus wants to be a team owner. He had it all planned out how we'd buy more cars and line up drivers and get serious about racing. Then maybe he'd buy me a garage and we'd make some real money and we wouldn't have to run shine anymore. Now we've got to start all over and…"

"Is that all?" the relief was clear in his voice. "Hell, I can take care of that." True to form, Finn wasn't one to wait around for a good idea. Whatever came into his mind first would do just fine. To his way of thinking, the only reason he got caught was because he slowed down to rescue Dog, who now followed him everywhere.

Finn knew he was the best driver in the county, maybe even in the state. All he had to do was put the word out that he was available to drive and the jobs would come rolling in. Even without owning the car, a couple of good runs to Atlanta, and they would be back in business. He was off the porch in two bounds, ready to put his plan into action. Dog glanced at Skye and then followed Finn.

That very night, with Dog riding shotgun, Finn turned onto Highway 9, stepped on the gas and they headed to Atlanta with a load of shine in a cloud of red dust. Considering what had happened the last time he drove that road, Finn should have been scared, but he wasn't. The car was running fine— not as good as Skye's V-8, but good enough—and he watched the speedometer climb past 95. Dog looked straight ahead, on the watch for anything that might get in their way. Behind the wheel was the one place in the world where Finn felt at peace and in total control.

That's when it dawned on him. The road was deadly quiet. Revenuers didn't chase him on every trip, but something was different. Things were *too* quiet. He made the run to Atlanta and back in record time. He was so proud of himself he could hardly wait to tell somebody his story. He saw the red glow of his father's cigarette on the porch. "Hey Pa, guess what! I just made a run to Atlanta and there wasn't nobody else on the road. Not a fed, not anybody. It was spooky."

"That's because the feds were busy over here bustin' up a stash house. You know that old storeroom off the Fellowship Hall in back of the Baptist Church? Well, somebody's been usin' that to store their shine and the feds got every drop. Course they didn't know who it belonged to. That's what has got everybody upset. How did they know to look there in the first place? That wasn't no accident. Somebody tipped 'em off, probably collected a reward too." That definitely took some of the shine off Finn's adventure.

Out in the early days of the West, something like that would have been referred to as "a hanging offense," ranking right up there with horse-stealing or cattle-rustling. Nobody was meaner or lower than a thief who stole a man's livelihood.

Sean, Finn and Dog sat together pondering the seriousness and the consequences of such an action. The idea that one of their friends might have betrayed them was unthinkable. "You got to be a lot more careful, Son. Seems like now-a-days you never know who's watchin' you and just waitin' to turn you in. Damn, it's a sad situation when you can't trust nobody. I'm gonna call it a day and turn in." Sean left Finn sitting on the porch alone with his thoughts.

Suspicion is a terrible thing. Once it takes hold, nobody's safe. A woman shows up two Sundays in a row wearing a new hat, and everyone wonders what she's been up to. A farmer buys a new tractor, and everyone wonders where he got the money.

Finn knew his pa was upset, but as soon as he heard Sean's story, another idea popped into his head. If the feds were otherwise occupied, he figured he could make a second run to Atlanta and earn enough money to make up for what he owed

Gus and Skye. They would surely be pleased by that. As usual, his idea immediately turned into action. Since he had a car handy, he loaded it with shine from the last run they had made and headed south for the second time that night.

The next day he met up with Gus and Skye. "Here," he said, handing over the money. "That oughta make up for the lost shine and help us buy another car. Maybe not a new V-8, but Skye, you can take care of that." Finn was pleased that his plan had worked out so well. At first things were a little awkward, but Gus wasn't one to hold a grudge and the kids quickly got back in sync.

The mysterious raid on the Baptist church was the topic of conversation throughout Dawsonville. Junky Brown and Skye were at the garage when Homer and several other local agents brought their cars in.

"Homer, was you in on that raid?" Junky asked.

"None of us were. There's a new bunch of agents in from up north, Chicago mostly. They're braggin' that they're gonna wipe out moonshining, not just here, but in Tennessee, North Carolina, all over the South. From what I hear, they're gonna make Sherman's raid look like a Sunday school picnic."

"Why send them down here? Don't the big bosses in Washington think you guys are up to the job?"

Homer lit a cigarette. "Way I figure it is this, now that Prohibition's been over a while, they got too many agents on the payroll. Got no speakeasies to raid, no more gangsters to shoot, so they're movin' south. I heard that Skinner guy say the only way to get the job done was to chop the head off the snake; wipe moonshiners out once and for all."

Based on Homer's information, the group decided the best course of action was to lay low, a lesson every Southerner knew from Brer Rabbit stories. But there was another side to Brer Rabbit. He was a trickster. Somebody was always trying to catch him, but he out-foxed them every time. It was those stories that appealed to Skye, Gus, Finn and the rest of the young trippers.

It was Curtis Slone Jr. who got the ball rolling. "Y'all know that stash they found at the Baptist church? Well, it was one of ours. Since Pa is on the Board of Deacons, he figured nobody would ever look in that old storage room. No way the feds found that by accident."

As the teenagers saw it, the Yankee agents were dead set on destroying their families and their time-honored way of life. Something had to be done.

"We need to stop 'em."

"Teach 'em a lesson."

"Make 'em look stupid."

Someone suggested they run an empty car down Highway 9 and when the feds stopped it, they wouldn't find anything. That would be a good story to spread around the county.

"Lemme drive it," Curtis said. "Since it was our stash, I reckon I'm the one that oughta go."

Discussion followed and although Curtis wasn't the best driver around, he could drive fast enough to fool the feds. Besides, he wouldn't be in any danger, because technically he wasn't doing anything wrong.

It was a good plan, but it wasn't enough for Finn.

"I think we oughta try to make back some of your pa's money. What if me and Gus each take a load of your pa's shine and make a run through Gainesville. Make up for what you lost and stay out of trouble 'cause the feds won't be watchin' over there." The next night, they put that plan into action.

Normally the federal agents worked in the wee hours of the morning because that's when the trippers were most active. However, they figured another raid in broad daylight was just what they needed to put the fear of God into the locals.

Late in the afternoon of the following day, the feds—minus Homer and the other local agents—knocked on the downstairs door of the jail. Sheriff Hamilton was not home and his wife and children were ordered at gunpoint to stay inside and keep away from doors and windows.

The feds went directly to the abandoned outhouse behind the jail. It was almost falling down and certainly not a place anyone would think to hide something valuable. Apparently the feds knew exactly what they would find. They poured the shine down the toilet hole and treated the whole thing like a big joke.

Just as they expected, the commotion quickly drew a crowd. When Sheriff Hamilton got home, everyone wanted to know what he knew. Turns out, he knew nothing about the raid or the stash. Clearly the feds had a source of information and everything pointed to someone local. Suspicion floated in the air as thick as April pollen.

Shortly after midnight of the same day, the trippers got ready to go. Gus and Finn loaded their cars and headed toward Gainesville. With help from some of the other boys, Curtis loaded some old tires in the trunk of his car so it rode low and from a distance looked like it was loaded with shine. They took out the back seat and covered the empty space with blankets just for effect. Then Curtis headed down Highway 9.

Curtis wasn't driving more than about 60 miles an hour; after all he *wanted* to get caught. However, once he saw the headlights in his rearview mirror he went fast enough to give the feds a run for their money. Finally he saw a roadblock and slammed on the breaks stopping just short of another car parked across the road.

Get out!" Skinner shouted.

Curtis obediently got out of the car and put his hands up. "I don't know why y'all stopped me. I ain't doin' nothin' wrong."

"Shut up." Skinner, who seemed to be in charge, was a head taller than the others. He had a scar over one eye and a mustache. He approached Curtis and the boy stepped back just in time to avoid the rifle butt aimed at his face.

The rest of the feds broke open the trunk and cursed when they found nothing but tires. When they snatched the blankets off the back seat and found that empty, they hesitated as if not quite sure what to do next.

"I told y'all I wasn't doin' nothin'," Curtis said. "Guess y'all are just barkin' up the wrong tree. We had an ole dog like that once and…"

Curtis never finished his sentence. Skinner hit him with his rifle and the blow dropped him to the ground. "Listen to me you goddamn wiseass, I'll teach you to have some respect for the law." Before anyone knew what was happening, Skinner shot Curtis.

That sent a jolt of lightning through the other agents. They instantly wrestled the gun away from Skinner. "You crazy bastard, what the hell's the matter with you? The boy wasn't even armed!"

"Shit! I don't know how they handle things down here, but that's the way we handle criminals up in Chicago. Besides, that'll teach the rest of these stupid hillbillies not to mess with federal law enforcement." He yanked his arms free from their grasp. "Let's get outa here and for God's sake keep your damn mouths shut. He was coming at me and I shot him. That's it."

***

It was nearly daylight when Finn and Gus got home and pulled into their separate driveways. Both houses were dark which wasn't too unusual considering the hour. However, the front porch light was on at the Calhouns and Skye was sitting on the steps crying.

Gus saw her first. He made it across the yard in less than ten seconds. Finn was right behind him. Skye stood up and embraced them both. "Thank God you're home. Are you OK? I was so worried. It took you so long…I mean you were late and I thought…I thought maybe they caught you too."

"What do you mean 'too?' Remember, we drove down through Gainesville? We weren't anywhere near Highway 9," Finn said.

"But Curtis was and they shot him."

"Shot him?! Why? He wasn't haulin' nothin'," Gus said.

"I know. Some hunters found him lyin' beside the car. The trunk was open and the car doors were all open too. They found some blankets on the ground and they wrapped Curtis in them and brought him to Doc. The feds have all gone crazy."

Finn couldn't believe the plan had gone so wrong. They were just supposed to be playing a trick on the feds. Nobody was supposed to get hurt.

"As soon as folks heard what happened to Curtis, they all went over to Doc's. Half the town is there now," Skye said. "I came back here to make sure y'all were OK." She stood up. "Come on, we gotta go to Doc's."

Gus put his arm around her shoulders. "Skye, we're fine. We don't need to go to Doc's."

"You don't understand. I'm not worried about y'all anymore. It's Curtis. Doc's been workin' on him ever since they brought him in. He's tryin' to save his life."

CHAPTER FOURTEEN

Folks living in the north Georgia mountains were a hearty, independent lot. They had survived the journey from the old country. They had subdued the rugged land in the New World. They had squeezed a living out of the hard, red clay. As moonshiners, they found a way to support their families and live with the destruction of their stills, the spilling of whiskey and the loss of a moonshine car from time to time. They were hardworking, opinionated and a bit standoffish. But when it came to family, they were united. The unwritten law was you don't mess with family!

The group crammed into Doc's waiting room stayed through the night. They prayed for the best, but they planned for the worst. They would take care of the situation one way or another.

Shortly after daybreak Doc gave them the news. Curtis had lost a lot of blood, but by some miracle the bullet hadn't damaged any vital organs. He would live. The women went home. The men lingered.

Old man Slone was standing at the back of the room. He was of average height and average weight, in fact, everything about him was average. But at that moment, he was a man possessed. "We got to put a stop to this. First it was that kid up in Gilmer County, then Finn and now my boy. On top of that, we ain't got no idea who tipped off the feds. They got us lookin' suspicious at all our neighbors. It ain't right. We got lucky this time, but sooner or later somebody's gonna get killed."

Angry voices bounced around the room. "Let's make sure it's them, not one of us."

"We ain't gonna take this lyin' down."

"They want a fight, let's give 'em one."

"I got a couple sticks of dynamite left over from blowin' up some tree stumps. We could send the whole lot of 'em straight to hell. Be too many pieces for anybody to ever find."

"Lots of huntin' goin' on this time of year. Accidents happen."

"Gotta be a hundred places we could set up an ambush…"

Tempers in the room were rising to a dangerous level. It was Duncan who finally spoke up. "I understand how you fellas feel, but we're not just dealin' with a couple of trigger-happy outsiders. Like it or not, they're *federal agents.* We could bring the whole U.S. gov'ment down on our heads."

The group was clearly between a rock and a hard place. They had to do something, but Duncan was right, tangling with the federal government was a bad idea no matter how they approached it. On the other hand, Duncan knew his friends and neighbors well enough to know they might agree to do nothing at the meeting and then turn around and do *something*—probably something stupid—on their own.

"I know I'm not the only one who's done time in Atlanta. Six months was about all I could stand and that was just for makin' shine. If they arrest you for killin' a federal agent, they'll probably hang you on the spot. And don't think you won't get caught. Them Treasury boys got long memories. It's not worth takin' that kind of risk. There's gotta be a better way." The better way walked in the door without even knocking. Sheriff Hamilton made his way through the crowd.

"Looks like I got here just in time. How's Curtis?"

"He's gonna be laid up for a while, but he'll live," Duncan said.

"Glad to hear it. You boys can simmer down 'cause the situation is under control." He held up a hand to forestall any arguments. "Sometime in the middle of the night two of them federal fellas came knockin' on my door. Got me out of bed and hauled me over to Junky's. When we got over there, they showed me this guy, Skinner. He was sittin' on the ground lookin' considerably worse for wear. They had got him handcuffed to the rear axle of a Ford Junky'd been workin' on."

The long and the short of the story was that all three of the feds were headed back to Chicago. According to them, Skinner had gone rogue and they hadn't signed on for any killing. After they got him more or less under control, they'd called their bosses up north and were instructed to bring Skinner back in handcuffs.

The night finally ended and the next day was bright and cold. Curtis went home to his family and as folks sat down to Thanksgiving dinner, they counted their blessings. Curtis was on the way to recovery. The Chicago feds were gone. The war in Europe was a long way off.

Folks in Dawsonville felt safe because the Neutrality Act meant the United States would not get drawn into a war overseas. The war was 3,000 miles away and it stayed that way until two events changed the world forever.

A stunned population listened as President Roosevelt announced, "Yesterday, December 7, 1941—a date which will live in infamy—the United States of America was suddenly and deliberately attacked by naval and air forces of the Empire of Japan.

"The attack on the Hawaiian islands has caused severe damage to American naval and military forces. I regret to tell you that very many American lives have been lost. Since the unprovoked and dastardly attack by Japan, a state of war has existed between the United States and the Japanese empire."

Then, four days later Hitler and Mussolini declared war on the United States. It was a fatal mistake! That decision voided the Neutrality Act. The full force of America's industrial and military might was now focused on winning the war both in the Pacific and in Europe.

The Scots-Irish of the North Georgia mountains were torn between their deep love for America and their equal distrust of anything involving the government. After a lot of soul searching, many families decided to wait until their men were called up. When they were really needed, they would gladly go. In the meantime, families found themselves coping with wartime shortages and planning for a lean Christmas.

Tires were rationed immediately, followed by cars and gasoline shortly after that. Sugar was the first food item to be rationed because it was needed to make chocolate bars which were included in every box of C-rations.

The government hadn't been able to legislate or prosecute moonshiners out of business, but it could certainly starve them out. Whiskey-making required three things: sugar, rubber and gasoline. Take those away and family moonshine businesses could not survive for long. The future looked bleak from every angle.

Winter rain clouds hanging over the mountains added to the sense that dark days were ahead. Whenever folks got together, the main topic of conversation was always how to get by without the moonshine industry that had sustained the community for hundreds of years.

"We could always go back to makin' whiskey like my pa did, just usin' sprouted corn. That way you don't really need sugar for fermentation," Duncan said.

"Yeah, but that takes so much longer, you can't make enough to sell," Sean pointed out. "And even if you had enough shine, you can't get enough gas to haul it to Atlanta. Ain't no way to make this work."

As if to add insult to injury, that night a storm hit in full force. Trees were such a natural part of the landscape that most people never looked all the way to the top of them. Hundred-foot pine trees were head and shoulders above ash and beech which looked down on mountain oaks and magnolias, which in turn looked down on crepe myrtle and smaller trees and shrubs.

A 60-mile-an-hour wind turned gentle shade trees into lashing, roaring giants that threatened everything in their path if they fell. And then there was the rain.

Moonshine stills were designed to go undetected, which meant no straight lines, no protective structures. Making shine required attention and timing was critical. Being outside and dealing with the elements was just part of the job.

But this was no gentle shower, the raindrops were big as quarters and driven by the powerful wind, stung when they hit bare skin. Hundreds of tiny creeks that supplied water for stills overflowed their banks, picking up anything in their way and rolling it downstream. The old folks called these rains gulley-washers.

Downed trees meant downed power lines and loss of electricity. People stayed inside, lit oil lamps and candles, listened to the wind growling high up in the crown of the trees and the rain pounding on every roof. There was nothing to do but hunker down and wait.

There was no let-up in the storm. It was cold and dark and the rain continued for days. Folks began to wonder if maybe God had changed his mind and decided to try another flood. Then on the seventh day, just like in the Bible—or an MGM musical—things changed. The rain stopped, the electricity came back on and the sun came out.

Old folks always said, "It's an ill wind that blows no good." As industries began to convert their facilities to wartime production, new factories opened up. That meant new jobs and new opportunities for folks at home. Anyone who wanted to work could easily find a job.

Junky hung a banner over the front of the garage which read, "We used to make 'em fast, now we make 'em last." He turned a lot of the car repairs over to Skye. He had his hands full repairing washing machines, refrigerators, irons and even radios. New appliances—like new cars—were scarcer than hen's teeth.

Junky kept an old horse tank filled with water that he used to find holes in inner tubes. He'd slap on a patch, put the tube back in the tire and send the customer on his way good for a few more miles at least. He almost single-handedly kept Dawsonville rolling during the war years, mostly because he never threw anything away.

When the dirt tracks closed, Junky scavenged them for discarded cars with reusable parts. He called them never-knows. "Can't hardly get new parts anymore and you never know when you might need an old part to replace an even older one."

Bell Bomber in Marietta was hiring workers to build Boeing B-29 airplanes. The pay was good and they provided on-the-job training. "The whole thing is set up like Henry Ford's assembly line," Junky said. "They're looking for good workers, people they can trust to do things right every time, 'cause people's lives are gonna depend on it."

Within a week, Duncan and Sean had been taken on at the aircraft plant. They took the local bus down to Marietta every Monday, worked all week and came home on weekends. They stayed at a boarding house near the plant. Working inside, doing the same thing over and over, answering to a supervisor and adhering to a strict schedule took some getting used to, but the pay envelope at the end of each week eased the pain. Eventually more than 28,000 Georgians ended up working at Bell Bomber making B-29s.

Mattie and Emma were determined to make 1941 a good Christmas in spite of everything. For once they had cash money to spend on presents. There just wasn't much to buy.

Mattie knew a family out in the country who raised turkeys. They were more than happy to sell her two birds for some extra cash. By pooling their ration allotments, Emma managed to bake a couple of pies. It was a merry Christmas and for that day at least, nobody talked about the war. However, they couldn't help but wonder where they would be when Christmas 1942 rolled around.

CHAPTER FIFTEEN

The auto industry stopped making cars at the beginning of 1942 and almost overnight retooled their facilities to make tanks, trucks, jeeps, airplanes, bombs, torpedoes, steel helmets and ammunition. American industry had a profound effect on the war, and by the same token, the war had an equally profound effect on America. In 1942 eating leftovers became a patriotic duty and wasting food was a mortal sin.

Readers had a good laugh at the article in the *Dawsonville News* about a man in Memphis who was granted a divorce because his wife made him a one-dish meal of leftover beans, sardines and salmon, topped with stale cake.

Everything from hairpins to gasoline was rationed. Emma was good with numbers, but she admitted trying to figure out the rationing system was beyond understanding. Even people trading coupons and stamps on the black market were never sure they had made the best deal.

Kids stopped playing hide and seek and, like Little Orphan Annie, went on scavenger hunts in order to collect tin cans, paper, toothpaste tubes, tinfoil peeled from chewing gum wrappers, rubber bands and even bacon grease.

Just in case anyone questioned the benefits of collecting scrap, posters made it abundantly clear. One old radiator equaled seventeen .30 caliber rifles. One lawnmower equaled six three-inch shells. One rubber tire equaled twelve gas masks. One shovel equaled four hand grenades.

Even characters in the funny papers joined up. Smilin'
Jack became a pilot in the Air Force, Joe Palooka joined the
Army and Terry and the Pirates fought the Japanese. Even
Dixie Dugan and Tillie the Toiler got into the act.

Superman, however, failed to make the cut. He was
classified 4-F because instead of reading the eye chart in front
of him, his X-ray vision looked right through that chart and
the wall behind it and he read the chart two rooms over. He
spent the war promoting the Red Cross and V-bonds. Popular
songs dropped moon-June-spoon lyrics for more patriotic titles
like *Praise the Lord and Pass the Ammunition* and *This is the
Army Mister Jones.*

Detroit and other big cities beckoned and the young men
in Dawsonville hit the road determined to make as much
money as possible before they got drafted. Skye considered
herself lucky. Her single friends were sad because, as the song
said, all the men in town were "either too young or too old."

Junky realized he had to do something to keep Skye from
leaving for the big city, so he promoted her to supervisor and
hired two 15-year old assistants for her to train. He figured
they would at least stay until they were 18.

Mattie and Emma joined the church ladies as they rolled
mountains of bandages and knitted thousands of socks and
scarves to send overseas. They helped plant every available
patch of dirt in Dawsonville with beans and tomatoes. Victory
gardens sprouted up everywhere from small towns, to Park
Avenue terraces and patches of dirt in parking lots in major
cities.

Because the military wouldn't take convicted felons,
Junky hired two retired moonshiners to help with his growing
repair business. When Homer Webster joked about Junky
hiring ex-cons, he was banished him from the garage for two
weeks. That was a hardship because without stills to smash

and trippers to chase, Homer spent a good deal of time hanging out at the garage gossiping with other men who found themselves at loose ends.

With their menfolk working in Marietta all week, Emma, Mattie and Skye often ate supper together. "Emma, if all this had happened when we were girls, do you think you woulda left home to go work somewhere else?" Mattie asked.

"Mattie, have you forgotten that we were both married and havin' babies by the time we were 15? And that we each started a second family after 40. Now, if you're askin' me if I wanted to run off to seek my fortune at 14, the answer is no."

"Yeah, I know, but things are different now. The men are workin' down in Marietta and Skye's got a real job and we're just sittin' here rollin' bandages and stuff. Don't that bother you?"

"Well, no, it didn't bother me at all. But now that you've brought it up, I guess I'll have to worry about it."

"It's just that… "

"It's just that between the two of us we've raised thirteen kids and sent more than our share of boys off to war. Don't you think that's enough? Far as I'm concerned, I've earned the *right* to do nothin' for a while."

Mattie let the matter drop, but Emma and Skye both knew she wasn't done. Then suddenly Skye asked, "Oh my God, Aunt Mattie, you're not pregnant again, are you?"

"At my age?! It's just that I got a letter from a friend over in Rome who works at the Army Hospital over there. They're talkin' about settin' up a Nurses' Aide Corps. Seems like they figure there's gonna be a lot of wounded soldiers who'll need more extensive treatment, that's what she said, 'more extensive treatment,' than they can get at a regular Army hospital. They're gonna start hirin' pretty soon and I just thought maybe we could drive over there... just think about it, that's all I'm sayin'."

Emma rolled her eyes to heaven. She wondered how long Mattie had been pickin' at that particular scab.

After Emma and Skye went home, Mattie decided she wanted a cup of good strong tea made with tea leaves not a tea bag. She found a tin pushed to the back of a pantry shelf. Making tea, instead of just pouring a cup of coffee, was a total waste of time in her prewar life. Now she had time to pamper herself a little. She got down her favorite porcelain mug, sat at the kitchen table, held the cup between her hands to warm her cold fingers and enjoyed the aroma of the tea.

With nothing specific demanding her immediate attention, she walked around looking at her house with a stranger's eye. It was a good house, warm in the winter, lots of open windows to keep it cool in the summer. Mattie knew not everyone understood about moonshining, but it had been good to her and her family. She finished her tea and looked for something to occupy her hands and her mind. She had never been able to just sit doing nothing.

She picked up her sewing basket. Without thinking she reached for her thimble and as she slipped it on her right-hand middle finger, childhood memories came back. The silver thimble was all she had left of her mother.

Mattie grew up the oldest girl in a family of six. From the beginning her mother counted on her to take care of the younger children. After she got married, Mattie had her own children to look after and then the grandchildren came along. Seems like taking care of folks was all she had ever done, but that suited her just fine. She was good at it, not everybody was.

Mattie had told Emma she was just thinking about going to work at the Soldiers' Hospital, but the truth was she had already decided to get a job there whether Emma went along or not.

***

Emma could not understand why some folks went out of their way to borrow trouble and Mattie was a prime example. She'd lived through the hard times, buried two babies, raised the rest up just fine, sent the older boys off to war and now she was waiting for the government to call up the one left at home. On top of that, she was looking for something else to worry about.

It just didn't make sense.

Emma's mother had been like that too. Emma, however, learned better when her Granny Bee came to live with them. Emma was ten and was just beginning to understand—and appreciate—sarcasm.

"Child, your ma is sufferin' from the worst case of the "gottados" I have ever seen. She's gotta do this and gotta do that and she's convinced if she don't do it all, the world will come to a screechin' halt. Well, it won't. Sometimes you just need to get out of the way and let the world take care of itself. When you get a little older, you'll realize that's why the good Lord created moonshine." Granny Bee always punctuated those lectures by either taking a swallow from the bottle she kept in her apron pocket or by puffing on her pipe.

Emma adored her grandmother and vowed to be just like her when she grew up. Of course, that gave her mother something else to worry about. Whenever Emma got in trouble—and the times were many—Granny Bee always took her side. She was the one who taught Emma how to drink shine, but only in moderation or when nothing else would ease the pain. Granny Bee also taught Emma to dance and flirt, to enjoy life and leave the gottados to somebody else whenever possible.

Emma might have been a thorn in her mother's side at home, but her teachers all loved her. She had an instant grasp of math, remembered everything she heard in history class and loved to read. Emma was an A student, but she didn't see any reason to share that information with her mother. She rather enjoyed being the "bad girl" in the family.

However, someone had to sign her report cards, so Emma confessed to Granny Bee, who was happy to keep her secret. Normally moonshine kids dropped out of school after the sixth grade, but on the last day of school, the principal called Emma into his office and handed her a sealed envelope to take home to her parents. Her mother expected the worst, so she waited until Emma's father got home.

The letter, as it turned out, was a recommendation from the principal that Emma be allowed to stay in school and finish her education. She would be among the few children in the county to finish all twelve grades. Without blinking an eye, Granny explained that since Emma was doing so well she had signed her report cards and seen no reason to mention anything. Emma's parents were too dumbfounded to object.

In order to maintain at least part of her reputation, Emma and Sean got married at Christmas of her senior year and she was secretly four months pregnant when she graduated from high school. Her parents suspected nothing, Granny was smug and Emma and Sean were delighted.

Emma shook her head remembering how hard she had worked just to drive her mother a little bit crazy. Now the shoe was on the other foot because her friend Mattie had caught the "gottados" and Emma knew she was going to drive her crazy about the hospital thing. "Well, alright, I'll go," she said to herself, "but if Mattie thinks I'm goin' all the way over there and waste my education messing with germs, blood, guts and bedpans, she's got another think coming. Maybe I'll just take over running the place. That'd serve her right."

***

It seemed everyone was looking for a way to support the war. President Roosevelt frequently used radio broadcasts to communicate with the country. He challenged American companies and workers. "It is not enough to turn out just a few more planes, a few more tanks, a few more guns, a few more ships than can be turned out by our enemies. We must out-produce them overwhelmingly, so that there can be no question of our ability to provide a crushing superiority of equipment in any theatre of the world war."

American companies took those words to heart and literally performed miracles. The average Ford car had some 15,000 separate parts. The B-24 Liberator long-range bomber had 1,550,000 parts and at the Ford plant in Michigan, one came off the line *every 63 minutes!* Chrysler made fuselages and became the largest tank factory in the country. General Motors made airplane engines, trucks and tanks. Packard made Rolls-Royce engines for the British air force.

Shipyards from Maine to Mobile turned out tonnage so fast that by the autumn of 1943 all Allied shipping sunk since 1939 had been replaced. Liberty Ships, the "Ugly Duckling" workhorses of World War II, were built in 13 states. The early Liberty Ships took about 230 days to build, but during the war, the average production time dropped to 42 days.

In addition to the staggering war production, throughout 1942 American troops were landing in Great Britain by the thousands. They were stationed everywhere from Scotland to Cornwall and all parts in between. For the most part they were young citizen-soldiers, full of piss and vinegar and righteous indignation at the unprovoked bombing of Pearl Harbor. They were anxious to get in on the war and at that point they still thought they were invincible.

For more than two years, the Brits had almost single-handedly been fighting the Germans. They had seen buddies wounded and killed. They were glad to see the Yanks, but they could do without the Mighty Mouse here-we-come-to-save-the-day attitude. The Tommies made an effort to hold their tongues because they knew the first taste of combat would change the Yanks' minds about the glory of war.

The War Department made an effort to ease tensions. They prepared a small pamphlet called "Instructions for American Servicemen in Britain." It contained advice such as, "Don't be a show off," and "NEVER criticize the King or Queen. The British don't know how to make a good cup of coffee. You don't know how to make a good cup of tea. It's an even swap." It ended with this directive. "It is always impolite to criticize your hosts; it is militarily stupid to criticize your allies."

The womenfolk in Dawsonville woke up each day and thanked their lucky stars their men hadn't been called up yet. Against all odds, they celebrated Christmas 1942 at home, but they knew time was running out.

CHAPTER SIXTEEN

True to her threat, Emma went with Mattie to the hospital and from the day she arrived she did indeed take over. After she got the bookkeeping in order, she moved on to what was euphemistically called the sunroom. The windows were so dirty the sun could hardly get through and what little light did get in was quickly swallowed by the washed-out gray walls. Men slumped on couches and slouched in wheelchairs like formless bundles of dirty laundry.

"God, this place would gag a maggot!" Emma announced at the top of her voice. She had heard a young boy use the phrase just before his mama boxed his ears. She rather liked the sound of it and was pleased to find a situation it fit so well. She and Mattie discussed the situation on the way home and the next day they showed up with a dozen half-full cans of paint in various colors.

As usual Emma took over. She didn't ask for volunteers, she issued orders. If she heard murmurs of "it's just like back in the army," she ignored them.

"Go find two ladders. Get the brushes and those stir sticks out of my car. Put these newspapers down on the floor. Open the cans and stir up the paint." She assigned three men to a wall, one on the ladder, one standing and one in a wheelchair. Each wall was to get a different color. "Get busy."

That taken care of, she turned to the windows. "Go find two big buckets, fill them half full of water and bring them back in here. Get that ragbag, the newspapers and the vinegar bottles out of my car. Mix the vinegar and water half-and-half. Wash with rags first then dry with newspaper. Get busy."

By the end of the day, the patients had transformed the room. The afternoon sun poured through the sparkling clean windows and bounced off the colorful walls. It was a good start.

The next morning Emma and Mattie were shocked to see that someone had written all over the newly painted walls. Emma was about to go on the warpath when Mattie noticed that the scribbles on the walls were actually cartoons of the patients, wounds and all.

As the GIs arrived in the sunroom, they were upset too, until they realized what they were seeing and then they started looking for themselves and laughing! It was the most beautiful sound Emma or Mattie had ever heard.

It was Mattie who finally discovered the artist, a shy young man by the name of Hector Lightfoot. He had lost both legs below the knee. "Hector, these are wonderful," she said, "but how did you draw the ones high up on the wall?"

Hector laughed. "Big Mo put me up on his shoulders. He held on to my stumps so I wouldn't fall. It was great. I ain't never been that tall before."

Mo was a sturdy farm boy who had lost an eye in the fighting. His picture showed a patch over his missing eye, but his good eye was looking at one of the nurses and the gleam was unmistakable.

That was the beginning. The second miracle happened by accident. On visitors' day a youngster about five was left on his own while his mother went to visit her son in the wards. The little boy started talking to one of the patients who habitually sat alone hiding the hook where his left hand had been. He refused to speak at all.

"What happened to your hand, mister?"

The young man instinctively pushed the hook farther under the blanket, but he didn't respond. The boy didn't seem to notice. "I wanna know what happened to your hand."

"It got blown off by a bomb."

"Wow. Did it hurt?"

"Not at first, but then, yeah, it hurt like a son-of-a...gun."

"Was you scared?"

"Most of the time, I was."

"Did you pray? Sometimes I do that when I get real scared. What's your name?"

"Eli."

"I'm Jimmy. Pleased to meetcha." They shook hands.

Emma was amazed. Most people made a point of ignoring the injuries, but she realized the natural curiosity of the boy gave the patient a chance to talk about what happened without sounding like a crybaby. From then on, she encouraged the families to bring young children with them. Babies were especially popular. Lots of the men just liked to hold them.

The patients were urged to write letters once a week. However, most patients treated that chore like slow torture. Mattie volunteered to do the writing for them, but it didn't help. "Got nothing to say," was the usual response. Mattie came up with a solution, a fill-in-the-blanks letter. They could fill in the words, or copy the letter over. Their choice.

A typical letter might go like this. "I am feeling... Please send me some... The best thing about this place is... The worst thing is... Yesterday I had to laugh when... I have a new friend whose name is... We talk about... all the time. The thing I miss the most is... The food here is ..." She was careful to include places to say good things and places to get some things off their chests. Before long the men were writing on their own.

Emma realized that the war had torn these men apart and made them old before their time. Underneath though, they were still young men, so she invited Skye to visit. "Do *not* wear those overalls. Put on something pretty and let your hair hang down."

Just looking at Skye was a treat. But the icing on the cake was when she apologized for having grease under her nails and they discovered she knew about cars. They couldn't have been more excited if she had shed her clothes and danced naked on the table. Skye could talk about cylinder heads, engine blocks, transmissions and carburetors with the best of them. In fact she put most of them to shame. They loved it.

On top of that, when Skye came, so did Dog. He was devoted to her, but way down in his canine heart, he missed the masculine touch he remembered from Finn. Men petted differently and sounded different and smelled different. "This is a great place. Everybody wants to pet me. If nobody stops me, I'll just wander into all the rooms and say hello to everybody." Dog went into the wards and nuzzled the hands of soldiers lying in bed. The doctors and nurses just shook their heads and looked the other way. The men couldn't help but smile at Dog's big, happy, fuzzy face.

As a result of Skye's visits, Junky decided to come with her one day. They arrived in a 1940 Ford V-8 fitted with a supercharged Cadillac ambulance engine, a real whiskey car. He parked in the back of the hospital, raised the hood and waited while patients who could walk helped those who couldn't.

They crowded around while Junky gave them a crash course in how to soup up an engine. He won a special place in heaven when he pointed to Eli's hook and said, "You got one up on me, Son. You're never gonna get burned on a hot exhaust pipe. With that thing you can handle stuff nobody else would touch. That'd make you an asset to any garage. If you want a job, come see me when you get released."

Junky went on to tell them that Skye was one of the best whiskey mechanics he had ever seen and said she knew all kinds of tricks for getting more power out of these flathead V-8s. Bore them, stroke them, add hotter cams and bigger carburetors, whatever it took to boost the engine to roughly 500 horsepower.

"Both my husband and my twin brother were trippers and they loved this 1940 V-8 because it handled real good at high speeds." Skye said. "That's mostly because of its torsion bar."

The men nudged each other. "How many women do you suppose even know what a torsion bar is?"

"You see most of the time trippers are drivin' with nothin' but moonlight along dirt-road switchbacks. They'll get up to 100 miles an hour and they're carryin' 100 gallons of highly-flammable liquid in their trunks and back seats. Come over here and Junky'll show you." At that point, Junky opened the trunk and showed them how it could be loaded with 100 to 132 gallons of moonshine.

The sounds of battle had left some of the men skittish, so Junky warned them of the noise, but if anyone was interested they were welcome to get behind the wheel and crank up the engine. Some men went back inside, but most of them stayed. Noise wasn't so scary when you were the one making it.

After Junky and Skye's visit, Emma racked her brain to think of something to top that, so she organized a band. Not just any band, but one tailor-made to the Soldier's Hospital. No fancy-schmancy instruments, only things easily available and cheap. A bucket turned upside down and a couple of dowel rods made a fine drum. Add wire brushes for a jazz vibe. A washboard and thimbles and some wood blocks filled out the rhythm section.

A metal bedpan and a couple of case knives added some high notes. One shy kid from the mountains played the spoons and was glad to give lessons. Another patient played an empty moonshine jug. It wasn't exactly a wind instrument, but it made a nice noise.

One of the last patients to join the band was a kid who said he played a vacuum cleaner hose. Emma was skeptical. "Just close your eyes, Ma'am, and tell me what you hear." What she heard were the big fat notes of a tuba. "You're in," she said.

Throw in a harmonica and a fiddle to carry the tune and add the twang of a Jew's harp—or juice harp to some folks—and the band was in business. To everyone's surprise, at the next rehearsal, Mattie showed up with a wash-tub base and joined the group. Emma announced their first concert and a celebration with hot dogs and fire crackers. The band didn't do so well on ballads, but they really rocked the joint on *Yankee Doodle*.

Shortly after that, Emma was at the Piggly Wiggly when a worn-out looking woman with several children hanging onto her skirts reached out and shook her hand. "I just wanna thank you for the shine. When my man was fightin' the cancer, that was the only thing what gave him any relief. I'm much obliged."

She was gone before Emma could respond. It took a while, but Emma finally figured it out. The woman had mistaken her for Mattie. Emma couldn't get the woman's sad face out of her mind and whenever she thought about her, she got a bad feeling, like an itch she couldn't scratch.

With wartime sugar rationing, hardly anybody was making shine any more. Almost all the moonshiners in the county had packed it in and were working in war production of some kind. But just because nobody was making shine didn't mean there wasn't still a need for it. And that's when Emma got an idea. She would make shine.

Clearly she would need some help, so naturally she talked to Mattie who confessed she had been thinking about the same thing. They decided to clean up the little still the kids weren't using any more. They didn't start out to keep the enterprise to themselves, but the more they worked on it, the more they realized having a secret was fun.

Emma figured out how to get around the problem of rationed sugar. "We'll go back to the way my grandpa made shine. He used sprouted corn to make its own sugar. Natural fermentation takes longer and it wouldn't work if we needed to make a lot of whiskey fast, but we don't."

In the simplest terms, if they arranged the right amounts of the raw materials in the right order, applied heat and then cooled the steam back into liquid, Mother Nature would do her part and they'd have shine. No store-bought sugar needed.

They already had a list of loyal customers. They would take care of them and hold back enough shine to give away to folks who really needed it. The Soldiers' Hospital received their first donation.

The one thing Mattie wasn't prepared for in working with wounded soldiers was the fact that rehabilitation involved pain. There was no way around it. To get better, patients had to go through what they called "the hard stuff."

The nurses who supervised the exercise sessions pushed the patients beyond their limits and Mattie saw some of the young men throw up when the pain of moving a joint or stretching a muscle got to be too much. What most surprised her was seeing the nurses who were hard as nails with the patients sobbing after a session. Everybody, patients and nurses alike suffered.

The men who had been through it tried to help the new ones by explaining they just needed to hang on long enough to get "over the hump." They promised the pain would taper off and the exercises would get easier. "You just have to be patient."

Neither Mattie nor Emma put much store in being patient. "Emma, we just gotta do something," Mattie said. The next morning she came to work carrying a vile-looking brown bottle which she said contained tonic. After a patient finished a hard session, she'd pull out the bottle and a long-handled kitchen spoon.

"Tilt your head back, open your mouth, hold your nose if you want to, and swallow it down all at once. It's gonna burn, but it'll do the trick. Then go lie down for a couple of hours."

The dosage was always the same, two spoonfuls, one after the other. Maybe it was the burning sensation as the tonic went down, maybe it was the power of suggestion or the deep sleep that allowed sore muscles to relax. Whatever it was, it worked! Mattie's tonic helped more than one young soldier get "over the hump." The women were proud that they could contribute something valuable to the war effort.

THE WAR: OVER HERE
AND OVER THERE

(1942 – 1945)

*"You can always count on the Americans to do the right thing,
after they have tried everything else.*
Winston Churchill

CHAPTER SEVENTEEN

Every day in 1943 was a gift. Then, on September 23, the postman delivered the letter everyone had been dreading for over a year. "Greetings." That one simple word brought the war home to Dawsonville. Men were told when and where to report for induction followed by basic training, then a two-week furlough before shipping out at the end of December. They were given a week to get ready.

Finn couldn't wait to get to the war. Gus, on the other hand, had a lot more to leave. Because he knew the way Finn felt, Gus was left with no one to talk to. He didn't want to sound unpatriotic, but he didn't want to go to war either. He decided to walk back to Duncan's old still and try to think the problem through.

He was sitting there with his head in his hands when Skye walked into the clearing. Without a word, he stood up, took her in his arms and kissed her with an urgency she hadn't felt before. Just days ago they had all the time in the world. Now it was gone. Everything was moving double-time. Gus felt older. Skye felt excited. She ran her hands under his shirt and felt the warmth of his skin.

"If she's impatient, she'll help you." He heard Miss Rita's voice and thought, "Oh my God, this is it." In an instant, Gus forgot the war.

He untied the ribbon holding Skye's hair, then he ran his hands through the soft curls. "Slow," he told himself, go slow.

He took her face in his hands and kissed her, working his way down her neck as he unbuttoned her blouse.

She didn't stop him and when his fingers touched her breasts, his resolve to go slow deserted him all together. He wanted to touch her everywhere all at once. "Skye, I want to be with you... *now.* I mean, all the way." He pulled at her skirt and was about to undress her right there in front of God and everybody.

"Lord help me," Skye thought. "This is it. This is when I'm supposed to say no, but it feels so good I don't want him to stop." It took all the will power she could muster to grab his hand and stop him. She tried to catch her breath. "Gus we can't do this here. What if somebody comes along? We need a place to be alone."

Gus started counting to 100 and tried to hear what Skye was saying. It sounded like no, but it definitely didn't feel that way. "I thought this was what you wanted."

"I do. Oh, I *really do,* but not this way. I want our first time to be, well, I don't know, not like this." She looked at the smashed still and the briars and brambles sprouting up everywhere. "I want to be in bed with you, in a room where we can do whatever we want and then..."

Gus only hesitated a minute then blurted out, "Let's get married. Then we can be together every night until I have to leave." He rushed on, sounding like Finn with one of his wild ideas. "We could do it after church on Sunday. Everyone will be there anyway..."

Skye had stopped listening after "together every night." "OK," she said.

For a moment they stood in stunned silence, each lost in their individual thoughts about what was about to happen. Skye suddenly wondered where she could find a wedding dress with just two days' notice. Gus wasn't thinking about wedding dresses, his thoughts were elsewhere.

It was amazing how fast the idea turned into reality. Maybe Finn's approach to life was right after all. Sunday morning—with Finn as best man and Mary Beth as maid of honor—Sean Calhoun gave his daughter Skye Calhoun to be married to Angus McLagan. She wore a white dress made by Emma and Mattie. They had the reception in the basement of the Methodist church. Everyone was relieved they weren't required to drink lime sherbet floating in a sea of ginger ale, better known as Green Baptist Punch.

Mary Beth might not have been impressed with Finn and his snakebite when they were kids, but now she saw him in a whole new light. The two of them lingered after most of the other guests left. Thinking something like that might happen, Mary Beth had prayed about it ahead of time. As far as she was concerned, the Lord had told her it would be all right just once since Finn was going off to war. After he left, she could go back to being a virgin.

Junky gave the newlyweds the key to the spare room over the garage as a wedding present. Gus carried Skye over the threshold and immediately took off his shoes and socks. Then he picked Skye up and carried her to the bed. They managed to slowly undress each other, but after the touch of skin on skin, there was no way to slow down.

"Next time I'll go slow," he whispered. Skye wasn't complaining. Gus seemed to know exactly where and how to touch her. She had no idea she could feel so good in so many places all at once. Skye laughed, that oh-God-that-feels-good kind of laugh, that joyful noise Gus was hoping to hear. He laughed too. True to his word, the second time Gus took his time and followed Miss Rita's instructions to the letter.

It was afternoon before Skye and Gus finally got up. As they were walking to the McLagans, they saw Doc. "Morning Gus, morning Skye. Or should I say good afternoon Mr. and Mrs. McLagan?"

Skye blushed slightly. "Gus, you go on ahead, I want to talk to Doc a minute. Don't worry, I'll be right there."

"Skye, is there something I can do for you?"

"Yes. I want you to give me that woman's address in Atlanta." Doc looked worried. "Gus told me all about it." Skye let him suffer a minute more. "I want to send her a thank-you note," she said with a knowing smile. This time it was Doc's turn to blush.

A week later Gus and Finn reported for induction. Gus sailed through the physical exam and was assigned to Services of Supply, the Quartermaster Corps.

Finn was rejected because he had flat feet. However, there was no way he was going to be classified 4-F. He got into an argument with the doctor and ended up pleading his case to the captain in charge. "Son, if you can't walk, you can't march and if you can't march you *cannot* be in the United States Army."

Finn wouldn't give up. "There's gotta be something I can do. I been walking all my life and I ain't had a problem, but if you say I can't walk, OK, I can't walk. But, listen Doc, I can *drive* like a son-of-a-gun. There's gotta be vehicles in the Army and somebody's gotta drive 'em."

"So you want to get behind the wheel of a deuce-and-a-half and go hot-rodding..."

"Oh no Sir. I'm fast, but I'm careful. I've been driving since I was a kid and I ain't never spilled a drop..."

"STOP!" the captain ordered. He looked at Finn, then studied the file lying open on his desk. "You're from Dawsonville, is that right?"

"Yes, Sir."

"Did a lot of driving down Highway 9, did you?" Finn nodded. The Captain smiled, "Well, Son, I think Uncle Sam might be able to use your services after all. You have just become a part of the American Field Service. For your information, that's the voluntary ambulance service." He stood up and looked Finn in the eye. "I want to make sure you understand you will be driving our most precious cargo. You got that?"

"Yes, Sir."

"In that case, welcome to the Army."

The next hurdle was basic training. They got their heads shaved, were given shots for every disease known to man, were issued uniforms and learned how to make beds and pack footlockers. After basic, they each received two more weeks of specialized training, then finally they got their orders and headed home for two weeks to enjoy Christmas and say good-bye to their families.

Finn and Gus weren't the only ones leaving, so the whole town threw a huge going-away party. Friends and neighbors bundled up and visited from house to house eating, drinking, singing, dancing and telling their young men good-bye.

The crowd finally ended up at a big bonfire in the vacant lot between the McLagans and the Calhouns. A large banner stretched between their two houses said, "Good Luck and God Bless Angus McLagan and Patrick Seamus Calhoun." Folks looked confused. "What about Finn? Where's his sign?"

"You'll have to ask Emma about that," Sean said. "She named him that, but I made it clear I wasn't havin' me only son called Paddy by the likes of those who don't know any better." So, of course, for the rest of the evening, Finn was called Paddy by one-and-all. Finally things quieted down a bit and someone called for a story. "Sean, tell us one of your Irish stories."

"It will be my pleasure to educate you sorry lot with a story about the greatest Irish hero who ever lived, Finn MacCool, me son's namesake. Now let's see, I reckon I could try to recall one wee story." Sean never sounded more Irish than when he was telling an Irish story. The audience laughed. They had been listening to Finn MacCool stories from Sean all their lives.

Sean cleared his throat and began. "Twas in the North of Ireland, a most beautiful place, with hills, windin' rivers and lakes scooped out by giants. And rocks! Some of them so heavy all of y'all together couldn't lift one.

"But that made no difference to Finn MacCool, who was one huge, great giant. He wasn't afraid of anything in Ireland, but he was a trifle uneasy about Benandonner, another giant who lived in Scotland. They used to throw insults at each other across the causeway. One day Finn gathered up a great store of six-sided stones. He planted them deep in the water and built a perfect road. 'Come across that if you dare!' he yelled at Benandonner.

"And do you know what happened? Benandonner took the dare. As the giant got closer, Finn realized he was a lot bigger than he looked standing across the bay. Finn knew right away he had bitten off more than he could chew. So he did what any right-thinkin' Irishman would do, he went home to ask his wife for help.

"Now everybody knew his wife—I'm gonna just call her Emma—everybody knew she was a lot smarter than ole Finn. Without a moment to spare, she shoved him into a great empty tub normally used for washing clothes. She threw a couple of sheets over him and stuck a petticoat on his head to look like a baby's cap.

"When Benandonner arrived, Emma invited him in. 'Sure and it's a pity Finn's not home. Make yourself comfortable, but be careful not to wake the wee baby.' That was Finn, of course, lyin' in the washing tub.

"Then Emma fried up some griddle-bread, and put the iron griddle between the slices. When Benandonner bit into it, he broke three front teeth. In order to soothe his gums, she gave Benandonner a gallon bucket of shine.

"When he finished the shine, she invited him to come over and take a look at the wee baby. Well, Benandonner was feelin' a bit woozy from all that shine, and when he saw Finn lyin' there suckin' his thumb, he got a shock. If *that* was the baby, he was pretty sure he didn't want to meet the father.

"Just then, Finn jumped up, threw off his disguise and chased Benandonner out of Ireland. He threw a handful of clay at him, but he missed and it fell into the Channel. They call it the Isle of Man now. Then Finn started tearing out the stones he had used to build the bridge. And Benandonner did the same thing across the bay. They just left the ragged ends on either side. My great, great, great, great grandfather swore he saw them and that proves this story is one hundred percent, absolutely true."

The crowd cheered and passed the moonshine jars around again. "Now Duncan, you've got to stand up for the Scots. We know you've got at least one story."

Duncan stood up looking a little sheepish. Truth be told, that was exactly what he had, one story. It was a poem he learned from his grandfather when he was a boy and it was anchored in his memory as only childhood rhymes can be. "Tiz *The Dancing Lass of Anglesey* I'll be reciting.

"Listen my friends to a tale of the time when battles were fought and yet none would be killed.

The victor was chosen by dancer's skill and not by the measure of most blood spilled.

In Scotland long ago, a king was ashen pale with fright
He trembled to think that 15 men would claim his lands that night.

They were coming to dance his lands away, with pounding steps and graceful sway.

Each was a dancing champion with steps so firm and strong
None of the King's own champions could dance as fine or long.

'I'll lose my gold. I'll lose my lands,' the king worried and wrung his hands.

'I cannot gain the victory 'till I find the lass from Anglesey. None can dance as well as she.'

He sent north and south and east and west to find the one who danced the best.

'Go forth, my Lords, and bring to me the Dancing Lass of Anglesey.

They say she dances the time away till flowers bloom and wheat crops sway,

Till everything dies and fades away, till nothing can stand anymore.

She dances the season, she dances the time, she dances the tides, the ageless rhyme.

With delicate feet she keeps the beat, till none can stand anymore. She'll dance them to the floor.'

Well, they found her on a distant hill and brought her before the king

'If you'll dance for me,' he said, 'I'll give you anything.

'I'll give you a mill and lands,' he said, 'and my bonniest knight for you to wed.'

She replied, 'I'll take your mill. I'll take your land, I care not for a knight to take my hand.

'So keep your bonny boy, I'll dance just for the joy.'

And so came them all to the great king's hall and she danced them one by one.

With delicate feet she kept the beat till none could stand anymore.

She stepped, she twirled in a dancer's world, till they lay in a heap on the floor.

When the 15 knights were all undone, she danced the king's men one by one.

And then she took the king and danced him to the floor.

She leapt about the heap of men who could not fight any more.

So she gathered their swords and their silver buckles and out the door went she.

For none could dance as long or strong as the Lass from Anglesey, The Dancing Lass from Anglesey.

Oh, I wish that it were in modern times, a battle could be fought and yet none would be killed.

The champion would be chosen by dancer's skill and not by the measure of most blood spilled."

In the hush that followed, Duncan hugged Gus and there was many a tear in many an eye that night.

The next morning every whiskey car in Dawsonville and the surrounding county was lined up to make one last run down Highway 9. Sheriff Hamilton, Homer Webster and the rest of the local revenuers led the parade. Finn drove, his parents sat in the back seat and Dog happily rode shotgun. Skye rode with Gus and his family. The rest of the cars were filled with friends and family. Their destination was Union Station in Atlanta.

When they reached the station, Dog walked proudly by Finn's side as they went through the big building filled with soldiers. The McLagans and the Calhouns made their way to the tracks where the train waited patiently.

There was a lot of hugging and kissing and then another round of hugs and kisses. Dog waited while everyone said good-bye. Finally Finn knelt down to say good-bye to Dog, then he stepped onto the train. Dog followed. Everyone laughed. Finn got down and so did Dog. Finn tried to board again and Dog was right behind him. "I like this new game," Dog thought.

The third time Finn insisted that he stay with Skye. She knelt beside him and explained that he couldn't go with Finn this time. So he stayed, but he kept his eyes on Finn. When the boy disappeared, Dog howled. Skye tightened her grip, then there was a lot of noise and Finn was gone.

Dog broke free and tried to run after the train, but Skye caught him. He was very confused. "Where is Finn? Where is everybody going? They can't leave." Dog hesitated a minute then he ran to the end of the platform and howled at the train again, but it didn't stop. "I don't understand," Dog thought. He barked at the train once more and then he sadly turned around. "I guess I better go back because I've been lost once and I don't want to get lost again." He hung his head and slowly walked back to meet Skye.

When they got to the car, Dog hesitated again. Since Finn wasn't driving, he didn't know where he belonged. Skye climbed into the back seat and patted the space beside her. Reluctantly, Dog obeyed. On the way home, he put his head on her lap and she petted him. "It's not Finn, but I guess she'll have to do until he comes home again."

They were all in for a long wait.

CHAPTER EIGHTEEN

The boys were on their way and World War II began in earnest for the citizens of Dawsonville. Like they had done since Pearl Harbor, they listened to President Roosevelt's radio broadcasts and hung on each and every word from, "Good evening, friends," until the last notes of the national anthem died away. So far, the reports had just been about the course of the war, but now the news was personal.

FDR and the news broadcasters casually mentioned divisions of men. Emma looked up the word and found out that a division was between 10,000 and 18,000 men! She was absolutely shocked, especially since the entire population of Dawson County was less than 5,000.

Douglas Edwards on WSB radio and Edward R. Murrow on CBS both reported that a million and a half Americans were being sent to England to help the Allies who had basically been fighting alone.

A week after the boys left, letters began to arrive. Gus, as was his nature, paid attention to everything and his first letter was full of facts. "I started this letter on the train, but now we're here at Camp Kilmer in New Jersey. This place holds nearly 40,000 troops!! I reckon that's more than all the people in Georgia.

"Once all the training is over, they'll put us on ferry boats to take us to the embarkation piers, probably Pier 54 in New York City, and then on to the troop transports. Me and Finn are trying to stay together, but because we've got different jobs, we'll probably be separated. Since I'll be working in supply, I don't think I'll have to go to the front. It'll be our job to stay behind the lines and make sure everything like fuel, food, supplies, weapons and ammunition gets to the guys who need it.

"I'm kind of worried because some guys say crossing the North Atlantic this early in the year can be rough. It'll probably take about six days, maybe more if we have bad weather or have to avoid German U-boats. I sure don't want to get seasick.

"I miss everybody. Once we get settled, we'll have an APO, that's Army Post Office address, and you can write to me. I'll sign off for now. Love, Gus."

"Skye, what does your letter say?" Mattie asked. Skye hesitated. She unfolded her letter and scanned it quickly. "Well, he says he misses me and he loves me and... he promises to keep his shoes and socks on all the time." She looked up and smiled innocently.

Duncan and Mattie exchanged looks. "That sounds... sensible," Duncan said.

Finn's letter was totally different. "You will not believe we're going to sail right up the North Channel between Scotland and Ireland. We'll be real close to the Isle of Man and maybe I'll see Finn MacCool's bridge.

"Gus and me are probably not going to be able to stay together for long. Since I'm going to be driving an ambulance, I'll be right close to the front lines. Don't worry about me. I'll just pretend the Germans are revenuers and I know I can outrun them.

"Tell Doc I'm learning different kinds of bandaging and how to give morphine shots. I'm learning everything I can. Never know when it might come in handy.

"Everybody's got a nickname. Somehow they found out I was a moonshiner, so now everybody calls me Shine. Ha! Ha! They call Gus, The Professor. That's because he remembers everything he reads in the training manuals.

"I can't wait to get out on the ocean. Some of the boys think it's funny that I've never seen an ocean. When I ask them if they've ever seen a moonshine still, they shut up.

"Everybody wants to know what moonshine tastes like. I tell them it's like swallowing lightning. The boys from South Carolina, Kentucky and Tennessee back me up on that. We make it sound as bad as possible.

"When we get to our duty station, I'll probably get a Dodge ambulance. I was hoping for a Ford, but I don't reckon I'll have much choice.

"Well, it's chow time and they feed us pretty good, so I don't want to be late. Give my love to everybody. Love, Finn. PS: Tell Dog I miss him too."

Dog had attached himself to Skye and had become the mascot of the garage. "This is a good place to explore new smells, a safe place to sleep and there's always somebody to pet me. All in all, I think it's a good place to wait for Finn to come home."

The warnings about the North Atlantic crossing proved to be accurate. For the first couple of days, Gus was seasick but eventually he got his sea legs. With typical teenage humor, the lucky ones divided their fellow passengers into two groups: the Upchucks and the Uprights.

The crossing took about a week and the troops were anxious to move forward as soon as they landed. There was real excitement in the air because everyone knew something big was coming. On the other hand, it was cold and rainy and the drills were carried out using live ammunition. Welcome to the war.

In some places, whole fields were covered with jeeps, tanks, trucks, bulldozers and piles and piles of supplies. In the midst of all the activity, Gus found time to write home. No more long letters. Now everything had to fit on V-mail, one sheet of paper that folded to become its own envelope. Gus kept his letters short, one for family, one for Skye.

"Working with the Quartermasters is kinda like packing up everything in Dawsonville, loading it on a ship and sending it halfway around the world. Then somebody else unloads it, puts it on trucks and sends it off to a dozen other places where another somebody has to check it off a list and put it all away again. We handle everything from guns to razor blades. When a GI reaches for something, it's got to be there. All the items have to be listed just exactly right or somebody who needs ammunition might end up getting toilet paper instead. My sergeant says I'm a natural because I pay attention. Time to go. Love, Gus."

He knew his parents shared their letters with Skye, so he didn't waste space telling her about his work. "I'm pretty sure somebody here reads our mail, so I can't really say what I want to say. Just know that I think about you and about us all the time. From the time I took off my shoes until I put them back on, I remember every detail. I love you.

"It's cold here and we're living in tents. I sure wish you were here to keep me warm. All the guys talk about their wives and sweethearts. When I tell them how pretty you are *and* that you know all about cars, they think I'm about the luckiest guy in the Army. I agree. Please send me a picture in your next letter. I know my dad took some with the Kodak at the wedding. I just wish we'd get started so we could get this over with. Never forget that I love you. Gus"

Finn paid no attention to the shortage of writing space. If he was in the middle of a thought, he just started another letter. "I'm still getting medical training. I haven't seen an ambulance yet, but trucks and jeeps are everywhere. I thought these guys were supposed to speak English, but now I'm not so sure. Over here, cars don't have hoods and trunks, they have bonnets and boots and the pavement isn't the road, it's the *sidewalk*. But the weirdest thing is tea. Nobody over here has ever heard of ice tea, in fact, they can't imagine why anybody would want to drink cold tea.

"When they unloaded the ship at the dock, the workers had this tank in a big net, which is how they unload stuff. Anyway they had a crane that hauled it out of the ship and swung it over the side to the dock. When it was about half way over, somebody yelled 'tea time' and they just left it hanging up in the air while they all went off to have tea and crumpets, whatever they are.

"Everybody knows something is up and the waiting is getting on everybody's nerves. I wish they'd get on with it.

"Love to everybody. Tell Dog hello."

The main holdup was the weather. The invasion required a full moon and clear skies to expose the German underwater defenses. It also had to coincide with low tide and the landing site had to be within easy range for the British Spitfires and the American Thunderbolts. The last hurdle was the Channel itself. Rough seas and high winds could scuttle the operation before it ever got started.

For Gus, June 3 started out like every other day: reveille, chow, plan of the day. His sergeant hardly glanced up as the troops filed in and found seats. Then abruptly he came to attention. "Officer on deck!"

"At ease, gentlemen, take your seats. I have been asked to distribute a letter dictated by General Eisenhower in which he says, 'You are part of the greatest fighting force the world has ever known and we are on the eve of the most extensive amphibious invasion ever conceived. I wish each of you God's speed.'"

"Damn," Gus said. "I'm gonna send this home to Ma. She's never gonna believe I got a letter signed by General Dwight D. Eisenhower. Who knows, he might do something important someday."

A wave of excitement had gone through the room. Sgt. Wheeler watched the scene and shook his head sadly. He was a lifer, career Army. He'd seen action as a young man in the last war and he was only too well aware of what was to come. He thought of the group as his boys and he knew that more than half of them would not make it off the beach.

"For God's sake, pipe down and don't be in such an all-fired hurry to get your goddamn heads blown off." He knew it was no use. They were young, they were trained, they were armed and more to the point, they were bored and spoiling for a fight. This was their moment, their time to test themselves against The Enemy. They were too young to know they could die... or worse.

Wheeler bowed to the inevitable. "Alright, you heard the man. Trucks are waiting. Go back to your quarters, pack up your gear, and report back here on the double." A war cry went up and the crowd stampeded toward the door.

It wasn't until they started the hundred-mile trip across the English Channel that Gus and the rest of the men learned they were going to land at Omaha Beach and that they would be the second wave to go in. "Thank God," Gus thought and was immediately ashamed. It was common knowledge that most of the first wave would be killed as soon as they hit the beach.

The pre-dawn darkness was filled with the steady roar of thousands of planes headed across the Channel. The air was saturated with noise from the aircraft and the naval gunfire hitting the beaches.

Gus soon learned there are different degrees of fear. Everyone was afraid of dying, but Gus's immediate fear was having to go over the side of the ship, climb down a slippery rope ladder and drop the last several feet into a landing craft bobbing up and down in six-foot waves.

The men in the first group began to unload and Gus watched helplessly as one of his buddies lost his grip, slipped and—weighted down with his 75-pound pack—sank instantly into the dark water and drowned. Those supervising the loading hardly missed a beat.

Gus was ordered over the side with the second wave an hour later. Although his hands were stiff and cold, he was determined not to drown getting off the boat. Troops were packed shoulder-to-shoulder into the high-sided landing craft. There was no way for them to see what was directly in front of them. It took about three hours to reach the coast. When the transport doors opened, Gus got his first view of the beach and what lay ahead.

The Germans had the high ground and were raining machine-gun fire down from concrete bunkers on top of the cliffs 100 feet above the beach. There was no time to think. Gus stepped off into chest-deep, blood stained water, waded to the beach and then ran for his life across 200 yards of open sand. The beach was covered with blood and the dead and dying men of the first wave who had landed an hour earlier.

Gus took cover behind some burning tanks and disabled artillery. At one point he realized he was crouched behind a pile of bodies washed up against the concrete dragon's teeth put there by the Germans to rip the bottoms out of tanks.

Tears were streaming down his face. "Goddamn, it's not supposed to be like this!" Even with all the noise of the bombardment, the screams of wounded men calling for help cut through everything else.

At one point Gus reached out to help a man with several cameras around his neck drag a wounded soldier to cover. "What the hell is he doing with cameras out here?" he wondered in the instant before he spotted an opening and made another dash up the beach. By late afternoon tanks and trucks started to move off the beach in a more or less orderly fashion. Gus just hoped Finn was part of that group.

As a matter of fact, Finn hadn't landed yet. Like everyone else in his unit, an awful roar startled him out of a sound sleep. He looked out and the sky was full of planes, thousands of them all headed toward France. Then he heard the sound of explosions from across the Channel. It was happening. The invasion had begun.

There was nothing the ambulance outfit could do until the beaches had been cleared of mines. So Finn and his buddies watched and waited as their ambulances were loaded onto a ship ready for the crossing.

That night families all over America listened as FDR said, "My Fellow Americans: When I last spoke with you, I knew that troops of the United States and our Allies were crossing the English Channel. The invasion has come to pass with success thus far."

Roosevelt's words might have been truthful up to a point. But families listening back home knew they were far from the whole story. By the end of that first day, thanks to the big guns on the Navy destroyers, the Nazi batteries had been wiped out and most of the wounded had been evacuated from Omaha Beach. The real story, however, was hidden in the numbers. By official count, 2,500 Americans were killed. The killed, wounded or missing on both sides was a staggering 425,000.

Sergeant Wheeler's estimate was not far wrong.

CHAPTER NINETEEN

Mattie sat quietly holding the last letter from Gus dated May 30. She kept reading one line over and over. "I thought since I was in supply, I'd be behind the lines, but I just found out the Quartermasters will be part of the invasion force, so I guess I'll hit the beach along with everybody else."

"...hit the beach," my God, he had made it sound like a vacation, but Mattie knew better. Emma knew better too. They had both been warned by their sons not to expect letters for a while, but they completely forgot all about that in the anxiety following D-Day.

It was hard to keep track of what happened when, because neither Gus nor Finn was good about dating their letters. To make matters worse, weeks could go by with no letters at all and then a whole bunch would be delivered on the same day. Postmarks couldn't be counted on to keep things in order. The best the women could do was to listen to the current reports on the radio every night, read the newspapers every day, track developments on Emma's map and hope for the best.

Emma complained loudly about the newspapers using what she called cotton words like "advances" and "break out" and "defensive action." They took up space but they didn't actually give you any hard facts. Emma wanted to *know*, to somehow see for herself. What she really wanted—what they all wanted—was instant communication. But that just wasn't available.

For Mattie it was as if the war was on a different planet, a different world all together. But no, today was Wednesday in Dawsonville and yesterday had been just an ordinary Tuesday, except over there it was D-Day and there was nothing ordinary about it.

For want of anything better to do, Mattie and Emma had decided to go to Wednesday night prayer meeting at the Baptist church. The church was nearly full—unheard of for a mid-week service. Apparently lots of folks figured a little extra prayer couldn't hurt.

Toward the end of the service, Doc showed up. He and the preacher talked quietly for a moment. Then Doc faced the congregation, "Y'all may remember some time back I treated a young boy from up in Gilmer County. Feds beat him up pretty bad, broke his arm and left him out in the woods. His family brought him to me 'cause I was the closest doctor. Kid's name is Emmet Baker. Well, his family's been hit by tragedy again, only this time it's his little brother, Bud, who's in trouble.

"His daddy carried him into my office yesterday, I mean literally *carried* him in. Seems like the boy started feeling bad the night before and they thought he just had the flu. He woke up crying in the middle of the night saying his legs felt like pins and needles sticking in them. By the next morning he couldn't walk.

They laid a featherbed and all the quilts they had in the back of their wagon, hitched up the plow horse and drove down here. I examined the boy the best I could and I'm pretty sure he's got polio." That word alone was enough to terrify the congregation.

"We don't know much about polio. Nobody's sure what causes it and there's no cure. It usually hits kids about Bud's age—he's nine—but sometimes adults get it too.

"Best thing we can do is to get Bud to someplace where he can get special help. Now there's a new place up in Hickory, North Carolina. They're having some good results, but they've got an outbreak in their own county, so they're treating mostly folks from their area. Then there's Warm Springs here in Georgia. I want to remind those of y'all who've got small children, to keep 'em close to home and no crowds. If they show any signs of the flu, come see me right away. Now the Bakers' are gonna need..."

Before he could finish the sentence, Edith Mae Howard, president of the Baptist Women's Missionary Union, stood up. "We all know the Lord never sends us more than we can bear, but that poor family has surely had more than their fair share of grief. I propose, and I know the other members of the WMU will pitch in, to make sure that the Baker family is well fed and taken care of while they're here. We'll gather up some clothes and make up some covered dishes and take them over. Just to be on the safe side, Doc, we'll leave everything on the porch."

Mattie felt Emma stiffen and she knew—even if no one else did—that Edith Mae was in imminent danger of being bundled up and left on the porch herself. Mattie patted Emma's hand. "Take it easy, Emma. It's just her way. Don't let your Irish temper get out of control."

Emma pulled away. "Damn it, Mattie," she said under her breath, "what good is havin' an Irish temper if you won't ever let me use it?"

Mattie smiled. "Doc, I'm sure the church ladies can take care of gathering up food and clothes. Emma and Skye and me will make sure Bud gets down to Warm Springs as quick as possible. Where are they stayin' now?"

Sometimes, there's nothing better to solve one problem than to take on another problem. At least helping out the

Bakers was a situation the community could do something about... unlike the war.

"They're over at the old Wilcox place. They've got kin around, but once they heard Bud had polio, nobody wanted to take him in," Doc said. Edith Mae leaned over, smiled and nodded at Emma as if to make a point. Emma made a move in her direction, but Mattie caught her before things got out of hand.

The next morning Skye told Junky about Bud's condition and explained that the Bakers needed to borrow a car. Junky said he had just the thing, a big 1940 Custom DeSoto. He took the back seat out and used a mattress and the featherbed and all the quilts from the Bakers' wagon to make a place for Bud to lie down. Compared to riding in the back of a wagon on the bumpy dirt roads, riding in that DeSoto would be like sailing on a cloud.

Emmet, Bud's oldest brother, had been a tripper before his run-in with the feds. Since they broke his arm he hadn't been hauling, but he was more than capable of driving the DeSoto, so his dad could take the horse and wagon back home. The Baptist ladies packed several picnic baskets for the trip to Warm Springs and one for Mr. Baker to take home.

Mattie knew enough about the treatment at Warm Springs to know that this wasn't going to be just a weekend trip. The family would need supplies for a much longer stay. She packed as many cans of Spam as she could find, some Mason jars of tomatoes, string beans, black-eyed peas and okra from her pantry and added a couple of pans of cornbread.

Emma found a road map and marked the route with a red crayon. She went over it several times with both Emmet and his mother until she was sure they could get to Warm Springs without getting lost.

Both the Baptists and the Methodists decided to take up a love offering. When the Baptists announced that they had raised $9.25, the Methodists passed the plate again and came up with $10.50. Just before she turned the Baptist envelope over to the Bakers, Edith Mae dropped in another $2.25 to bring the Baptist total to $11.50 and give them bragging rights around the county. Christian charity be praised! The Bakers got a grand total of $22.00. It wasn't a fortune, but if they stayed with kinfolks and were careful, it should be sufficient for a month.

Junky filled the car's tank with gas and put a five-gallon can and a couple of cans of oil in a wooden box that he tied to the back bumper. He also put a tool kit in the trunk and gave Emmet some extra gas rations he had collected. The family thanked Junky and Emmet said he was sure he could handle whatever might go wrong with the car along the way.

Early Saturday morning the town gathered to see young Bud on his way to Warm Springs. Doc called ahead to make sure someone was expecting them and that the family would be taken care of. Both congregations congratulated themselves on their good works and to show their appreciation, Mattie, Emma and Skye put in an appearance at both churches the following morning. They drew the line at going to Sunday school.

Another week passed with still no mail from overseas. However, Doc got a call from a colleague in Warm Springs to assure him that young Bud had been admitted and was settling in and getting acquainted with the other patients.

June 19 finally rolled around and like millions of other subscribers, Emma was waiting for the mail and her copy of *Life* magazine. And there it was, D-Day in black and white on the cover. The pictures and captions that filled the 50 pages of the magazine gave American families a ringside seat and their first glimpse of the D-Day landing.

It is a good bet that most of Dawsonville was captivated by a picture of a young soldier protecting his rifle and trying to keep his head above water as he lay on his belly on Omaha Beach. His face was clearly visible. Skye touched the soldier's face and looked at Emma. "You reckon his mama's lookin' at that picture too?" Alone at home, Mattie stared at the picture so long she felt she could almost step into the frame and reach out to help the boy.

***

Robert Capa shifted his weight slightly in the crowded landing craft headed for Omaha Beach. He was one of four civilian photographers credited by the United States to land with the troops. He looked at the faces around him. He had a hard time thinking of them as men because most of them were still in their teens. Soldiers, that's what they were, one and all. At 30 he was an old man by comparison. He was also in uniform and he had a life preserver. But in place of a weapon, he had three cameras slung around his neck and a watertight pouch inside his shirt.

Not for the first time, he wished there were some way to capture the noise all around him because it was as tangible as steel and pressed in on his body from all sides. In his years of shooting other wars, he had learned to wade through the noise like the soldiers around him were wading through the chest-high water. Doing his best to keep his camera dry, he focused and began taking pictures.

When he made it to the beach, he realized by following the troops, he wasn't seeing faces. So he turned his back to the enemy guns. He watched as a young soldier stepped off the landing craft. When the boy reached the beach, he was hit three times in the shoulder. Capa clicked his camera as the soldier fell into the water. In the next instant, he ran to help.

As he reached for the wounded man, a tall, thin soldier also reached out to help. Together they dragged the boy to cover behind some damaged equipment. It happened so fast, Capa didn't see the face of his helper, but he heard him say, "We gotcha, Bubba," and immediately identified his Southern accent. Before he could speak to him, the soldier was gone and Capa went back to work.

For an hour and a half he continued to shoot pictures under fire. Eventually he handed off the pouch with four rolls of 35 mm film to a courier. It was his job to get the film safely across the Channel and deliver it to John Morris the picture editor at *Life's* London Bureau in Grosvenor Square.

Morris was working against a tight deadline. As quickly as possible, the film was developed and contact prints ordered. For some reason the first three rolls were blank. However, the final roll of black and white prints was quickly transferred to Prestwick International Airport in Scotland, and then on to Newfoundland and Washington D.C. Finally it was hand-delivered to Time-Life headquarters on 31st Street in New York City. *Life's* general manager stopped the presses to get the photographs on to the cover and into the June 19 issue, the one Mattie, Emma, Skye and half the country held in their hands that Monday morning.

CHAPTER TWENTY

In the early days of the war, young Alvin Fox loved his job. His bum leg sometimes gave him trouble, but he forgot that when he saw the smiles on the faces of his friends and neighbors as they reached out to get the letters he carried.

A week after delivering all the *Life* magazines, Alvin's mail bag was bulging with letters people had been waiting for since D-Day. Skye was the first person he saw when he left on his rounds. He had a letter for her, so he took the time to go through his mailbag and hand it to her on the street. Her blue eyes sparkled and he fell asleep that night remembering that smile.

Skye sat down on the nearest bench and carefully tore open the V-mail envelope. "Dear Skye, I love you. I made it. I'm alive. Before D-Day I thought of a thousand things a day to write about, but now none of that seems important. The only thing that matters is that I made it through the landing without a scratch! I got the picture in your last letter. Thanks. Now I can prove to all the guys how pretty you are. God I miss you.

"They're keeping me busy. Even with all the guns and the bombs and the noise, tons of stuff were unloaded on the beach, so I got put to work right away. It was chaos. Mostly I was just directing traffic. I helped another guy drag this wounded kid to cover. At first I didn't believe we'd ever make it off that beach, but we did.

Gus's letter continued but more than half of it was blacked out. From what she *could* read, Skye figured out that Gus was probably headed to Paris, which was about 175 miles from Omaha Beach.

"I'll write again as soon as I can. I love you. Gus"

Gus's letter to his parents came the next day and it was a little bit different. "Dear Ma and Pa, I'm alive, but I've never been so scared in my life. We had to wade through water up to our chests. When it dries, the salt makes your clothes stiff and itchy, but at least I didn't get hit. It's a miracle because when we got to the beach we were like sitting ducks. The Krauts were dug in on cliffs above the beach.

"Even after seeing all the blood and the dead bodies, the worst part was the noise. Back home, noise was just part of the fun of racing. Everything is different over here. The noise of the bombs and big guns felt like someone banging on your chest from the inside and trying to bust your eardrums at the same time.

"I can still hear explosions and gunfire, of course, but now they're farther away. I spend most of my time checking off equipment and directing traffic. We Quartermasters manage to eat pretty good, if you like C-rations. Don't worry, I'm fine. Love, Gus."

Alvin finally delivered a letter to Emma and she was so happy she grabbed him and planted a big kiss right on his mouth. The poor boy turned seven shades of red and whirled around so fast he nearly spilled all the mail in her front yard. Emma just laughed. Rather than rip the letter open at once, she walked into the kitchen, poured herself a cup of coffee, kicked off her shoes and sat down to read.

"Dear Everybody and Dog, My Irish luck is holding out. I'm fine. The landing was nothing like I thought it would be. I didn't have to wade ashore, I drove! Before we left England, we waterproofed the ambulance with black, sticky gunk. It's called Cosoline, or something like that. We put it around all the spark plugs, the battery, the distributor cap and then we sealed an extension to the tailpipe so it stuck up about five feet above the roof. We sealed the doors and windows except on the driver's side. Once we got all that done, they loaded us onto the ship to go across the Channel headed to Omaha Beach.

"When we got there, we went from the ship to a big landing craft. It took us as far in as it could go and then John Deere, that's the nickname for the medic who rides with me, crawled in the driver's window and I crawled in after him. Stinky, the cook, and a couple of other guys were already inside. Finally we sealed the window with the same black gunk and then I drove off into the water. I mean *under* the water!

Stinky kept saying, 'Keep her going, Shine, just keep her going.' I put it in four-wheel drive and drove about 100 yards before we came out into the air again. I've never been so glad to see the sky in my life!

"We picked up as many wounded guys as we could get in the ambulance and drove up the hill into a field. We were so glad to be alive, we got out and kissed the ground. Then we scraped the gook off everything and headed to the nearest aid station. That was our first run. I just wanted you to know I'm OK. I miss you. Tell Dog I miss him too. I'll write more later. Love, Finn."

When they finished reading their letters Emma wanted to call their men in Marietta. However, Mattie reminded her that the men would still be at work. Besides, the long distance rates didn't go down until after 6:00 so they should wait. At 6:05 they called the boarding house and the landlady answered.

When she heard the news she hollered up the stairs for Duncan and Sean to come quick. Sean grabbed the phone.

"It's Emma. We got letters. They're alive, both of them. They made it through. Hot damn!" he said as he handed the phone to Duncan.

Emma repeated the message and by the time they hung up everyone was laughing and crying together. Sean confessed he had a jar of shine in his room and the landlady gladly waived her no-drinking rule. The other three boarders were invited to join in and a grand time was had by all.

The next morning before they left to drive to Rome, Mattie and Emma mailed short letters to each of the boys to tell them they had both made it off Omaha Beach.

CHAPTER TWENTY-ONE

Duncan, how much money you got?"

Duncan put down his coffee and checked his pockets. "Two dollars and...seventy-three cents. Why? You wanna borrow some?"

"Lord no! That's the problem. I got too much." Sean sat down in one of the metal chairs on the front porch of their boarding house, put his coffee cup on the floor and breathed out a long, tortured sigh. "I tell you what, this whole money thing is keepin' me up at night. I just don't know what to do about it. I always figured if we had enough to pay our property taxes, keep food on the table and clothes on our backs, we were doin' fine. I worked hard and made enough money to pay my bills. Now we're doin' all that and we still got some left over! It's terrible."

Duncan took a breath, but before he could get a word out, Sean was off again. "Every time I try to think it through, my thoughts get all in a knot. It was hard times when I was growin' up, but it got better. Then I got married and Emma took over worryin' about the money.

All those years that you and me was in the moonshine business, we did good. We spent money to make money. Bought the land, paid to get the corn ground, bought the sugar, bought the stills, bought a car or two, paid for the gas and tires, lost a couple of loads, but all in all we made shine, we sold shine and we paid our way. I understand how that worked. But this is totally different."

Sean stopped just long enough to light a cigarette. Duncan drank his coffee and waited.

"Short of payin' for our room and board here and buyin' bus tickets, we ain't spendin' any money, but every week I get a pay envelope with wages and I take it home to Emma and I reckon you do about the same thing. Now I know this about our wives. The two of them could squeeze a quarter out of a nickel. That's the way it's always been.

But now, I'm workin', Emma's workin', Skye's workin' and Finn is sendin' money home every month. You and Mattie are both workin' and I bet Gus is sendin' his pay home too. What in the world are we supposed to do with what's left over?" Duncan waited some more.

"Back when the Depression hit, I used to feel sorry for those ole boys what had so much money they had to put some of it in the bank and then the banks lost it all. If they'd kept it at home, it woulda been safe. I know one thing. I'm not givin' my money to no bank. But keepin' it around the house don't seem like such a good idea either. Most of the folks I know are real good about stretchin' a dollar, but when the leftovers start to pile up…"

Duncan waited to see if Sean had actually come to a halt. He hadn't.

"I was listenin' to the guys at the plant talk about investin' their money. But as far as I can understand, that means givin' my money to somebody else to make more money, but if he loses it, there's nothin' I can do because I gave it to him in the first place. Now that *really* don't make any sense. I'm tellin' you, Duncan, I never had any idea havin' money could be such a burden." He shook his head sadly.

Apparently Sean had finally run out of steam. "To tell you the truth, Sean, I've been givin' our situation considerable thought myself." He took a long, slow drag off his cigarette, "There's a lot of kids who went off to war like ours did and God willin', a lot of them are gonna be comin' back. But they won't be kids anymore and they ain't gonna want to live at home.

"Take Gus, for instance, he's a married man now. Him and Skye are gonna want a place of their own. So here's my idea, we take a look around for a couple of little old houses in Dawsonville and we buy 'em, fix 'em up and rent 'em out.

"Bell Bomber is a good place to work, but the Army ain't gonna need bombers forever and even if this plant goes to makin' regular planes, I don't wanna work on no assembly line for the rest of my life. If we owned a few houses, then they'd be makin' money for us and we wouldn't even have to tend 'em every day like we did with our stills. Whatchu think?" Duncan gave Sean plenty to time to work it all out in his mind.

"We'd use some of the leftovers to buy the houses, right?"

Duncan nodded.

"And we'd collect the rent?"

"Right."

"What if something got busted?"

We'd take care of it."

"By ourselves?"

"Mostly. Or we'd hire somebody to do it. I was thinkin' about hirin' Curtis Jr. Remember he's the kid that got shot up by the feds?"

"Oh yeah, but who'd pay him?"

"We would, 'cause it'd be our property. Emma and Mattie could set it up so we put away part of the rent money to make repairs."

"But don't that mean we'd just keep on makin' more money?"

"Yeah, but don't forget, we won't be gettin' paid here anymore and the girls will probably lose their jobs too. And we'd have to pay for the upkeep on the houses."

"So we wouldn't make too much money, right?"

Duncan wasn't sure exactly how much Sean considered too much, but the important thing was to get him thinking in the direction of buying houses. "Just enough to get by with maybe a *little* walkin' around money left over."

Sean smiled. "So the leftovers wouldn't be pilin' up so much, right? Damn, Duncan, I think that's a great idea. When do we start?"

"We start by talkin' to Emma and Mattie. If they approve, then we start lookin' for real estate."

"Real estate?!" Sean looked worried again. "That sounds downright...prosperous. Duncan, remember we don't wanna get too prosperous, or I'll have to start worryin' about the leftovers again."

"Listen, Sean, rentin' houses would just be kind of a start-up. If we do have some leftovers, we could use that money to help the kids. I have a feelin' this racing business is gonna cost somebody money sometime."

"We won't get rich?"

"How in the world could anybody get rich drivin' around in circles? Don't worry about it."

Sean's way of looking at business was giving Duncan a headache. He told himself to relax. He had no doubt Emma would convince Sean that being a successful businessman was not an entirely bad thing. That weekend they presented the idea to the women who quickly approved the plan.

Having settled that and knowing that the boys came through the invasion all right took a load off everybody's mind.

The war was going better too. The nightly news reported that the Allies and Free French had entered Paris. Mattie and Emma scanned pictures in *Life* hoping to see Gus or Finn in the sea of American faces. No luck.

They did get letters. Even in the middle of the war, the boys were still talking about driving. "Dear Ma, Pa and Skye. You will not believe that I am now driving a shower truck. After men have been in the field or on the front lines for weeks, you can't imagine how glad they are to see our shower trucks roll in. Everybody turns in their dirty clothes and gets a *hot shower* and clean clothes from the inside out. They keep their boots. The guys come out clean from head to toe with big smiles. It's great.

"We try to get showers to them whenever we can pull troops out of the line, about every two weeks or so. We patch the uniforms just like hand-me-downs back home. Showers and clean clothes may not seem very important, but believe me, after living in the mud and gore for weeks at a time, they are! It's one of the best things I do and I wanted you to know about it.

"Sorry to take up most of my letter talking about dirty clothes. The war is still going on, but there's not much I can tell you about that. I'm still doing OK. I miss you. I love you. Gus"

Finn never wasted time or space on salutations. He just started right in. "I got a brand new, four-wheel drive Dodge Power Wagon with only five miles on it. I painted "White Lightning" on the side. It's one of the few that's got a heater and they tell me I'm gonna really be glad of that come winter.

"Me and John Deere ride together and most of the time we're driving without lights...just like back home. We got two little bitty triangle spaces on the headlights. They don't help you see any better, but they do let the other guy know you're coming.

"Sometimes the only way we can find the wounded is to follow the gun flashes and the noise of the shells. We load up, drive, unload and then do it all over again. We don't get a chance to sleep much and when we do, we just sleep in the ambulance. But it could be a lot worse. I could be one of the guys in the back instead of the driver. Love to everybody and Dog, Finn."

Finn kept his letters light. He wrote about food and that units were always glad to feed a medic. He wrote about the skinny little dog he rescued. He named him Mutt and the dog rode with him in his ambulance. However, he asked the family not to read that part to Dog because he might get his feelings hurt. He wrote about the P08 Luger he took from a dead German soldier. Since most medics choose not to carry any weapons, it was just for self-defense.

What Finn didn't write about was the war. The real war. From the minute he drove onto Omaha Beach, he had been in the thick of it. At first the sight of a dead body sickened him, but he'd gotten over that. It was the wounded, the ones torn apart, that he couldn't forget.

It wasn't his job to decide who would survive and who wouldn't. It was his job to put them on a litter, load them up and drive. But it didn't take a genius to know that a man with half his stomach blown away, who was trying to put his insides back in his body, wasn't going to make it.

Still, Finn tried to give them hope. "Stay with me, Buddy, this is your lucky day. My name's Shine. Back in Georgia, I drove moonshine in a souped up Ford V-8 going a hundred miles an hour in the dark, down twisty red-dirt roads and I never lost a drop. I'm the best damn driver you're ever gonna meet and if anybody can get you to the aid station, it's me. This here's John Deere. He's a medic and we're gonna get you through. You just hang in there. Mutt and ole White Lightning over there will have you on your way in no time." He did his best to sound convincing.

Sometimes ambulance drivers had to deal with pieces of bodies. On one occasion a farmer found a man's head and Finn volunteered to help find the rest of him. Nobody else was willing to go. The men in Finn's unit didn't understand. The dead soldier was out of harm's way. He didn't feel pain any more. He wasn't cold or hungry or afraid. He was free. Wherever he was, he was out of the war and in a better place.

For Finn, the burn cases were the worst. A man could live without an arm or a leg, but how could anyone survive without a face? And who would want to? How could he go home to his family looking like a Frankenstein monster? But Finn had no choice. He loaded them all into his ambulance and drove.

Finn treated the Dodge like another member of the team. He called her Dodge Baby. From the time he drove off the ship into the Channel and Stinky yelled, "Keep her going, Shine, just keep her going," that's exactly what Finn did. He put her in four-wheel drive and together they made their way through the dark and the rain and the mud and the blood and guts of the battlefield to the nearest aid station. And then did it all over again.

CHAPTER TWENTY-TWO

"I got a new job," Gus wrote. "To keep the Germans from sending reinforcements to Normandy, we bombed the French railroad system to smithereens. That stopped the Germans, but now we got another problem. A whole bunch of divisions are headed to Paris and without the railroads, we got no way to supply them.

"So the Army created the Red Ball Express. We got two one-way routes: one from Cherbourg in the south going north to Chartres and a return route back to Cherbourg. The trucks and the roads were marked with red balls. No civilian traffic is allowed. Each one of our trucks has two drivers because we run 24 hours a day. One sleeps while the other one drives. Most of the drivers came from the black non-combat units. I'm running out of room so I'll put the rest in another letter."

The next installment began, "The way I got involved is that my sergeant asked me if I could drive and knew how to fix a truck. I told him if it wasn't busted too bad, I could probably take care of it. Next thing you know, I'm part of the Red Ball Express. I got a co-driver named Lincoln Bedford. He's about my age and believe it or not, he comes from a little town close to Daytona Beach.

"We're supposed to drive in a five-truck convoy escorted front and rear by jeeps. But me and Linc take off as soon as our truck is loaded. Our trucks used to have governors set at 56 miles an hour, but I fixed that and I showed the other drivers how fix theirs too. No need to make ourselves an easy target for the German Luftwaffe.

"Linc likes to play with numbers and he figures by the time we're done, the Red Ball Express will have delivered about 62,250,000 tons of supplies, more or less. Pretty impressive, huh? I guess all that driving on Highway 9 paid off after all. Well, I've got to go, I'll write more later. I love you. Gus."

Once the port of Antwerp opened and the French railroads were repaired, the Red Ball Express was disbanded. Gus and Linc shook hands and promised to look each other up when they got home.

In November, Gus was transferred to a railhead depot in Gouvy, a small village near the Ardennes Forest on the Belgium-Luxembourg border. A few weeks later, newspapers back home were full of stories about the attack launched by Hitler on December 16. His idea was to split the Allied armies by a surprise attack through the Ardennes. The attack caught the Americans completely off-guard and initially the Nazi troops pushed through the Allied line in what the papers called the Battle of the Bulge.

One morning Gus saw American units retreating through Gouvy. "Hey, where are you guys coming from?"

Their position had been overrun and by noon Gus and the rest of the men could hear machine gun fire from all sides. Thinking it was only a matter of time before they were overrun too, the officer in charge decided to evacuate. However, their escape route was blocked by three burning tanks, so they turned around, headed back and prepared to defend Gouvy the best they could.

The CO took a look around. "Listen up. If we're gonna stay here, then by God we're gonna do our job. We may not be able to get *out*, but the troops are still counting on us. So, we're gonna send supplies to any unit that can get a truck *in* to us. If I know our troops, they'll find a way." And they did.

When the word spread that the Quartermasters at Gouvy were still in business, it became a rallying point. Before long, soldiers who had gotten separated from their units started to show up. They were a motley group, but they didn't hesitate to fight against the German tanks and infantry swarming all over the area. Having reinforcements lifted everyone's spirits and the situation didn't look quite as hopeless as before.

Under the cover of darkness, American truck drivers began to arrive. With food, medical supplies and ammunition as a reward, they came in empty and left fully loaded. Perhaps the most important thing they carried was hope.

The expanded Quartermaster group went on the offensive. The Nazis were surprised to find they weren't just dealing with a bunch of storekeepers, they were up against a fighting force.

Thanks to the Quartermasters, American soldiers in the area continued to be well supplied. While their trucks were loaded, drivers got a hot meal and a cup of steaming hot coffee. That went a long way to revive spirits.

Several days into the battle, the CO received a message ordering them to "resist at all cost." There was a moment of silence as he looked at the rag-tag troops before him. Then someone in the back of the room yelled, "Shit, Sir, I thought that's what we *were* doing." The men laughed and went back to work.

Late in December, the garrison at Gouvy finally did have to evacuate. They torched what little was left of the ration dump and left not a moment too soon because within two hours the village was overrun by a large German force.

Early on Christmas Eve, the Quartermasters reached First Army Headquarters. News of their heroic efforts has preceded them and they were cheered by fellow GIs. The troops were justifiably proud of themselves. They had certainly earned the right to be called the Fighting Quartermasters.

Gus, and some of his buddies headed toward the mess hall looking forward to a hot meal. They were laughing and talking and congratulating themselves on a job well done. Suddenly a wounded German soldier came out of nowhere and lobbed a grenade in their direction. His aim was bad and he was so weak it didn't go very far, but it went far enough.

Gus saw a blinding flash of light and heard a very loud noise. For a moment or two, he had no idea what had happened. Then he felt a burning pain all along his right side. When he looked down, his shirt and pants were torn and bloody. His friends were picking themselves off the ground.

"Are you hit?" he tried to say. They seemed to answer, but he couldn't hear them.

He made an effort to walk, but he hadn't taken more than a few steps before the blackness closed in like a curtain being drawn across his eyes. He was powerless to stop himself from falling. For Gus, the war was over.

CHAPTER TWENTY-THREE

Skye felt like a round peg in a square hole. She just didn't fit anywhere anymore. For as long as she could remember she had been part of the kids with Gus and Finn. Now they were gone. Most of the girls she knew from school had long since gotten married and started having babies. The single girls in town had jobs at Bell Bomber in Marietta. Her mother and Mattie were busy with the Soldiers' Hospital.

She was a married woman, but that didn't quite feel right either. She and Gus had a honeymoon and then he was gone. She still lived with her parents and slept in the same bed in the same room she'd always known.She loved her job at Junky's and in the beginning she thought it was great that everyone treated her like one of the boys. They still did, but at the end of the day, they didn't invite her to join them for a beer. And if they had, she wasn't sure she would have gone. But Dog went.

She just wasn't sure where she belonged. Maybe it was just the holidays. The only thing she *was* sure of was that she had a bad case of the blues.

Early in November she and Mattie had carefully packed Christmas boxes for both Finn and Gus. Each one included a fruitcake that had been soaking in moonshine since mid-summer, long johns, gloves, wool scarves and wool socks, all practical, thoughtful things. Unfortunately there was no way to pack hopes and dreams and prayers. They sealed the boxes and sent them on their way.

A couple of weeks later, they got a letter from Finn thanking them for his box and telling them all about his plans for Christmas. "Your Christmas package was great. There are four of us guys sharing a room off the garage where our ambulances are kept. The other driver, Elwin Richie, is my best friend. We call him Gator because he's from Florida. When I told the guys you sent me a fruitcake, they turned up their noses, but when I opened the tin and they smelled the shine, boy, did that change their minds.

"The Army does its best to make Christmas dinner special, so we've decided to share our packages and have a Christmas Eve *breakfast*. We got four fresh eggs from a French family who lives close to one of the aid stations. Each one of us is going to get a fried egg. That's a big deal because you can't fry powdered eggs."

Skye had to laugh because obviously Finn had forgotten that he didn't like fried eggs.

"KC, Gator's medic, got a jar of Kansas City bar-b-que sauce and if you fry Spam and put enough or that stuff on it, it's not half bad. Mutt likes it. John Deere knows where to get cheese and bread. French cheese isn't like Velveeta at all, but once you get used to it, it's pretty good. Gator's mom sent him a wooden box with six big Florida oranges all packed in newspaper. We each get one and we're going to give the other two to the French family who gave us the eggs. We're all set.

"Since I have a heater in my ambulance, I'm sharing the long johns. Wear them a week, wash them out good and pass them on. Everybody is really glad when their turn comes because it's freezing cold around here. We see a lot of guys with frostbite. The smart ones keep a pair of dry socks in their helmet liners and change them a lot. Frostbite can be really bad. When our socks get wet, we dry them out on the engine exhaust.

"I'm on call, so I gotta go. Merry Christmas, thanks for the gifts and I love you. P.S. Love to Dog too, Finn."

Skye finally had to admit it wasn't just the holidays that were making her sad, it was the fact that they hadn't heard from Gus in nearly two months. It had never taken him this long to reply. She and Mattie both checked the mail every day.

To make matters worse, there wasn't much work at the garage. Folks weren't spending money to fix cars this close to Christmas. To fill the time, the crew collected old toys and fixed them up good as new for kids on Christmas morning.

Skye thought something new might make her feel better, so she ordered a red taffeta dress from Sears. It didn't help much, but she wore it when she went with Mattie and Emma to the Christmas party at the Soldiers' Hospital.

Edith Mae Howard and the WMU pitched in to help out. They brought their best covered dishes and prize-winning desserts. That let the kitchen staff take the day off.

Christmas is all about children, so the hospital staff was encouraged to bring their families to the party. Even pets were invited. Dog sported a big red bow. "Since I know everybody around here, I guess it's my job to show the other dogs how to behave," Dog said to himself.

Big Mo dressed up as Santa and gave out candy. Edith Mae played the piano and everyone sang along on their favorite carols. The band performed, but they stayed away from the more melodic selections. However, they did a rousing job on *Jingle Bells*. Then Edith Mae surprised everyone by breaking into a very un-Baptist, honky-tonk version of *Boogie Woogie Santa Claus*.

It was the grandchildren who salvaged Christmas 1944 for the McLagans and the Calhouns. They came in from all over Dawson County. By Christmas Eve, both houses were full of kids sleeping on pallets, which was so much more fun than sleeping on a bed.

Very early Christmas morning the kids all went running around yelling, "It's snowing! It's snowing!" As soon as someone opened the back door, Dog darted outside. He bit at falling snowflakes, kicked up mountains of snow and lay on his back, looking like he was trying to make snow angels. "I love this stuff! I'm going to stay outside all day."

The grandkids momentarily forgot about the snow in their rush to open presents. It was all their parents could do to get them to eat breakfast, but finally they were allowed to go outside and immediately set up a massive snowball fight with Dog right in the middle of the action.

Skye and Mattie went into the living room and waded through wrapping paper, boxes, ribbons and bows. They set aside everything that could be saved until next Christmas. The rest of the day was spent in the kitchen cooking, in the dining room eating and then back in the kitchen cleaning. That night everyone in both houses fell into a happy and exhausted sleep. Christmas was over.

There were no decorated trees with lights and presents and joy and laughter for the troops in Europe. However, just like the North Georgia mountains, it was snowing in France in one of the coldest winters anyone could remember. The Allied troops spent Christmas day fighting to stop Germany's last great counter offensive, the Battle of the Bulge.

Citizens of Dawsonville listened to WSB and read the account of the battle in the newspaper. They felt equal parts of pride and fear for what might have happened to their loved ones. It was clear that the courageous action of the Allied forces that Christmas was what finally broke the back of the German war machine.

Sometime after 9:00 at night on December 28, the phone rang at the McLagans house.

Everyone froze. Late night calls could not bring good news. Duncan finally answered.

"Sir, this is the Southern Bell Telephone and Telegraph Company. I have a telegraph for Mr. Duncan McLagan. It will be delivered tomorrow. Do you want me to read it to you now?"

The blood drained from Duncan's face as he turned to Mattie and Skye. "It's a telegram. They want to know if I want to hear it now."

The women both nodded. Hesitantly, Duncan spoke to the voice on the phone. "Will you read it very loud, please? We're all trying to listen at once."

The young man complied. "Merry Christmas. (stop) I survived. (stop) In Belgium hospital. (stop) Having shrapnel removed. (stop) It's signed Gus." When he didn't get a response, the caller asked, "Did you hear me, Sir? He says he survived."

"Yes, yes we heard! That's wonderful. Thank you, young man. Merry Christmas to you."

"You're welcome and Merry Christmas to you too, Sir."

***

There had been rumors and scuttlebutt but it wasn't until the spring of 1945 that U.S. troops liberated the first Nazi concentration camp, a sub camp of Buchenwald. Eisenhower, Patton and Bradley viewed the horrors and word of the atrocities spread throughout the Allied forces as well as newspapers and magazines back home.

As horrible as the death camps were, the headline news on April 12, 1945 was the death of just one man, President Franklin Delano Roosevelt. Radio programs were interrupted and newspaper headlines announced the news to a shocked nation.

Along with thousands who lined the tracks along the funeral train route, the McLagans and the Calhouns drove to Atlanta to pay their respects. The stopover was brief, only 40 minutes. Then the train slowly pulled out of Union Station on its way to Washington and finally to the funeral at Hyde Park.

The country hardly had time to catch its breath before the latest news from Berlin took over the headlines. On April 20, Hitler's birthday, Soviet artillery began shelling Berlin and the bombardment did not stop until the city surrendered. Ten days later, Hitler committed suicide and seven days after that, Nazi Germany officially surrendered.

On May 8, 1945, at 9:00 a.m. Eastern Standard Time, President Truman announced, "This is a solemn but glorious hour. General Eisenhower informs me that the forces of Germany have surrendered to the United Nations. The flags of freedom fly all over Europe. Let us not forget, my fellow Americans, the sorrow and the heartache which today abide in the homes of so many of our neighbors—neighbors whose most priceless possession has been rendered as a sacrifice to redeem our liberty."

And so after six long years the war in Europe was finally over.

GETTING BACK ON TRACK

(1945-1950 and beyond)

"There are only three sports: bull fighting, motor racing and mountain climbing; all the rest are merely games."
Earnest Hemmingway

CHAPTER TWENTY-FOUR

In a fluke that only military bureaucracy and red tape could create, Gus and Finn ended up on the same troop ship coming back to the States. The seas were rough and Finn saw a guy struggling to keep his balance on crutches. He went to help and found Gus. Finn, who had spent the war helping to lift 200-pound men on to litters, threw his arms around Gus and despite the difference in their heights, lifted Gus off the floor. They hadn't been in touch since before D-Day, but the missing time evaporated. Once they started to talk, it was almost like old times.

"What's with your leg?" Finn asked.

Gus sat down at one of the long mess tables where he could stretch his right leg out straight. "Long story."

"Long trip," Finn smiled.

Gus hit the highlights of the situation at Gouvy. "We were mostly all Quartermasters, you know. Hell, nobody expected us to be a fighting force. We were pretty much cut off, but the trucks kept coming in and we weren't gonna let our guys go hungry or run out of ammo, so we kept filling the trucks and sending 'em off until we were ordered to evacuate. We had almost made it back to First Army HQ when this half-dead Kraut throws a grenade. He wasn't even aiming at me. Just dumb luck, but it tore up my leg.

"The doctors at the hospital took a whole bunch of shrapnel out of my leg, but my knee is still messed up. Hurts bad sometimes, but that's what aspirin is for, right?"

Finn smiled and thought, "There was a time not too long ago when Gus would have said 'shine' not aspirin. Guess we've all changed since we've been away."

"Anyway, here I am. What about you?" Gus asked.

Finn took a minute to answer. "Not much to tell. You know, do your job, try to stay alive." He paused. "I had a dog, named him Mutt. He was nothing like Dog, just a scrappy little old thing. Me and the guys kinda adopted him. I gave him to a French family we'd traded stuff with. They had kids." He paused again. "You gonna have to keep the crutches?"

"I hope not. They told me if I used my leg, things would get better. Trouble is, I never know when my knee's gonna pop out, you know, get out of line. When that happens, the pain is pretty bad. Sometimes it hurts just to bend it and I'm worried..." Suddenly Gus stopped realizing he didn't really intend to discuss this problem with anybody.

"Man, I've seen guys shot up a whole lot worse than you and they manage just fine."

"It's not that. I can walk OK most of the time, but I just can't count on it. Sometimes it won't hold my weight, just gives out."

"Oh I get it. You're worried about how you're gonna perform in bed," Finn said matter-of-factly. "Does the rest of your equipment work?"

"Yeah."

"Then you've got nothing to worry about. Just lie back and let Skye take care of everything. She's a woman, she'll figure something out. There was this French girl got hold of me once and I'm telling you, I didn't do a damn thing and she plum wore me out. Like I said, you ain't got nothin' to worry about."

Gus looked at his friend with new interest and hoped to God he knew what he was talking about.

The boys decided to wait until they actually landed in the States before telling their folks they were on their way home. Finn introduced Gus to several guys from Brooklyn who promised to show them the sights of Manhattan. "I know you're anxious to get home, but the folks don't even know we're on our way," Finn said. "I'm tellin' you this is a once-in-a-lifetime opportunity." Gus started to decline, but after some further persuasion, he agreed.

The troops came home to a hero's welcome. With the general euphoria about V-E Day, their uniforms and Gus's crutches, they were treated like royalty in every bar, restaurant and night club they visited. Even taxi drivers offered rides off the books.

After the blackouts and bombed out buildings in Europe, the lights of New York City were a beautiful sight. Beautiful, but overwhelming. Stores were beginning to decorate their windows for Christmas and crowds of shoppers added to the general excitement. The boys insisted on going to Macy's to shop because they knew "the girls" would like the fancy boxes almost as much as what was inside. And gift wrapping was free!

They squandered $6 for orchestra seats to see Ethel Merman in "Annie Get Your Gun," went to the top of the Empire State Building and marveled at the subway system. Great as it all was, Gus and Finn finally said good-bye to their buddies, called their folks and headed home. As if the city had held out one last surprise, they couldn't help but gawk at the star-studded ceiling of Grand Central Terminal on the way to catch the Southern Crescent for Atlanta.

Once on the train, passengers were eager to buy them drinks or invite them to join their table for dinner. It had been a long time coming, but as 1945 came to a close, the whole country was celebrating. Every little town was bright with lights. There were no bomb craters and no scorched fields. America seemed untouched by the war.

The morning the boys were due to arrive, there was a flurry of activity in Dawsonville. Even Dog was on the alert. Something was going on because everyone was up early, but they didn't go off in different directions like they normally did. The McLagans got in their car and the Calhouns did the same.

Skye signaled for Dog to get in, but he was hesitant. "The last time something like this happened, Finn went away. It could happen again and I might lose someone else." Dog finally got in the car, but just to make sure everyone stayed put, he sat with both paws on Skye's leg all the way to Atlanta.

Sure enough they went back to that big building. Dog did not like anything about this at all. Skye walked close beside him through the big lobby and then down to the noisy place he remembered. It was at that point he spotted his friend a long way off. Cecil B. Demille couldn't have staged it any better.

Finn was taller, but Dog knew him in an instant and the crowd parted as he and Finn ran toward one another. When Dog jumped up, put his front paws on Finn's shoulders and gave him a big doggy kiss, everyone applauded. Finn grabbed Dog's fuzzy ears and buried his head in his soft fur. "Oh Buddy, am I glad to see you!"

Dog grinned. "I'm glad to see you too."

Finally, Dog settled down and Finn went to greet his parents. Poor Gus almost got lost in all the excitement. He hung back to let Finn have his moment and to give himself a minute to get down the train steps with his crutches. He hadn't mentioned them in any of his letters. Mattie and Skye spotted him about the same time and they hugged him so hard they nearly knocked him over. Duncan hugged him to.

Then Skye spun him around and gave him a welcome-home kiss that promised better things to come. That prompted another round of applause.

When they got to the car, Duncan asked his son if he wanted to drive. Gus just shook his head. Duncan took the hint and did his best not to watch Gus and Skye in the rear view mirror.

Finn was only too glad to drive home. Dog proudly rode shotgun. Finn was home, God was in his heaven and all was right with the world.

When they got to Dawsonville, Gus expected his dad to take them to the upstairs room at Junky's Garage. Instead they pulled up in front of a small house with holiday lights all over the front porch.

"It's ours," Skye said. "Well, it really belongs to our families, but they fixed it up so we could have a place of our own for you to come home to." Gus hugged his folks and waved as they drove away. Then he turned to Skye, "I wish I could carry you over the threshold, but I'm afraid I can't handle that."

"All that matters is that you're home." Skye was glad to have him home, but now that they were alone, neither of them knew quite how to behave. The last time they were together was their honeymoon, but this was different. Gus wasn't sure how he would perform and Skye didn't know what to make of his hesitation. To stall for time, Skye said, "It was a long trip, you wanna take a hot shower?"

"Yeah, that sounds like a good idea."

"Now what?" she thought. For a minute she thought back to their first time and how they had laughed together. "Maybe that's it. If I can make him laugh, we'll be fine." Like Finn, it might not have been a great idea, but it was all she could come up with at the moment.

When Gus got into bed, he expected to find Skye waiting for him, but she wasn't there. A moment later, he heard honky-tonk music and Skye appeared in the doorway wearing everything in her closet. As Gus watched amazed, she started to strip, one piece at a time. Coats, jackets, scarves, gloves, blouses, skirts, undershirts, slips, bras, stockings. The finale was when she stepped out of a pair of his boxer shorts. She looked so sexy and so ridiculous, he couldn't help but laugh. Finn had said Skye would know what to do and she did, and she did, and then she did it again. Gus fell into a happy, exhausted sleep. God, it was good to be home!

Families welcomed their men home by pulling out all the stops for Thanksgiving. Emma and Mattie planned a combined family dinner even though they knew better. It is a widely known fact that Southern females are genetically incapable of attending family dinners without bringing their specialties, even if that meant ending up with four green-bean casseroles, three identical Jell-O salads and multiple plates of deviled eggs.

Seems like they had no sooner washed and put away the dishes from Thanksgiving, than it was Christmas morning. Everyone knew the drill. Take your time, untie ribbons, slide packages out and don't tear the paper. And the boxes! All those beautiful Macy's boxes had to be preserved for future use.

Dog enjoyed rooting under and around all the piles of paper and ribbons. However, he viewed the stack of boxes with suspicion. There were too many of them and he feared at any minute they might join forces, so he pounced on the largest one and tore it to pieces. When the ladies came into the room, Dog looked up expectantly. "See what I did to that dangerous box? He can't hurt anybody now." Dog couldn't understand why they were not properly impressed. His best efforts went unrewarded.

CHAPTER TWENTY-FIVE

Fitting back into a pre-war routine was like trying to fit back into an old pair of shoes that hadn't been worn in several years. Duncan and Sean were in their 60s and rebuilding their moonshine business was more than either of them was willing to tackle.

Like Rosie the Riveter, Emma and Mattie had discovered they could function quiet well outside the family. Skye wasn't just that kid at Junky's anymore. She was the one folks came to for new ideas and solutions. No one got out of the war untouched. Gus's wound was visible, Finn's wasn't so easy to see. They were all trying to find their way into a new year.

On the bright side, in 1946 thousands of returning veterans were eligible for money from the GI Bill. When the local school board decided to tear down the old high school, Finn cheered. Then he got an idea and signed on as part of the work crew. The main part of the building housed the classrooms, but the auditorium was in a wing by itself. Finn got a loan and bought that part of the building.

"Finn, what the hell are you up to?" Sean asked.

"Don't you worry, Pa. This idea is a lot more practical than tryin' to set up an animal hospital in the basement."

"Yeah and let's not forget how you nearly blew the roof off the house trying to make dynamite out of fireworks."

"Come on, Pa. That was a long time ago. I was a kid and besides it was just an accident. It didn't do any *real* damage.

I'm tellin' you this idea is gonna work out, you just wait and see."

Finn's plan was to leave the stage and the seats in place and add a new façade. To get started, he hired Curtis and they added a lobby with a popcorn machine, a projection booth at the back of the balcony and opened Dawsonville's first picture show. Admission 25 cents.

They were four blocks from the town square, but Finn was sure folks would come. They did and bought popcorn—10 cents a bag—and Raisinets, Jujubes, Milk Duds, Goobers, Junior Mints and of course, Coca-Colas. Folks usually spent more money on treats than they did on the price of the movie.

Finn remembered Dog's first meeting with Emma and decided getting her involved would be a very good idea. Emma was more than happy to trade bedpans for Hollywood glamour. She became the manager. They decided to open with *Anchors Aweigh*, starring Frank Sinatra, Kathryn Grayson and Gene Kelly. To appeal to the men and boys, Friday night was reserved for mysteries and Saturday was devoted to westerns like *Dakota*, with John Wayne, Walter Brennan and Ward Bond.

At first Wednesday was a slow night because of prayer meeting, but Curtis solved that. "Miss Emma, my mama goes over to Dahlonega on Wednesday nights 'cause the picture show over there gives away a different piece of china every week. She wouldn't miss it for nothin'." Wednesday became dish night and attendance definitely picked up, at least at the movies. The picture show was an immediate success and Finn was praised for having a good idea after all.

While Emma was busy in Dawsonville, Mattie continued to work at the Soldiers' Hospital until all the patients were discharged or had been transferred to hospitals closer to their hometowns. Eli was still hanging around on the last day.

Mattie knew that soldiers with amputations were sometimes reluctant to go home.

"I got no place to go. What little family there is lives way over in Texas and I was never close to them. Not sure what I'm gonna do now," Eli said.

"Didn't Junky say somethin' to you about workin' at the garage?"

"You reckon he was serious?"

Mattie smiled. "I've never seen Junky be anything but serious."

The next day when Skye and Dog came to work, they saw Eli standing outside. Dog came over to say hello and Skye called Junky over.

"Glad to see you're out of the hospital, Son. You still interested in goin' to work?"

Eli broke into an easy smile. "Yessir, I sure am."

"When can you start?"

Eli laughed. "Right now I guess. I came by here first to see if you'd have me and then I was gonna look for a place to stay."

"I got a room upstairs. It's not much, but the rent's cheap."

"That would be... great."

"You'll be workin' with Lewis till you kinda get the feel of things. By the way, do you know anything about cars?"

"Yessir. I worked in the motor pool before...well before this."

Lewis rolled out from under a car and Eli was surprised to see that he was a black man. Apparently Junky was willing to give everybody a fair shake. Lewis came over and he and Eli shook hands.

"I can do that too," Dog said and held up his paw. Eli was glad for an excuse to lean over and shake hands. He hoped nobody noticed the tears in his eyes. When he lost his left hand, he figured the best part of his life was over. Now here he was with a new job, a room of his own and a place he might be able to make friends.

Junky wasn't the only one hiring new staff. Doc decided to expand his practice. With all the young men coming home, Doc anticipated a growing practice delivering babies. He hired Mattie to be both his nurse and his office manager. A few of his older patients still worked on the barter system, but the younger ones paid in folding money and some actually made appointments.

Working with Finn at the picture show, Emma realized he was not the happy-go-lucky kid he had been before the war. He ate supper with the family, most of the time. And he slept at home, some of the time. But he spent most of his time driving around the back roads looking for a place to race.

Junky did his part to help out. He hired a bulldozer, graded the track, repaired the bleachers and replaced the missing chicken wire that had somehow found its way to a nearby farm. His was one of the more organized tracks. Most didn't have bleachers or chicken wire. Spectators were free to stand as close to the track as they could get in spite of—or maybe because of—the danger.

Everyone was getting involved in new adventures except Gus. Skye felt bad about that and decided to take matters into her own hands and talk to Junky. "I know it wouldn't be a good idea to have Gus workin' here, besides he's better at drivin' cars than fixin' them, but I've got an idea." When she said that, she realized she sounded just like Finn.

"What I was thinkin' was that maybe we could open a car dealership—Ford of course. I think Gus could get a GI loan to help start the business and I'd be willin' to put in some money too. Gus needs something to do and if *you* asked him, I'm pretty sure he'd be glad to manage the place. Who knows, he might even sell a car or two."

Gus was surprised when Junky approached him with the idea, but since he didn't have anything else going, he agreed. With the loan, they bought the old Key Furniture Store and Showroom on the west side of the square around the corner from the garage. Junky, Gus and Skye would be the owners and Gus tried to look excited when the sign for JGS Motors went up, but he just felt useless. After being in charge of millions of items during the war, all he had now was one 1946 Ford. Even if they added another model or two, it wouldn't help.

On his first visit to the showroom, Duncan soon realized something was wrong and it didn't take long to see that Gus was bored. He knew that after what his son had done in the Army, the showroom wasn't enough.

The next day Duncan dropped in again. "Listen, Son, I've got a little problem and I need your help. I might have somebody interested in buyin' that little rental house you and Skye are livin' in. What do you think about buildin' a new house for the two of you? I reckon the GI Bill might help with that too."

"You want me to build a house? I don't know nothin' about that."

Duncan laughed. "Guess you'll have to hire somebody to help you and then you'll just have to figure it out. Reckon you can handle that?"

The light in Gus's eyes told Duncan that he was on to something. "You could talk to Curtis Junior. After he got shot by the feds, he stopped drivin' but he's pretty handy. He worked with Finn on the picture show and he's been helpin' Sean and me take care of the rental houses for a while."

Gus took charge. He was on call if Junky needed him, otherwise he was on his own. With Duncan's help, he bought a piece of property, hired Curtis and a couple of other veterans and they were in business.

However, he realized that somewhere along the line he'd lost sight of his dream to be a race team owner like his idol Mr. Raymond Parks. It was the only thing he had ever really wanted to do, the only thing he'd ever wanted to be.

It is a fact that everyone in a small town knows everybody else's business, past, present and sometimes even into the future. If a third cousin on your mother's side went out for a pack of smokes and never came home, everybody knew about it and it was fair game for speculation even years after the event. Mountain folks are as quick to cheer a winner as they are to shake their heads and bless the hearts of those who mess up.

So, of course, Gus—like everybody else in Dawsonville—knew the complete history of the Parks family, beginning with Benjamin Parks, who discovered gold in Lumpkin County in1828. All Dawsonville school kids knew about the Georgia Gold Rush, but it was more recent history that interested Gus. He had heard the other drivers talk about what a successful businessman Parks was and Gus was convinced he and Mr. Parks were somehow connected. After all they had a lot in common.

Raymond was the oldest of 16 children. Gus was the youngest of six brothers. At 14, Parks left home to seek his fortune and became a whiskey tripper running shine from Dawsonville to Atlanta. Sorta like Gus. He also served a year and a day in a federal penitentiary. Like Gus's dad. And he was involved in the Battle of the Bulge in World War II. Sorta like Gus.

Parks owned the '34 Ford Finn's hero, Lloyd Seay, drove in his winning race at Lakewood back in 1938. And he owned the Oldsmobile that Gus's friend Red Byron was racing at the time. Parks had attended the NASCAR meeting in Daytona. Like Gus.

As far as Gus was concerned, it all added up. Parks was the first team owner in car racing and Gus wanted to be just like him. All he had to do was to sit down with Mr. Parks and find out exactly what he needed to do to make that happen.

The only problem was Parks didn't live and work in Dawsonville any more. He spent most of his time in Atlanta. Gus made a point of looking in at the Pool Room every day figuring that would be the one place Parks would visit if he came to town.

It took a couple of weeks, but finally Gus's patience paid off. It was easy to spot Mr. Parks because he was the only man in the room wearing a hat, a sparkling white shirt, a tie and a tailored suit that even Gus could tell didn't come from Sears or JC Penny.

Gus squared his shoulders and approached the table. "Mr. Parks would you mind if I sat down with you for a minute?" Parks nodded and Gus took the chair facing him. He introduced himself and quickly outlined his background. Gus mentioned Skye and Finn and told Parks how he started out driving shine and how they built their first still.

"We saved enough to buy our first car, but...well, the feds got it and the load of shine too, so we had to start over. Then I got drafted and I was in the Army quartermaster corps. I went in with the second wave on D-Day. I did some time with the Red Ball Express and then got transferred to the quartermaster garrison at Gouvy. I was a sergeant by then." Gus stopped. He realized he was talking too much. "Then I got wounded and here I am."

"Gouvy? Were you part of the Fighting Quartermasters?"

"Yessir," Gus said proudly, "I was."

"What are you doing now?"

"I'm learnin' how to build a house and drivin' when I can. Finn's a way better driver than me. I guess I think about it too much."

Parks nodded. Reached for his coffee and waited for Gus to continue.

"What I'm gettin' at is I've always wanted to do what you do, own a team, but I don't know how to get started. I was hopin' you could give me some advice." Gus took a notebook and a pencil out of his pocket and waited.

Parks glanced at the notebook and smiled. "First of all, it takes money to own a team. Lots of money. You'll need a profession other than racing...or moonshine. You any good at building?"

"I'm learnin' as I go along and I like being in charge of a crew and supplies and all."

Parks told Gus about the different businesses he owned. "You got any other income?"

Gus explained that everyone in the family contributed to the racing fund. Skye worked for Junky Brown and she would be their master mechanic. He and Finn put in part of their winnings and Finn added money from the picture show. Junky would supply Fords as long as he could put his name on the car.

"My pa, Duncan McLagan, and Mr. Sean Calhoun, Finn's pa, are getting into real estate and they're willin' to help us too. And Mrs. Calhoun has been teachin' me how to keep books." Gus thought he had the whole thing pretty much under control.

Parks took his time, finished the last of his Bully burger and drained his coffee. "It sounds like this is shaping up to be a family business. I believe in keeping things in the family, *but* what you need to understand is that it will be a *business*. Not fun and games. When people give you their money, they have a right to expect you to be responsible...for everything. That's what being a businessman means. Are you sure you want all that responsibility?"

Gus was busy scribbling notes. "What does 'everything' mean?"

"Well, you have to manage the money, keep the books, do all the paperwork, buy the cars, get insurance, work with your master mechanic, get a pit crew together, hire the best drivers and treat them fairly. And that's just for openers. There'll always be things that come up that you can't control, but you're responsible for those too.

"One other thing. Quit driving. You want to be an owner, be an owner but you can't be both. Think like a businessman. You'll be the head of a company now. If you get yourself killed, everybody loses their money and they're all out of a job. Are you sure you're ready for this?"

"It's way more complicated than I thought, but I still wanna give it a try." Gus put away his notebook and thanked Mr. Parks for his help.

They shook hands. "Good luck, Son."

Gus patted the notebook. This hadn't been nearly as much fun as taking notes with Miss Rita. But he wasn't studying on fun, this was serious business and clearly he had been blinded by the white shirt and the nice suit. He'd never thought about owning a team in terms of responsibility. Slowly, he headed home. He had a lot to think about.

CHAPTER TWENTY-SIX

"Your pa still makin' shine?" Finn asked Curtis.

"Yeah, he's stayin' real busy. Since most folks 'round here have cut back to just makin' enough for home use, he's picked up a bunch of new customers."

"You still drivin'?"

"No." His tone of voice made it clear that was all Curtis intended to say on the subject.

"Well, you tell your pa if he ever needs a driver, he can count on me."

That's how it started and pretty soon Finn was back making regular runs down Highway 9 to Atlanta. Once in a while, he was chased by a revenuer, but he outran them with no problem. He was fearless.

As soon as he could afford it, Finn went over to Junky's showroom and bought a new Ford V-8 from Gus. Might as well keep it in the family. His next stop was the garage where he turned the car over to Skye for her to work her magic. Once the car was ready, he and Dog went searching for dirt tracks. It didn't matter what condition they were in, or if they were offering prize money, Finn just needed to drive, with or without moonshine.

Nobody wasted time worrying about safety. Like most drivers, Finn did tape over the headlights to keep glass from flying and put a screen over the grill to keep dirt and rocks out of the radiator. He got a football helmet and some goggles, tied himself to the car with a piece of rope and used an old leather belt to cinch the doors to the frame tight enough to keep them from swinging open during the race. Because Dog went where Finn went, he rigged up a harness to anchor Dog to the passenger seat. That was it. They were ready to race.

When Finn was racing, his mind was completely focused: drive to the limit, look for an opening, take a chance, move up, make the other guy move over, stay in control. Crashes only happened to other drivers. He loved the noise because it was so loud he couldn't hear himself think. It left no room for memories of the war.

For those who had access to a car, racing was wide open. Every kind of car was eligible: coupes, hardtops, sports cars, convertibles. If a driver had a car—bought or borrowed—and could find a track, he could race. In some cases, there was prize money, usually there was not.

Sometimes promotors managed to take up a collection from the spectators—sorta like a love offering at church—because when you came right down to it, most drivers did what they did for the love of it. When the green flag went down, cars flew around the track until the checkered flag dropped or until they spun out or crashed, whichever came first.

Most drivers hated Lakewood Speedway in Atlanta because it had originally been a horse track and the turns weren't banked. Cars frequently spun into the lake. Gus loved it.

The old Daytona Beach-Road course was unique. Just surviving on that track was an accomplishment. It started at the far south end of Ponce Inlet and ran two miles north on the beach. The south straightaway ran two miles down highway A1A.

"It's the turns that'll kill you," Gus said.

"Not me!" Finn said and laughed.

The beach sand was hard packed, but after the first lap, the soft sand in the turns was nothing but ruts. Heavy cars bogged down. Tow trucks stood by ready to pull them out of the way. Drivers made it through the turns any which way they could, sometimes on just two wheels.

In addition to enjoying the drivers' stunts, fans quickly latched on to Dog. They loved to see him roar by sitting in the passenger seat, his eyes fixed on the track ahead. It was wild, wide open, dangerous, reckless fun. The drivers loved it. The fans loved it. The promoters loved it.

So of course, it was only a matter of time before someone came along to organize the sport for the good of all or take all the fun out of it, depending on who was telling the story.

***

Junky never got letters. And yet, there it was lying in the middle of his work bench. Rather than open it, he poked at it with the box-end wrench he had in his hand. The war was over, so it couldn't be a draft notice, but there was something ominous about it. Better to just leave it alone.

When Skye came in, she noticed it immediately. "Hey Junky, you got a letter. Want me to open it?"

Junky took a little too long to answer and Skye took that as permission, ripped open the envelope and unfolded the letter. "My goodness, this is addressed to *Mr.* Brown, it must be something serious."

"You read it," Junky said.

"It says you are invited to a three-day meeting at the Streamline Hotel in Daytona Beach starting December 14 to work out the details for a new racing organization."

"Good God, we got too many associations now. The last thing we need is another damn organization makin' rules and tellin' us what to do."

Junky had a point. Racers, owners and promoters were dealing with a pile-up of seven different organizations plus the National Championship Stock Car Circuit.

"It says mechanics, drivers, owners and promoters are all invited to the First Annual Convention of the NCSCC."

"What idiot do you reckon thought all that up?" Junky demanded.

Skye glanced at the signature. "Bill France."

"Big Bill France? God help us!" Junky spat out the words.

They didn't call him Big Bill for nothing. He was nearly six and a half feet tall and weighed over 200 pounds. He was known to be a pretty good mechanic, a fair driver and a hard worker. He was also a world-class talker and his genius lay in promotion, organization and getting his own way. He has been instrumental in setting up the Daytona Beach-Road course.

France had a couple of false starts before he figured out how to make the race pay off. He was well on the way to building his dream of a nationwide presence for stock car racing, when World War II put the brakes on his plans. But now, after the war, he picked up where he left off.

"Wonder who else got a letter," Junky said. "What about Gus and Finn?"

"Not as far as I know," Skye said.

"Is Gus workin' at the showroom this morning?" Junky asked.

"Yeah. He usually works on our house in the morning but today he went to the showroom instead." Skye wondered why Junky cared.

"Think I'll walk over there and see if Gus has heard anything. Come on, Dog. I could use the company."

Skye, Eli and Lewis watched in amazement. Junky *never* left the garage during work hours. They had never seen him walk farther than from one job to another in the garage. And as far as they could ever remember, he had never paid any particular attention to Dog.

Gus had come in to sort out some paperwork he had been avoiding. It was so unusual to have a customer, it took him several minutes to notice the tall, lanky man looking over the Ford.

"You lookin' to buy a car?"

The man shook his head. "Naw, I'm just curious. My car's at Junky's getting some adjustments made." As he walked around the display model, Gus noticed he had a limp. "Car looks good," the man said, "but you know it's the same as the '42 under the skin."

"Yeah, '42 was a good car, but not quite as good as the '39. Best whiskey car ever made." The words were no sooner out of his mouth than Gus wondered if he'd spoken out of turn.

The man smiled and gestured slightly to Gus's cane. "Wounded?"

Gus nodded. "Grenade. Knee gives me trouble sometimes. You?"

"Bomb went off where it shouldn't. Shrapnel." The man extended his hand, "Byron, everybody calls me Red."

"Gus McLagan. I raced against you before the war. So you're still drivin'? How do you…"

"I wear a steel brace. My mechanic Red Vogt fixed it up so I can bolt the brace to the clutch. When I need to shift, I do it by shifting my body weight. "

"How's it workin'?"

Byron smiled "Hurts." He reached in his pocket and took out a bottle of aspirin. "This helps."

Gus smiled and pointed to a bottle of aspirin on his desk. "Me too."

"At least I'm driving. I've won a few races Bill France set up. Hope to keep doing that. Walk over to the garage with me and I'll show you how the brace works."

They ran into Junky and Dog as they walked out the door. Dog immediately went into the showroom, walked over and sniffed the tires on the Ford. Then he looked at Gus as if to say, "Don't worry, I know better."

"Well, Red, didn't expect to see you, but I'm glad you're here," Junky said. "Did you get a letter from Bill France about some big meeting down in Daytona?"

Byron nodded. "Yeah, I saw it this morning. Couple of the other drivers got one too and Vogt got one."

"What the hell you reckon France is up to?"

"I'm guessing he thinks we need to get organized. And he's right about that. I've been driving in his NCSCC and that's gone pretty good. Trouble is, France can have a heavy hand when it comes to doing things his way. Just how he's planning to organize everything kinda has me worried."

They walked into the garage and Junky pointed to Red's car. "It's over yonder."

Gus saw Skye with her head buried under the hood of another car. Gus started to slap her on the behind, but thought better of the idea. He knew Skye was a big fan of Red Byron so he tapped her on the shoulder. "Skye, I want you to meet somebody."

Red was obviously surprised to see such a pretty face where he had expected a good ole boy. Gus knew the look. "This is my wife, Skye. She's Junky's secret weapon. Great mechanic."

Red shook hands. "I've heard about you."

Skye smiled. "I've heard about you too." She liked his refined manner which was different from most of the drivers she met.

Red showed Skye and Gus how he bolted the brace on his left leg to the clutch pedal. They talked for a while and Red offered some suggestions to solve Gus's problem. It hadn't occurred to Gus before that there might be other wounded veterans having to adjust to a different world than they had known before the war. If he got invited to the Daytona meeting, he might meet some of them.

Although Gus's injury was to his right leg, Byron's solution got everyone thinking. One afternoon they were hanging around the garage when Doc dropped by. When Gus sat down and crossed his right leg over his left, the pain hit him. "That's it," Gus said. "That's when it hurts the most." He straightened his leg and the pain went away.

"Lateral weakness, left to right pressure," Doc said. "Centrifugal force during a race is gonna kill you. It's gonna hurt whenever your knee is forced to the right. What you need is something to keep your knee lined up straight."

"What you need is a panty girdle, a really big one," Finn said. That got everybody's attention.

"I'm not kiddin'. You can put it on over your pants. Pull it up just far enough so the leg part covers your knees. Then roll the top part down to get it out of your way. Your leg can't shift far. Problem solved."

"That's crazy! I'm not showin' up at the track with no panty girdle."

"Now wait a minute, Finn might be on to something," Doc said. "Maybe you could just wear one leg of the girdle… "

Gus threw up his hands.

"What if we could build some kind of hinged knee brace?" Eli suggested.

"Yeah," Junky said. "Something that would let you move your leg up and down, just not side to side."

"We could put a padded band around your thigh and another one just under your knee and put some support in between," Skye added.

The conversation continued as they worked out the details. "Just don't forget it was my idea about the girdle that got y'all thinkin' in the right direction," Finn said.

It took a couple of days, but when Gus tried the brace, it worked fine. He went with Finn to some of the small dirt tracks where he could test his knee and build up his courage. It wasn't like riding a bicycle, you did forget. Little by little he relaxed into his old habit of holding back, analyzing the other drivers and working out his strategy. Gus still used a cane off the track, but when it came to racing, he was back in business and just in time because the next day he and Finn got their Daytona invitations.

CHAPTER TWENTY-SEVEN

Gus was having fun and Finn was attacking life flat out on all cylinders. Bars, girls, juke joints and fine restaurants all had to deal with his craziness and the fact that where Finn went, Dog went. No use arguing about it.

On the frequent nights when Finn slept in a bed other than his own, he and Dog worked out a system. Finn left him a bowl of water, a dish of food and a nice old blanket for a bed.

"I'd rather have Finn here to open the door for me, but I'm perfectly capable of going in and out through an open window if I need to."

One morning about 2:00 a.m. Sean was jarred out of a deep sleep. He managed to get out of bed, shuffle down the hall and answer the phone. "Hey, Pa. How're you doin'?"

By this time Emma had joined her husband. Calls at that hour could only be bad news.

"Finn! It's two damn o'clock in the morning. Where the hell are you anyway? (pause) What are you doin' in Dahlonega? (pause) No, I don't wanna talk to the sheriff. I wanna talk to you and you better tell me what's goin' on right now. (pause) OK, I get it. You can fill in the details later." Sean shook his head and mumbled "eejit" under his breath. "Alright. We'll be there as soon as we can. By the way, are you hurt?

On the way to Dahlonega, Sean told Emma what little he knew. They had to wait for the sheriff to provide the details. It seems Finn and some friends had left a local bar and decided to use Dahlonega as their private racetrack. The idea was to see who could drive the fastest around the Courthouse Square *backward*. The citizens didn't appreciate the noise or the damage to bushes, park benches and flower beds in the area.

Since all the drivers were veterans, the sheriff was just holding them, not making any arrests. But he said none of them were sober enough to drive, so Emma was there to drive Finn's car home.

Finn and his friends listened in silence while the sheriff talked to the families. Finn looked a little sheepish as he left the police station. He started to get into Sean's car. "Not so fast. You're ridin' with me," Emma said. Finn considered asking the sheriff to lock him up, but it was too late.

Before Sean drove away, the sheriff pulled him aside. "Mr. Calhoun, I know your boy, Finn. I've seen him drive. He's got talent, but he's running wild. I fought over there and I know sometimes it's hard to leave all that behind you. But if he keeps up like this…"

"I'll talk to him, Sheriff. We'll get it straightened out."

Emma kept her eyes on the road and waited to speak until she was calm enough to sound rational. "Finn…" She stopped, took a deep breath and started again. "Honey, I know you're not a kid anymore. You've seen and done things I can't even imagine, but I'm worried about you. You were always my wild child, but there was a sense of fun in what you did. Now, to be honest with you, you're scarin' me. Is there anything I can do to help you? Would it make you feel better to talk to Skye? You two have always been so close."

Finn shifted uncomfortably in his seat. He knew he was messed up, but he wasn't sure how to make things better. His mother was right, he had seen and done things she couldn't imagine and he couldn't imagine trying to explain those things to her or to Skye. "Oh Ma, I'm just lettin' off steam. Nothing for you to worry about."

The next day Finn got more or less the same talk from Sean. He knew his parents were just trying to help, so he told his dad what he knew Sean wanted to hear. "It's like I told Ma last night, I was actin' crazy. I'm sorry and you don't need to worry, it won't happen again." Sean took him at his word and let the incident slide.

Gus found himself walking on egg shells. Finn was on edge because he was trying to stay out of trouble and Skye was seriously ticked off because she hadn't been invited to Daytona. In an effort to get the world spinning again, Gus took over. "Get your coats and come with me. We're going over to the Pool Room. My treat."

The place still looked the same. Pictures of dirt-track races, drivers and stock cars covered the walls. There was no menu. Mr. Gordon, the owner, kept it simple. Bully burgers—named for Bully Thurmond—or hot dogs, Coke or Dr. Pepper and French fries with everything. And because the veterans kept asking for it, ice cold milk by the glassful.

There was a pool table and old-timers came to eat, drink, shoot pool, watch Stacy and tell stories. Stacy was the short-order cook who worked behind the counter. She fired up the burners, and heated up the grill when she opened up in the morning and turned them off when she closed at night.

Like the trippers she served, she had only one speed—fast. She never wasted time adjusting the heat. The burners were set where she wanted them and the grill stayed hot. Her hands never stopped moving. Timing was the secret. Everything came out crispy around the edges but nothing ever burned.

When the lunchtime crowd came in, Bully Thurmond came in to help out. He never wrote down an order and he did fine until he got overwhelmed. Then he just gave everybody the same thing, a hamburger patty on a bun with coleslaw, onions, mustard, ketchup and pickles. Folks finally gave up and just ordered a Bully burger to save time.

As more people bought cars and took to the road for fun, business at the Pool Room picked up some. First-time visitors walked around looking at the photographs and sooner or later someone was bound to point to one picture and ask, "Who's that?"

On cue, the kids and the rest of the regular patrons stopped talking and Mr. Gordon stood up. "That's Lightning Lloyd in his #7 car up on two wheels sailin' through the north turn at Daytona. The crowd really loved that trick. His full name was Lloyd Seay. He's a local boy and Bill France, big promoter down in Florida, said he was the best driver he'd ever seen. Kid was a natural.

"Lloyd started drivin' shine for his cousin Raymond Parks when he was 13. He had this way of holdin' the wheel at the bottom with the palms of his hands up, like this," Mr. Gordon demonstrated. "He said that way he could make a 180-degree turn—we call it a bootlegger's turn—all in one motion.

"Anyway, back in '38 Lloyd heard about a race at the Lakewood Fairgrounds in Atlanta. He didn't have a car, but he begged Raymond to field him a modified moonshine car.

So Parks got together with Red Vogt, greatest mechanic ever, and gave Lloyd a 1934 Ford roadster to drive. He called that little black and silver car the Silver Bullet. It was his first race and he was drivin' against racers like Roy Hall—another one of his cousins—and Bill France and Bob Flock. That's some stiff competition and the kid won!"

"Tell 'em the good part," someone in the room prompted. "Oh yeah," Mr. Gordon acted as if he'd forgotten, "turns out the kid was drivin' with a broken arm!"

"How did his arm get broken?"

"To tell the truth, I can't rightly remember. But Lloyd grew up tough and he was never one to step away from a fight." Skye poked Finn in the side and smiled at him.

One of the other old-timers chimed in, "Hell, in one of the Daytona races, Lloyd flipped his car twice and still came in fourth! Man, ain't never been a driver like him!"

"Did he ever win any big races?"

Mr. Gordon and all the old-timers laughed. "Well, let's see. In August of '41, he won at the Daytona Beach-Road course. Then a week later he drove up to North Carolina and won at High Point Speedway. Then he took off for Atlanta, but he got there too late to qualify and had to start in last place. By the 35th lap, he grabbed first place and led the rest of the way to win at Lakewood on Labor Day. So he won three national races in three different states in 15 days."

"How come nobody's ever heard of him? Is he still racing?"

"Naw, that's where his story gets sad." Gordon paused, maybe out of respect for Seay's memory, maybe for dramatic effect.

"So what happened?"

"Lots of different versions. The Labor Day victory at Lakewood was the biggest win of Lloyd's career. Now the way I heard it, after that race Lloyd was tired and didn't want to drive all the way back up here to Dawsonville, so he stayed at his brother Jim's house near Atlanta. Early next morning Woodrow Anderson, another one of his cousins, came bangin' on the door demandin' money he said Lloyd owed him for chargin' a $5 bag of sugar for his moonshine still to Woody's account.

"Jim got involved, they got into a big argument, and Anderson ended up shootin' them both. Jim was shot in the neck and survived. Lloyd died on the spot. Anderson was arrested, tried and the SOB is doin' life down in Atlanta."

At this point the regulars got in on the story. "I remember the funeral. The church was full of all different kinds of people, moonshiners, trippers, race car drivers, promoters, fans, friends and half the county, most of who were related to Lloyd."

"Mr. Parks drove Lloyd's Silver Bullet in the funeral procession and folks all along the streets were crying. It was a terrible day."

"It's supposed to be a secret, but most folks know Mr. Parks designed this special headstone and had it installed. The grave is over yonder in the Dawsonville Cemetery.

"If you've never seen it, y'all ought to go take a look. You won't have no problem findin' it. It's tall and you can read his name real easy. And it says, 'Winner National Stock Car Championship, Sept. 1, 1941, Lakewood Speedway.' There's this raised section with his trophy and his Ford and a glass-covered picture of him in the driver's window. It looks like he's still drivin'."

"The next race at Lakewood was in November and they called it "The Lloyd Seay Memorial 100."

Mr. Gordon summed up, "Kid was only 21 when he was shot. Reckon if he'd lived he could have been so famous everybody woulda known his name."

Another old-timer from the back of the room spoke up. "You forgot to tell 'em about the si-reen."

Gordon laughed. "Oh yeah. Well, back a'ways I bought a siren for the fire house. After they got a new one, they gave the old one back to me. When Lloyd won his first race, I saw the siren just lying there and I grabbed an extension cord, hooked that thing up and let 'er rip. Loudest noise I ever heard.

"Didn't take long for the sheriff to show up to see what was goin' on. I told him about Lloyd and he just smiled. I mounted the siren on the roof and from then on, whenever Lloyd won, I cranked it up. After he died, it didn't seem right to use it for anybody else. I don't reckon any other driver from Dawsonville will be as awesome as Lloyd, but I'm keepin' it handy 'cause you just never know. Anything can happen."

Gus smiled. The kids had heard that story many times and hearing it again was comforting, like a favorite fairytale. They bundled up against the December wind and walked home remembering a time when a Bully-burger and fries could cure almost anything.

On Friday, December 12, the Dawsonville contingent headed for Daytona. Skye and Dog were left behind. They were more than a little bit annoyed that they hadn't been invited.

CHAPTER TWENTY-EIGHT

They came from everywhere: New Jersey, Rhode Island, New York, Ohio, Connecticut, Massachusetts and, of course, from Florida, Georgia and the Carolinas. Bill France wasn't wasting any time in setting up his new organization on a national basis. He had everything under control, even the weather.

The sun was shining and there was a gentle breeze off the ocean. Excitement was running high. Finally drivers, owners, mechanics and promoters all felt like they had found an advocate, someone who would stand up for their rights. Ultimately two dozen men found their way to the sea-green Art Deco hotel on South Atlantic Avenue.

No doubt about it, France knew how to please his guests. This was a business meeting disguised as a party with free food, free liquor and a group of bathing beauties France invited from a nearby modeling school.

The meeting was held in the Ebony Room on the roof of the Streamline Hotel. The view from the terrace was better than a vacation poster. The beach was beautiful and the Atlantic Ocean went on forever.

At 1:00 p.m. on Sunday afternoon, France called the meeting to order. "Gentlemen, the future of stock car racing is right here in this room. We have the opportunity to set it up on a big scale. First, we need a name, I suggest the National Stock Car Racing Association."

"Somebody's already using that," Red Vogt said. "How 'bout the National Association for Stock Car Auto Racing, NAS-CAR. You can actually say it, not like a bunch of strung-out letters nobody can remember."

NASCAR was in.

"What about promoters who promise big money and then run off with the gate receipts?" Bob Flock demanded. France had that covered by legal contracts, escrow accounts and law suits.

Contracts and enforcement were in.

Gus looked around and saw heads nodding. He wondered if he was the only one worried about where things might be headed.

"While we're talking about money," France said, "I've never thought winner-take-all was fair. With NASCAR, you'll get points for the number of races you enter, the number of wins, number of times you're in the top five, or top ten and your total winnings. At the end of the season, you'll get a bonus based on the number of points." This idea was greeted with confused silence.

"I know it sounds complicated," Finn said, "but nobody else has ever offered to pay us *after* a season. We got a chance to earn a little extra money. How bad can that be?"

The points system was in.

Ice cubs tinkled in glasses, overflowing ash trays were emptied and refilled and the group moved on to other topics. It was decided the first official NASCAR race would be in February. Modified cars only because Detroit couldn't make new cars fast enough. Strictly stock would have to wait a year.

The modified race was in.

"What about the tracks? They're banked every-which-way and they've all got different rules."

"To be sanctioned by NASCAR," France said, "they'll have to abide by our rules. That may not sound like much right now, but believe me when we go national, the name NASCAR is gonna put the fear of God in a lot of folks."

At that moment, France was putting the fear of God in more than one person in the room. He seemed to sense that he was losing his audience. "Let's break for dinner. Steak and lobster, drinks, all on the house."

The liquor flowed, the conversation got louder and folks naturally sorted themselves in clans: drivers and mechanics, owners, promoters and out-of-towners at different tables.

Gus and Finn sat with Red Byron, Roy Hall, Lee Petty, Red Vogt and the notorious Flock brothers Tim, Bob and Fonty. Raymond Parks had skipped the meeting. "I don't like meetings. Nobody ever says what they mean. People voting on things they don't understand. Gives me a headache."

As Finn and Gus listened to the conversation around the table, it was clear everyone was a little uncomfortable with one person having so much power.

"I don't understand how this escrow account is supposed to work," Finn said.

"Yeah, France was a little sketchy about where the bonus money was coming from."

They continued to voice doubts, but in the end, they decided it was too early to make a final judgment. When they reconvened the next morning, Red Vogt spoke up. "OK, we need one set of rules that all the tracks follow." There was general agreement until someone asked, "Yeah, but who's gonna *make* the rules?"

"We are," France said. "We got three more days to work out the details, but once we approve the rules, they're gonna apply to all NASCAR sanctioned races and they will be *strictly enforced.*"

Rules and enforcement were in.

Before France could continue, Red Byron raised his hand. "I know nobody wants to talk about this, but we got ourselves one dangerous sport. We need some safety precautions."

Safety was in.

"And," Byron continued, "we ought to have a way to help out when one of us gets hurt."

France had that covered too. "We've got a top-notch lawyer right here and I guarantee we'll have insurance and a benevolent fund as part of the final package."

Insurance and compensation were in.

That all sounded good, but Gus saw their wide-open sport being squeezed into a very narrow space. And he saw France as the only person controlling that space.

Toward the end of the third day, Lee Petty spoke up. "Assumin' we get all this worked out, who's gonna care? NASCAR's not gonna mean much unless we can get the newspapers and sports reporters to take us seriously. Right now *Speed Age* is about the only magazine that even mentions stock car races."

Once again France had that covered. "We're gonna have a publicity director and he's gonna send press releases about NASCAR to the hometown papers of every driver, owner and mechanic and to every sports editor he can get hold of. Mark my words, this time next year NASCAR is gonna be on sports pages all over the country."

Publicity was in.

At the end of four days a lawyer drew up the papers and NASCAR was founded as a private corporation with Bill France as president.

Some folks didn't think the idea would fly at all. Others decided just to bide their time. Nevertheless, it had been four history-making days and most of the participants were proud of what they had accomplished. They had a name, they had rules, they had compensation and they had an advocate.

Red Vogt, who had known Bill France a long time said, "You mark my words, the next thing you know, NASCAR is gonna belong to Bill France."

And that is exactly what happened.

CHAPTER TWENTY-NINE

Late one night, the phone rang. It was Finn. "Gus, Buddy! Can you come get me and Dog? We're at the Soldiers' Hospital over in Rome. The police are here too. We're havin' coffee. They're nice fellas." Finn was slurring his words and not making a whole lot of sense. "I offered to buy 'em a drink, not at the hospital, at the bar. Anyway, I told 'em my mama was workin' over here, at the hospital, not the bar. But now I can't find her. Nobody can find her. Do you know where she is? Anyway, I'd like to go home now, but the police won't let me drive. They think I'm drunk, but I don't think so. Anyway, could you come get me?"

Gus shook himself awake and did his best to relay the conversation to Skye. "He's talkin' crazy. He thinks his ma is still workin' at the Soldiers' Hospital. He ought to know better than that. She hasn't been over there for months. He sounds pretty drunk and he said the police were there, so I guess we better go get him."

By the time they arrived, Finn's wounds had been bandaged and he had a story to tell. "Me and Dog was in this bar where we go a lot. We were just sittin' there mindin' our own business when this wiseass tells the manager he ought to throw that flea-ridden, mangy ole mutt out, referrin' to Dog. Well, of course, that made me mad, but I didn't do nothin'. I just kept drinkin'.

"That's when his buddies decided to get in on the act. They were laughin' and sayin' my whole family probably had fleas, startin' with my mama. Well, y'all know I couldn't let 'em get away with that. I mean that was my ma they were talkin' about.

"Anyway, I went over to their table to give 'em a chance to apologize, but they just laughed at me. So I cold-cocked the SOB and that's when his buddies jumped me."

"How many were there?"

"Three. But Dog had one of 'em by the seat of his britches and I figured I could handle the other two. Goddamn it, Gus, somebody needed to teach those stupid punks some manners. You just don't go insultin' somebody's ma. It ain't right."

Gus shook his head. Finn was one sorry sight. He had a black eye, a fat lip and his nose was a little out of line. Dog, on the other hand, looked rather pleased with himself.

Finn couldn't help but turn the whole thing into a funny story, but underneath the humor Gus sensed a hint of rage. The bartender might have seen it too. He had smelled trouble from the beginning and called the cops, but not before Finn got hit over the head with a chair. The officers finally got there and took the wounded to Soldiers' Hospital because it was close by.

Finn showed no signs of remorse except that he hadn't done more damage to the loudmouth who started the whole thing. When they got ready to leave, Finn remembered his manners and thanked the police for showing him such a nice time. When Gus finally got him in the car, he fell flat on his back in the back seat and passed out. Dog sat on the floor with his head on Finn's leg. Skye followed in Finn's car.

From then on, Gus insisted they travel as a team. That way he could keep an eye on Finn. Skye went along to supervise the volunteer pit crew when she could get away from the garage. Now that he was back on the circuit, Gus heard other stories about Finn. Apparently he had spun into the water at Lakewood more than once.

The last time it happened, Dog got out of his harness and made it out through the window. He dog-paddled to the shore, climbed out, shook himself dry and gave Finn a disgusted look. The crowd cheered. "I'm getting too old for this kind of nonsense," he thought. Miraculously, he made it off the track and went looking for Skye.

Finn was dripping wet, but otherwise he didn't seem at all fazed by the fact that he might have drowned if some kids hadn't pulled him out. Again the crowd cheered.

Dirt tracks were narrow, but Finn was always the one to push his way forward to where three drivers were running door-to-door with only inches between them. One of his favorite tricks was to snag another driver's bumper and make him tip over. If Finn flipped in the process, so much the better. A massive pile-up of ten or more cars wasn't unusual. Drivers normally just sorted themselves out and got back in the race. The crowds cheered.

With the exception of getting dunked in the lake, Dog liked riding shotgun. When Finn was lucky enough to take a victory lap, Dog looked out his window and smiled at the crowd. That ended when Finn got broadsided. The impact threw Dog out of his harness. He landed upside-down, then right-side-up again, then wedged under the dashboard.

"That's it! I'm not racing with you anymore." In the confusion of clearing the cars off the track, Dog found his way to his pit crew. They laughed. "That dog's got more sense than Finn. No doubt about it." Finn missed Dog, but he went right on taking crazy chances. He loved the thrill and the crowds and the noise.

To him, the cars sounded like wild animals growling to establish their badass credentials. The thunder of 50 to 60 cars tuned to run flat-out filled up the air space and made it hard to breathe. There was no escaping it. Drivers accepted it and concentrated on winning and staying alive.

As usual Gus hung back and calculated the best way to get through the turns. Finn never slowed down. He maneuvered his lightweight Ford around the stalled cars. The crowds cheered.

On one of their trips to Daytona, Gus looked up Linc Bedford, his buddy from the Red Ball Express. Gus told him about their plans to build a racing team someday. "If we can get it together, you wanna drive for us?"

Linc looked at Gus as if he had lost his mind. "This ain't the Army, Gus. This is the South! There's no way that's gonna happen."

Gus thought a minute. "You're probably right but there's nothing that says you couldn't crew for us. Right?"

Linc grinned. "Yeah, I got a little garage across town, keeps me pretty busy, but I could always find time to work with you on the track when you're here. Who knows maybe one day somebody like me *could* race here."

"Maybe they could win too," Finn added. "Now wouldn't that just be a kick?!"

After watching Finn race for several laps, Linc turned to Skye, "Man, the kid is good, but he drives like the devil himself is chasin' him. Reckon what that's all about?"

Skye laughed off the remark, but she *had* begun to wonder if there might be more to Finn's recklessness than just putting on a good show. She talked to Gus about it, but since Finn seemed to be enjoying himself they decided to let it go. Besides, confrontation wasn't Gus's style. In fact he avoided it as much as possible.

Then one Sunday afternoon Finn suggested they go fishing. That was enough to set off warning bells in Gus's mind. As far as he knew Finn had never been fishing in his life.

Nevertheless, Finn showed up with borrowed poles, a coffee can full of bait and a cooler of beer. They went down to Flat Creek near the place they used to race when they were kids.

They found a comfortable place under a shade tree, sat down and baited their hooks. Since this had been Finn's idea, Gus waited to see what he had on his mind.

Finally, Finn asked, "Did you ever shoot anybody?"

That took Gus completely by surprise. At first he thought Finn was just fooling around, but he looked serious, so Gus decided to take the question seriously. "I don't know."

"How can you *not* know!?" Finn snapped. "Either you shot somebody or you didn't."

"Well, I shot *at* a lot of Krauts, but I don't know if I ever hit one. You know how it was."

Finn didn't answer right away. "Yeah, I know. We shot at the enemy, that's what we were supposed to do. But... I mean did you ever shoot anybody close up?"

Gus was beginning to get a little uncomfortable with the conversation. What in the world was going on with Finn? "Did *you?* Did you ever shoot anybody that way?" When Finn answered his voice was so low Gus wasn't sure he heard him right.

"Once."

"You shot a German?"

Finn just shook his head and continued to look straight ahead. Gus saw a tear running down the side of his face.

"Finn? Did you shoot a civilian?"

Again Finn shook his head.

"Then who?"

When he answered he almost vomited the words. "Gator. I shot my best friend over there. Gus, I shot him dead." He bent over and started to sob.

In all their years together, Gus had never seen Finn cry. "What happened?"

Finn was still sobbing. Gus opened the cooler looking for a beer, but he found a flask of moonshine instead. "Here, take a swallow of this," he said and handed it to Finn.

After a couple of swigs, Finn calmed down a little. "His name was Elwin Richie, but we called him Gator, 'cause he was from Florida. Remember I told you his ma sent us oranges at Christmas. Anyway, we were ordered out to make a pickup. They said this unit was under fire and had a lot of wounded. We left with Gator and his medic in his ambulance, me and John Deere in White Lightning." He took another swallow.

"When we got there, our guys were holed up in an old house, takin' heavy machine gun fire. We got close enough to load up the wounded and were about to leave when Gator's medic, K.C., saw a guy on the ground and went to help him.

In the middle of all the noise and the smoke I heard this huge explosion and a ball of fire hit the front of Gator's Dodge. I heard a scream and I thought it was the wounded in the back. I was afraid the whole thing was gonna blow up, so me and John Deere got them out the best we could. But the screamin' didn't stop so I ran around to the front of the ambulance.

"That's when I realized the Krauts had hit one of the jerry cans we tied on the front fenders. There were gas and flames all over and I looked around for Gator. Then I saw he was trapped in the cab. I tried to open the door, but it was red hot and it jammed. I was as close to him as we are right now.

"Oh God, it was so hot. I could smell him burning and he was begging me to shoot him. I just stood there. It seemed like forever. And he kept cryin' and beggin' and, and I shot him. I had this Lugar and I put it right to his head and I killed him. He was my best friend and I killed him.

"In all the confusion, nobody knew. John Deere, K.C. and I managed to get all the wounded into our ambulance and I drove away. We made it to the aid station. I reported that Gator's Dodge got blown up, but I never told anybody what really happened. I never told..." Finn started to sob again.

Gus had no idea what to say or what to do. So he did the only thing he could think of. He put his arm around Finn's shoulders and just let him cry.

Finally Gus said, "Finn, I don't think you killed him, I think you rescued him. You took his pain away. That's what you did, Finn. You made the pain stop. It was a good thing you did."

After that, they sat for a long time and watched the afternoon turn to night.

CHAPTER THIRTY

After that, Gus and Finn were a little awkward around each other until Gus finally brought the subject up again. "Listen, Buddy, you can trust me to keep your secret. I'm not even gonna tell Skye, but I'm glad you told me. Something like that is way too heavy for one person to carry around by himself."

At first Finn didn't respond and Gus wondered if bringing it up was the right thing to do. "Yeah, talkin' to you helped. I've been tryin' to run away from that ever since I got home. I keep goin' over it in my mind and wonderin' if there was something else I could have done. But there wasn't, Gus. It was the only way. I couldn't just let him suffer."

"I know. You did the right thing."

They didn't talk about it again, but little by little Finn seemed to come to terms with what happened. He would never be the innocent kid he had once been, but he was able to let go of the past and concentrate on the future. He even started enjoying himself again.

The bright spot on the horizon was the modified stock car race coming up in February. It would be the first NASCAR race ever run and it was getting a lot of attention. Gus decided it was time he put his grand plan into action, so he worked up his courage and called a family meeting. He knew if he was ever going to start a racing team, he had to get serious, he had to get started and he had to get both families onboard because he couldn't do it alone.

When he got everybody together, he told them about his meeting with Raymond Parks and he tried to remember everything Mr. Parks had told him. "He said it would take a lot of money and he asked me a lot of questions about how I thought I was gonna handle that. Then he told me I had to start thinkin' like a businessman. So that's what I'm tryin' to do here.

"The way I see it, the only way we can pull this off, is if we all work together. I've been thinkin' about this a while and here's my plan. Skye is a master mechanic, Finn's a great driver and Aunt Emma can help us get organized. I plan to drive two more years and rack up as many NASCAR points as I can. Then I'll cash in and let Finn take over the drivin'. And then some day maybe we'll be able to hire a second driver."

With everything Gus knew and all the times Finn had messed up, he was surprised Gus was willing to put so much trust in him. He made a promise to himself right then and there not to ever mess up again.

The next step in getting organized, was to stop collecting money in a moonshine jar and trying to do business that way. Gus asked Emma to help them open a bank account. "Mr. Parks said it would take more money that we could make racing, but with money from the picture show, the rental houses, the building business and each one of us addin' what we can, we should be OK. We're gonna have to mind our pennies, but I think we can do this."

Gus went on to explain that with a checking account, they wouldn't need to carry a lot of cash when they were on the road. It would also give them a way to keep track of where the money went. "Aunt Emma, Skye, Finn and me will be the only ones who can write checks on the account."

It had been a long time since the family had heard Gus so excited about the future. The only problem was he was so excited, he didn't see the hidden flaw in his plans.

In general, the whole family was in agreement, but Gus's announcement had put a crimp Mattie's plans. "I know Gus said we had to watch our money, but I'm doing it anyway," she announced when she and Emma were alone.

Emma was puzzled. "What does Duncan say?"

"I don't know. I didn't ask him. Emma, do you realize I'm nearly 60 years old and I have never done anything just because I wanted to. And because I could."

"I'm not exactly clear on how you think you can pull this off."

"I've been working for Doc now for more than a year and every time I got paid I saved out ten percent just for me. It's biblical, kinda like a tithe."

"Oh, so it says in the Bible that God wants you to own an electric washing machine?"

"No, it says that in the Constitution. I have an unalienable right to the pursuit of happiness and that's what I'm doing. Pursuing happiness."

"That's the Declaration of Independence."

"You sure it's not part of the Constitution? Anyway, I've saved enough and I'm going down to Sears and Roebuck and buy a Kenmore washer!"

"Lord help us," Emma thought. First it was moonshine, then it was run off to Rome to work at the Soldiers' Hospital and now this. God only knew what Mattie might get up to next.

Gus and Finn were taking the idea of team ownership a little more seriously. With the new rules and NASCAR points to be won, it looked like auto racing might amount to more than just a series of mind-numbing left turns.

Dog had been in on the family meeting and although he wasn't exactly sure what went on, he had some new plans of his own. He loved riding shotgun with Finn on the road, but once they got to the track and he heard the sound of the cars getting ready for the race, he flatly refused to get in the car. Just to make perfectly sure that Finn understood this new arrangement, Dog sometimes stayed home on race days. Finn was a little slow to catch on, but he finally figured it out.

Skye was surprised when Dog showed up at the garage on a day when she knew Finn was driving. Whatever the reason, everyone was glad to see him and Dog made the rounds wagging his tail and saying hello to his friends.

His old bed under Skye's work bench was gone, but Eli found an unclaimed back seat in Junky's never-know pile and set it up for Dog. "This is great. Nobody's gonna step on me and I can see everything that's going on."

Junky had always been a stickler for cleanliness in the garage. As he saw it, a clean engine ran better than a dirty one, so it only made sense that a clean garage produced better products. Cars took a beating at every race, but Junky saw to it that major repairs were made and when his cars showed up on the track sporting his name, they were always clean and shiny.

With Gus on the road so much, Junky needed someone else to manage the showroom. Duncan and Sean discussed whether or not they should apply for the job. "Now that we're all part of this new team-owner business, it might be a good idea for us to work for Junky. We could buy the boys better racing cars like maybe a Chrysler or even a Cadillac," Sean said.

"I'm not sure Junky would be too pleased to have us workin' in his Ford showroom and buyin' Cadillacs." Even so, they decided to talk to Junky about the job. The idea was for him to hire them both. They would split their time between the new car showroom and the used car lot that was filling up next door. It wasn't too long before word got out about the new management, and the showroom became *the* place to hang out and swap racing stories.

Almost everybody in town knew at least one story about the Flocks: Bob, Fonty, Tim and Ethel. A favorite was the time in Atlanta when the feds drove right onto the track with sirens screaming and lights flashing and chased Bob for a couple of laps before he drove off the track onto a side road and disappeared down the highway.

Some of the men remembered being at Daytona when Bob flipped his Hudson up-side-down and they got out on the track and helped him turn it right-side-up again. According to them he still finished in the money.

But the best story was about Jocko Flocko, a monkey that used to ride with Tim. Sean swore he was there the day the monkey got loose in the car. "Here's Tim tryin' to fight off the monkey with one hand and drive with the other. He finally gave the animal to the pit crew, and still finished third. I think that's where Finn got the idea to drive with Dog."

Working on the team ownership project was exciting. The anticipation of the first NASCAR race was exciting, but Gus and Skye trumped all that when they announced they would soon have a baby around the house. Finn, who was only half listening asked, "A baby what?"

Emma understood immediately. "When?" she demanded.

"End of April or early May. We're not exactly sure," Gus said, looking more than a little proud of himself.

Emma looked at her daughter. "That means you're four months along already! How did we miss that?"

"Coveralls," Skye smiled. "They not only keep you clean, they can hide a multitude of secrets."

Finn finally caught on. "You mean I'm gonna be an uncle again? He laughed. "That means you're gonna be Grandma and Grandpa, again. By the way, does Junky know about this?"

"Not yet. I'll tell him on Monday when I go to work."

"Reckon he's gonna fire you?" Finn asked.

"He better not try, not with our new business just gettin' started. I plan to work until I get so big my arms won't reach inside an engine."

"And what about after the baby comes?" Mattie asked gently.

"I figure I've got you and Ma to take care of that, or him, or her."

Never one to miss an opportunity to have a celebration, Sean brought out the moonshine and they drank a toast to the future. "Here's to the newest member our team, may he or she carry on the grand tradition of stock car racing for years to come."

CHAPTER THIRTY-ONE

In 1948, Detroit was still trying to catch up after not building new cars during the war years. For that reason, it had been decided to put the strictly stock race on hold for a year and make the first NASCAR race for modified cars. That was good news for drivers and especially good news for mechanics like Red Vogt and Junky and Skye. It would be their last chance to show off their skills in making fast cars even faster.

February 15 was hot and sunny in Daytona and 14,000 fans gathered at the Beach-Road course where they paid their $2.50 to be part of NASCAR history. Finn, Gus and 48 other drivers lined up at the start. The old course proved to be as tough as ever and mid-way though, half of the cars were out of the race.

The boys made a passable showing, but the glory of winning the first ever NASCAR race went to Red Byron in a Ford owned by Raymond Parks and tuned by Red Vogt. Gus made a point of congratulating all three of them. Byron was upset. "Damn those announcers, I wish they'd stop calling me a *disabled* war veteran. I may be a veteran, but I am *not* disabled or I wouldn't win. Why can't he just call me a race car driver?"

Gus laughed and went to join Skye and the pit crew. Her due date was about ten weeks away and she wasn't moving as fast as she usually did. Linc had come over to help out and Gus took the opportunity to talk to him. "We're really gettin' serious about our racing business, so anytime you wanna work with us, we'd be glad to have you. Right now we can't pay much, but we could cover your gas and expenses."

Linc said if he wasn't snowed under at his garage, he'd try to make some of the races. With that, the Dawsonville crew headed home.

While the boys were racing all over the country, Mattie and Emma spent considerable time speculating on whether Skye was having a boy or a girl. "She's carrying it high, so that means it's a boy," Mattie said.

"No, it's the other way around, that means it's a girl. Let's go ask Doc, he never misses."

Doc had a system. Whenever he was asked, he always said, "I think maybe it's gonna be a boy so I'll make a note right here on the chart." But he wrote "girl." That way, when the baby came, if it was a boy, Doc smiled and everyone one was happy. If it was a girl, then he'd say, "I knew it. See I wrote it right here," and his reputation continued to grow.

The end of April came, but there was no baby. The middle of May came and still there was no baby. Finally on June first, Skye called Junky and told him she needed to take the day off. Then she called Emma, Mattie and Doc and told them she thought it was time for the baby to come. Doc rushed right over and sure enough, two hours later Skye delivered a healthy six-pound boy. Once they made sure all his fingers, toes and other equipment were intact, Skye went to sleep.

That night Gus called from Nashville and his mother told him he had a son, Angus McLagan Junior. He immediately started spreading the news to everyone within shouting distance. It wasn't until he hung up that he realized he had completely forgotten to mention he'd won his first NASCAR race and Finn came in third. The two of them got together and headed for home.

For the next two weeks, Baby Mac was the center of everyone's universe, well, almost everyone. Dog wasn't so sure about this new human. For one thing, he didn't smell too good. Not like a real person. But apparently the other people planned to keep him around, so Dog decided to wait and see.

However, for the first time since Finn had rescued him and Emma had allowed him to stay in the house, Dog felt left out and he couldn't figure out why. That new person didn't do anything but make a lot of noise and still everyone thought he was wonderful. "If I made that much noise, they'd put me out the door. It's not fair." Dog decided to spend more time at the garage where his friends still paid attention to him.

Eventually the boys had to turn their attention to the next event, the Strictly Stock National Championship. The day before the race, they left Dawsonville headed for North Carolina, each driving a new car of his choice, supplied by Junky.

Most of the drivers didn't have that luxury. They drove the car provided by the owners or a mechanic or they drove their family car. Still others took a chance on finding a friend, relative, neighbor or someone just hanging around the infield who was willing to loan their car with no guarantee that it would be returned in one piece.

For the Charlotte race, Lee Petty borrowed a Buick from a neighbor, Glenn Dunnaway found a guy who had a Ford, but no driver. Tim Flock spotted a brand new Oldsmobile 88 in the infield and talked the owner into letting him drive the car. Beg or borrow, it didn't matter as long as you got in the race.

Fans might have skipped church in favor of the race, but they wore their Sunday best and started showing up before daylight. The line of cars stretched for miles along Wilkinson Boulevard. Gus and Finn told their families the best seats in the house were right at the start-finish line, as high up in the stands as they could get. Skye hated to miss the big race, but she stayed home for Baby Mac's sake. The rest of the family was in their seats early. The final attendance was 13,000, give or take a thousand or two.

The usual field of modified black Ford coups was nowhere in sight. According to NASCAR rules, these cars were all made after 1946 and were the best Detroit had to offer. There were Fords, Oldsmobiles, Hudsons, Lincolns, Kaisers, Buicks, Chryslers, a Mercury and one lone Cadillac. They were as bright and shiny as a new box of Crayons.

Fans were there to cheer for their favorite driver or their favorite car, which usually meant the model most like the street car they drove to work every day. Speedometers said these cars would do 100 or 120 miles an hour. Yeah, well maybe, maybe not. This was the time and the place to see if that was really possible.

More new NASCAR rules called for an inspection before and after the race. "That's just plain dumb," Finn complained. "What do they think we're gonna do, make modifications in the middle of the race!?"

Cars were allowed to paint a number on the door, add a piece of screen to keep mud and rocks out of the radiator and put masking tape over the headlights. Drivers could wear a helmet, goggles, tie themselves in place and lash the doors to the doorframes. That was it.

The cars lined up and the sound of the motors was like the roll of nearby thunder leading up to a storm. There was no official "gentlemen start your engines." That was to come later. On that June Sunday, all eyes were on the green flag and when it fell, the race was on!

For more than two hours, fans were treated to fender-banging, car-rolling, dirt-slinging, parts-flying, heart-stopping red-dust-covered fun. Half way through the first race he ever entered, Lee Petty rolled his borrowed Buick Roadmaster four times and ripped off all the doors. His family and the rest of the crowd held their breath until he climbed out unhurt.

The sun beat down and hundreds of funeral-home fans fluttered throughout the stands in a hopeless effort to create a breeze and blow away the dust. People weren't the only ones suffering from the heat. One by one, cars dropped out when their engines overheated.

Finally, Glenn Dunnaway and his borrowed 1946 Ford roared past the competition to win the race with a three-lap lead. The crowd cheered. They smiled, wiped their sweaty faces and headed home. But it was far from over for the drivers.

Then came the post-race inspection.

The officials had suspected something from the way the Ford handled in the corners. As it turned out, its springs had been stiffened, to give the car better traction. It was an old moonshiners' trick, but NASCAR said it was illegal.

Long after the stands were empty and the fans were gone, Bill France and the rest of the inspectors disqualified Glenn Dunnaway. They stripped him of his win and relegated his name to last place in the standings. He was blindsided.

The other drivers were equally stunned. "Bill, that don't seem fair," Gus said. "It wasn't Glenn's car. He had no way of knowing what the owner had done."

"He should have checked. Rules are rules," France said. "Everyone was warned the rules would be strictly enforced, so that's it." Without another word, he walked out of the room. There would be no negotiating. Dunnaway would get nothing. The win and the money went to Jim Roper who actually came in second.

The drivers—including Roper—stood in shocked silence. This wasn't what they bargained for. The men who had been in the Streamliner meeting had discussed the rules, even voted to accept them, but they expected France to be their advocate.

Finn wasn't about to let it go. "What the hell's goin' on with France? He was a driver, he's supposed to be one of us. Now he's soundin' like the Lord God Almighty! This ain't right, I don't care what France says."

The other drivers agreed, but there didn't seem to be anything they could do about it. Obviously NASCAR was the new world order and France's word was law.

"No way we're gonna let this stand," Finn said. "Glenn drove a good race, won it by three laps and deserves to go home with something to show for that." He grabbed an empty bucket and started to take up a collection. Gus added his bit. Everybody chipped in and Glenn went home with at least a pocket full of money.

The drivers couldn't do anything about the official records which forever listed Glenn Dunnaway in last place. But *he* knew, and the drivers who were *there* knew, he won. They all learned an important lesson that day. Bill France was indeed in charge and NASCAR was law.

As they were leaving the track, Gus saw Lee and his son Richard, looking a little lost. "Sorry about the car, but it's good you're not hurt. Y'all need a ride home or something?"

Lee shook his head. "Naw, we're gonna catch a ride with my brother, but thanks." He hesitated a moment, "You were a tripper back in day, right?" Gus nodded.

"Back then they told you to ditch the car, save yourself. Not anymore. Gotta save the car 'cause you can't win if you got nothing to drive at the end." With that, he walked away. Richard looked back and smiled.

The first official NASCAR Strictly Stock race was over and what a race it had been.

CHAPTER THIRTY-TWO

Skye finally went back to work at the garage and Emma and Mattie went back to their still. When the Soldiers' Hospital closed, they cut back on production but they continued to supply a few loyal customers in Dawsonville. Occasionally Mattie heard Doc talking about a patient who was in pain, but didn't have any money for medicine. They saw that those folks were taken care of too.

One afternoon following a summer storm, Emma found her path to the still blocked by an old white oak tree. As she was climbing over the limbs, she remembered a story in the newspaper and took a notion to try an experiment. She collected several small branches. When she got to the still, she called Mattie over.

"I was reading this article about aging shine. Usually they use a charred oak barrel to put the shine in, but this guy cut the wood into small pieces, charred it and put *the pieces* in the shine. I wanna try that, but I'm not sure how to go about charrin' the wood without burnin' it up."

Mattie solved that problem. When they got home, she grabbed her cast-iron skillet, dumped the oak chips in and heated them up. When the chips were blackened, she turned off the fire and let them cool.

The next time they made a run of whiskey, Mattie dropped a handful of the charred oak chips into one of the whiskey jars and set it aside. After that, every time one of them went by, they'd shake it. Over the months, the shine started changing color. Eventually it turned red and looked pretty much like the fancy bonded whiskey in the stores. Emma took it home and planned to have Sean taste it, but she forgot.

Mattie was picking up Baby Mac from Skye at the garage one day when Eli stopped her on the way out. "Miss Mattie, can I talk to you a minute?"

"Sure, Eli, what's on your mind?"

"I reckon you know this, but there's a pretty big TB sanitarium on the edge of town. Lots of the patients out there are veterans who got the consumption during the war over in Europe. They got no medicine to treat 'em, just good food and lots of bed rest. But it's hard to rest when you're coughing all the time. Anyway, I was wonderin' if maybe the tonic you brought to the Soldiers' Hospital might not help those boys get some relief. "

Mattie smiled. "I'll take a look, Eli, and see if I can find some for you. Thank you for lettin' me know." She and Emma discussed the situation and several days later, Mattie showed up at the sanitarium carrying a long-handled kitchen spoon and a vile-looking brown bottle of tonic. She talked to the nurses, several of whom knew her from the Soldiers' Hospital. They were glad to see her and when she explained the treatment, they were more than happy to help.

"Just two spoonful's at a time. Tell 'em to tilt their heads back, open their mouths, hold their noses if necessary, and swallow it down all at once. It's gonna burn, but it'll do the trick." And it certainly helped the patients get some sleep. Later in the year, streptomycin came along and finally offered a real treatment.

Not everyone in Dawsonville was feeling as useful and productive as the two grannies. Homer was depressed. He remembered the good old days when he could just pick any direction, walk into the woods, locate a creek or a stand of mountain laurel and be pretty sure he would find a copper pot still in operation. Then he'd bust up the apparatus and arrest the moonshiner. The biggest one he ever found was a 520-gallon silver cloud still. It was made out of galvanized steel and glowed like silver in the moonlight. Now that was a night to remember! It made him proud to be a federal agent.

Back then, he enjoyed his job. He was a revenuer and revenuers and moonshiners were sworn enemies. But they all lived in the same place and it was more a game of hide and seek. He'd catch 'em, they'd do time—usually a year and a day or less for good behavior—and when they'd get home, they'd fire up another still and the whole game would start all over again. It was Homer's job security.

The moonshiners and bootleggers lived on the frazzled edge of the law, but Homer understood they were just trying to make a living, not like those big-time criminals up in Chicago or New York. He and the moonshiners were even friends of a sort. He remembered letting Duncan go home to spend the night with his family instead of taking him off to jail. He trusted Duncan to show up at the courthouse the next day and he did because that's just the way things worked back then. Homer sighed. He needed to find a still. It didn't have to be a huge one, just a little 50-gallon one would be fine.

Sometimes, the Lord doth provide. Homer noticed the lights were on at Emma's house late at night and very early in the morning. Not a crime, but curious and with nothing better to do, he decided to keep an eye on things.

He suspected Emma was up to no good because she was seeing visitors and all of them happened to be men. Upon closer observation, he realized none of them ever stayed more than a few minutes and hell, nobody was that fast!

As it turned out, Homer knew most of the guests. The first one he recognized was Judge Edwin Dunbar. Then in turn he saw Sheriff Hamilton, Doc Fletcher, Brother Sizemore from up in Gilmer County and finally Edith May Howard's husband whose first name he could never remember. Obviously that line of investigation wasn't going to work, so he decided to forget about the men and watch Emma's comings and goings instead.

For a week or more, nothing happened. Then one morning she left early, stayed away most of the day and came home carrying two large grocery bags. Nothing unusual, but when the same thing happened the next two days in a row, Homer knew he was on to something.

His next move was to follow her when she left the house. He expected her to head into town, but she went the opposite direction. She walked across the local baseball field, made her way through the back lot of the hardware store and the lumber yard and then entered the woods that bordered on the creek. About a mile back in the woods, he smelled it. Shine!

"She's picking up shine from somebody's still sure as anything," he thought. He was careful to go slow because he knew moonshiners always set up multiple escape routes and he didn't want this one to get away. When he finally quietly stepped into the clearing, he couldn't believe his eyes. There were Emma and Mattie busy cleaning the kettle of a 50-gallon still. He saw four full gallon jugs, sitting beside a stack of grocery bags. Moonshining grannies! What was the world coming to?

He hesitated and something caught Emma's attention. When she turned around, she was looking right at him. He was the federal agent; she should have been startled by him. But instead she tapped Mattie on the shoulder and the two of them just stood there looking at him. For some reason he felt like he was the one caught red-handed.

"Homer," Emma said.

"Emma. Mattie. " He tried to sound official, but what came out was more like a glad-to-see-you-I-was-just-passing-by remark. He tried again. "What the hell are you two doin' back here?"

"Cleanin' up. You know how important it is to keep these things clean." Mattie took her cue from Emma and calmly went back to work. This was not at all the way things were supposed to happen, but yelling, "Freeze," didn't seem right either.

"We're about to finish up here, then you can walk us home," Mattie said.

Homer just threw up his hands and sat down to wait. When they were finished, Mattie put the last two gallon jugs in the paper bags and handed them to Homer. "If you don't mind carrying these, me and Emma can get the rest and we won't have to make another trip." She rewarded him with her sweetest smile.

Like a school boy carrying a girl's books, Homer did his best to keep his balance and follow the two of them to the edge of the woods. They walked on to Emma's where Mattie unloaded her grocery bags and then headed to her house next door.

Emma asked Homer to help her bring the jars into the house where she loaded them into an old cupboard in the back room. Then he followed her into the kitchen. "Can I get you something?" she asked. Then all of a sudden she seemed to remember something important in another room. She returned carrying another gallon of whiskey.

"As long as you're here, I wonder if you'd do me a favor. We were experimenting with this back in the woods and I brought it home to get Sean to taste it and then forgot. Lemme pour you a little bit and you tell me what you think."

As if he had been struck dumb, Homer sat and watched her. She got down two small glasses, poured each of them a shot and handed one to him. "Taste this and tell me what you think."

She tasted her own drink, put the glass down and looked at Homer. "Well?"

Homer took a swallow and let the amber liquid roll around in his mouth. He closed his eyes and let out a long slow sigh. "Bourbon," he said reverently. "Mighty fine bourbon."

Emma slapped the table in excitement. "I'll be damned it worked. Mattie'll be tickled."

"Where did you get this?"

"We made it. Just experimentin', you know. You think it's alright then?"

Homer drained the last few drops. "Maybe I should have another taste, just to be sure."

Emma happily obliged. Then she waited. More than once she had heard Sean say that good whiskey deserves time to be properly appreciated. So Emma poured another drink for them both and they sat in companionable silence for a while.

Homer finally put his empty glass on the table and found his voice, his official voice. "Emma, wait a minute. You do realize I caught you makin' shine?"

"Yeah." She nodded.

"And that's illegal?"

"Yeah, I know."

"And now I'm supposed to arrest you, both of you."

She just looked at him with a slight smile.

"And bust up your still."

She continued to look him in the eye as she sipped her bourbon.

"It's the law."

She topped off his drink.

"I need to do my job."

"I know," Emma said.

So the next day, Homer got the other agents together and they hiked back into the woods and busted up a still.

But it wasn't Emma's.

CHAPTER THIRTY-THREE

The year 1950 promised to bring changes. The shortages of the war years were over, and for the first time in a long time, folks were excited about the future. They had money to spend on all kinds of new cars and new labor-saving devices. The one thing that didn't change was summer in north Georgia. As usual it was hazy, hot and humid and everything was covered in red-clay dust.

The boys were enjoying a dirt-free weekend away from the racetrack so Mattie decided to fix supper for everyone. Skye was still at the garage finishing up a project with Junky, so Mattie kept her supper hot in the oven. As soon as they finished eating, Sean and Duncan settled in the living room to listen to "The Adventures of Sam Spade." Mattie was still sulking because her favorite show, the WSB Barn Dance, had gone off the air right after the first of the year.

Dog was sitting with his head on his paws in front of the radio. He looked for all the world as if he were hanging on every word of the program. At one point Baby Mac noticed Dog and smiled for the first time! Everyone made a big deal about that. "Oh he likes you," Emma said and petted Dog.

"I don't know what all the fuss is about," Dog thought. "Of course he likes me but now I guess I have to like him too. Maybe he'll be fun to play with...someday."

When Sam Spade was over, they turned off the radio. Finn, who was always full of the latest racing gossip, grabbed a flashlight to use as a microphone and started a running commentary in his best sportscaster voice.

"Good evening ladies and gentlemen, it's Finn Calhoun here to fill you in on what's been goin' on with NASCAR. First of all, as I'm sure you know, we got ourselves a fancy new name, thanks to Red Vogt. That would be Bill France, of course. Red Byron won the first official NASCAR race in Daytona. Those modified cars sure put on a show. Next up was the Strictly Stock race in Charlotte. Big news there is what happened to Glenn Dunnaway and how he got booted out of first place.

"In other big news, there was a 2,000-mile race across Mexico. It lasted last six days and paid $6,000. It's got a fancy name too, but we're gonna just call it the Mexican Road Race, for short. Three teams of our boys entered: Red Byron and Raymond Parks, Bill France and Curtis Turner and Bob and Fonty Flock. Sadly none of them were equal to 500-foot cliffs, loose gravel and the altitude. They were so high up cars and drivers were both gasping for air.

"Back here at home, there was more sad news. Seems like $5000 purses and year-end bonuses can't keep drivers from runnin' in unsanctioned races. So Big Bill stripped Red Byron, Lee Petty and Tim Flock of all their points! Let that be a warning' to you boys and girls, you better stay loyal to NASCAR or else!

"Latest news is that the new track up in South Carolina is offerin' a *$25,000* purse for the Labor Day race. Count those zeroes folks, that's twenty-five *thousand* dollars. That's gonna attract drivers from all over. I heard even Johnny "Madman" Mantz from way out there in Ca-li-for-ni-a may show up.

"Who knows? Anything can happen, so tune in again for the continuing saga of Bill France versus the world and more news from the inside track."

Duncan leaned over to Sean. "Lord God, that boy can talk! Reckon he oughta stop racing and start talkin' for a livin'?"

"Sure would be a lot cheaper."

The racing community was all talking about the way France stripped drivers of their points, which meant losing a lot of year-end bonus money. Gus wasn't a big fan of France and he agreed with most people who said France ran NASCAR like a dictator. On the other hand, France could always be counted on to help out a driver who needed a couple of bucks for gas to get home.

Knowing the drivers and the track owners the way he did, Gus had to admit France *needed* to be a dictator to hold it all together. He also knew that by now drivers should have learned better than to challenge France.

"Hell, Gus," Finn said, "it wasn't like Byron and them had a choice. NASCAR didn't even have a race that weekend, and they needed to make a living. Besides, everybody in the business knows NASCAR is governed by the rulebook, except when it's not. What is it they say, EIRI? Except in Rare Instances and I'll give you three guesses who decides what's 'rare' and what's not."

Throughout this conversation Dog and Baby Mac were lying on the rug in the middle of the living room. Baby Mac was carefully stacking blocks and then happily knocking them down. Dog was sleeping well away from the demolition zone.

"Daag," Baby Mac tried out the word.

Suddenly all attention was focused on the baby. Dog thought he heard the word in his sleep, but it didn't mean anything to him. Instinctively he moved farther away to stay just out of reach of Baby Mac's tiny hands.

"Daag," Baby Mac repeated, reaching for Dog.

Finn burst out laughing. "I guess that shows you guys who's important around here. Most babies start out with mama or da-da. Not this kid. I want y'all to remember his first word was Dog!"

Dog recognized his name immediately and opened one sleepy eye. Baby Mac was still a safe distance away, but just to be sure, Dog walked around to the other side of Finn's chair and lay down again.

Emma picked the baby up and slung him onto her hip. "Let's go look for Mama," she prompted. Baby Mac wasn't interested. Apparently one word a day was his limit. Emma looked out the window hoping to see Skye, instead she saw a car she didn't recognize. "Whose maroon Chevy is that?"

"Mine," Finn said. "I won it on a bet. Not bad, huh? I figure why buy 'em when you can win 'em? Right, Pa? I was hangin' out with that Curtis Turner fella and a bunch of his buddies. Y'all think I'm crazy, you oughta meet him."

According to Finn, Turner had a reputation for renting cars that he banged up so badly during a race the agency refused to take them back. When that happened, Turner just drove the car into the deep end of the swimming pool at his motel. Racers also said Turner once drove a pace car at race speed several laps around the track before the rest of the drivers ran him into the infield.

"That guy'll bet on anything and most of the time he wins. He can party all night and then drive just fine the next day. The way he figures it, he needs one hour of sleep for every hundred miles of the race. So for a 500-mile race, he just needs five hours sleep. That sounds like a plan to me, I'm gonna give it a try."

Gus shook his head.

"What!?" Finn demanded. "You're the one who's always tellin' me to pay attention. Well, I am. Like Lee Petty says you only learn by racing against drivers who are better'n you. So I'm learnin' from Curtis and I'm havin' a hellava time. You oughta try hangin' round instead of always bein' in such a hurry to leave. Don't you ever wanna just kick back and unwind after a race?"

"I do my unwindin' at home," Gus said as Emma handed Baby Mac over to him.

Finn laughed. "Well, since it's my sister you're comin' home to, I guess I shouldn't be givin' you a hard time."

"Damn right," Gus laughed too. "By the way, I did stay after one race and some of the guys were passin' around a bottle of what they claimed was home-made bourbon. They said they got it from Granny Shine. Do y'all know anybody by that name?"

Mattie and Emma exchanged quick glances and said honestly they had never heard of anyone by that name. They were searching for a new topic of conversation when Duncan innocently came to their rescue.

"Finn, what's the deal with the Labor Day races? Is Sam Nunis doin' one at Lakewood or is it gonna be that guy up in South Carolina?

"The 500 mile race *was* gonna be at Lakewood until Bill France heard about it. No way he was gonna let Nunis get ahead of him, so he decided to sponsor the one in South Carolina, which makes it an official NASCAR race."

Finn chimed in, "It's a huge purse and they're offerin' the winner $10,500! Can you believe that? No wonder everybody pulled out of Lakewood and signed on for Darlington. Nobody is gonna challenge NASCAR, not after what happened to Lee and Byron and them.

"Let's just hope France doesn't change his mind again. First he was in, then he was out, then he was in again. Who knows what he's gonna do next. I may sit this one out just to be on the safe side."

"Forget that," Gus said. "We both need to be in every NASCAR race. And with a purse that big, there's money to be won even if you don't come in first. So don't even think about sittin' it out. Just make sure to follow the rules so France doesn't take your points away."

CHAPTER THIRTY-FOUR

About that time, the conversation was interrupted when Skye walked in the front door. She always loved summer and never sweated, no matter how hot it got. But at that moment, she was a pitiful sight. Her hair was sticking to the sweat on her face and she hadn't changed out of her work overalls. Once inside, she just stood there. Her mouth was open, but no words came out. Her eyes were open, but she didn't seem to see anyone in the room.

"Skye?" Emma said. "What's wrong, Child?"

For several seconds Skye continued to stand perfectly still. Finally Emma reached out and touched her on the arm. "Skye?"

"It's Junky. He's gonna sell the garage and move down to Florida. That means we're all gonna be out of a job."

That announcement took everyone by surprise and they all started to talk at once. "Well, Mattie," she thought to herself, "you wanted them to talk about something besides cars and racing, now you got it. Be careful what you wish for."

Duncan finally managed to get a word in edgewise. "You mean to tell us that Junky is gonna sell the business his family has owned forever? And move to Florida? What's he gonna do in Florida? Fish?"

"He says his wife, Leeann, has been after him to move ever since he turned 65 and that was five years ago. She's got a sister down there and she thinks it's time for him to retire."

"What does Junky think?"

"He didn't pay her much mind until this guy from Atlanta came along and offered him a big wad of money to sell the garage."

"What about our jobs at the showroom and the used car lot? He gonna sell them too?"

"I guess not. Seems like it's just the garage."

"OK, so somebody else buys the garage," Duncan said. "Why do you think everybody's gonna get fired?"

Skye finally sat down and told them all she knew about the situation. Turns out, the guy didn't actually want to buy the business, he just wanted the land. He thought the location would be perfect for a new appliance store. According to him, appliances like washers, dryers, TVs and things were flying off store shelves and it didn't make sense that folks in Dawson County had to drive all the way to Atlanta to spend their money.

"Now just when we were makin' some real plans about the future, I'm gonna be out of a job and female mechanics aren't in real high demand you know. On top of that, who do you think is gonna hire Eli with his hook or Lewis? He's a good mechanic, but what other white man in this county is gonna give him a job? This whole thing is a disaster!"

"So how much did the guy offer Junky? Maybe *we* could buy the garage," Sean suggested.

"Eli and them think it was about $10,000. If that's true, there's no way Junky can turn that down." Skye answered.

"Gus, how much have we got in the racing account?" Finn asked.

"Should be about $2000. Since the picture show is makin' money and the rental houses and building business are doin' pretty well, maybe if we pooled our money we could come up with enough."

"There is no way we can come up with $10,000!" Skye was on the verge of tears. " You know what Mr. Parks said, it takes a lot of money to start a racing team. We counted on all of us working and now that's all falling apart. It's just not fair."

Gus put his arm around Skye. "Maybe there's still time. I mean he's not gonna sell the garage tomorrow is he? That's one part of the deal we don't know about. When is all this supposed to happen? Did Junky mention a deadline?"

Skye looked stricken. "That's the worst part. The guy is supposed to come back up here with his lawyer and they're gonna sign the final papers some time after Labor Day. That's just right around the corner. We don't have a chance. So unless somebody's got a way to turn $2000 into $10,000 overnight, we're out of luck."

Finn was thinking about a story he heard about Curtis Turner who bought a car from Lee Petty for $2000 and wrote him a check late on a Friday. He knew he didn't have enough money in the bank to cover it, *but* there were two races coming up over the weekend and if he could win both of them—which he was reasonably sure he could do—then he could deposit his winnings and that would cover the check.

The story was typical Turner. Nothing was ever simple. As it happened, someone taped the steering wheel in the car he bought from Petty. It was a common practice to give the driver a better grip. Unfortunately, whoever did it, wound the tape in the wrong direction. Turner managed to win the first race, but by then the tape had unraveled. It was in shreds and so were Turner's hands. No way he could drive the second race.

One of Turner's pit crew got a wild idea. He found Lee Petty, who was still at the track, and asked him if he would be willing to drive. Petty sized up the situation and agreed to help out. They re-taped the wheel, Petty drove, the car won and

Turner was credited with the win. He collected his winnings, deposited the money in the bank and Petty happily cashed the check on Monday.

Finn wasn't exactly sure how that story applied to this present situation, but that's what made stock car racing so much fun. Bad luck and good luck were all mixed up together. It was what every driver told himself at the start of every race. Anything can happen! What the hell, he might even win the race and collect the $10,500.

Finn might have seen a ray of hope, but everyone else went home carrying a little bit of Skye's problem with them. Gus picked up the sleeping baby, took Skye by the hand and they walked home in silence.

Skye threw herself down on the couch. Gus put the baby to bed and then headed to the kitchen. Skye was trying hard to shut out the world, so it took her a while to realize Gus was *working* in the kitchen. That was enough to jar her back to reality. "Gus, what are you doin'?"

"I'm makin' hot chocolate."

That was so totally out of character, Skye started to get up and investigate.

"Just stay where you are, I'll be right there," Gus said.

Skye didn't have the energy to argue. Minutes later, Gus came in carrying two large mugs and handed her one. "Be careful, it's hot."

She took a small sip and smiled. "What is this all about?"

"It's something Ma used to do. She kept a tin of this stuff hidden in the back of a cupboard and whenever something bad happened to one of us, she would make us a cup of hot chocolate. Nobody else got one, it was just for you and she explained that sometimes bad things happened. It might not be anybody's fault and you might not have done anything wrong. That's just the way the world was. But, it was important to remember that sometimes good things also happened for no reason at all. So I made you chocolate."

She reached out and touched his face. "I love you."

"I love you too." They made quiet, gentle love that night and fell asleep knowing that whatever came along, they'd face it together.

***

Next door Mattie and Duncan sat up drinking coffee and trying to figure out what to do. "I thought we were doin' so well," she said. "We got the boys home safe from the war, and Skye was happy workin' for Junky, and then the baby came. It wasn't like our lives when we first started out. Seems like back then there was always something to worry about. Sick kids and more kids and..."

"Yeah, the way I remember it, we just rolled along from one crisis to another worryin' about how we were gonna take care of everybody," Duncan said. "Feed 'em and send 'em off to school with clothes on their backs and shoes on their feet. But you know what, Mattie, in a way, we had it easier. When money got tight, we just set up another still. It was more work, but more shine meant more money and we always got by without havin' to borrow from anybody."

Mattie went to the pie safe, got out what was left of an apple pie and cut two generous pieces. Then she added some hot coffee to Duncan's cup and sat back down. She took a deep breath and looked at Duncan. "Speakin' of makin' shine, there's something I need to tell you. You remember when Gus asked if any of us knew a Granny Shine? Well, I do. I mean I am. What I mean to say is Emma and me are."

"Mattie, what are you talkin' about?"

Mattie started by telling Duncan how she used to leave shine for folks who needed it, but couldn't pay. And during the war years, she and Emma had used the kids' old still to supply their loyal customers who had always counted on their families to supply quality shine. While she was at it, she mentioned the tonic she took to the Soldiers' Hospital.

"It's not a big still and we only sell a little of it. We use most of it for good causes." That brought her around to their latest good cause, which was the TB sanitarium. Then she waited.

Duncan took a minute to digest that information. "So you never stopped! You have been makin' shine all this time? Mattie, how did you even know *how* to make shine?"

"For heaven's sake, Duncan McLagan! I've been workin' around stills since I was a kid. And who do you think tended the stills when you were doin' time down there in Atlanta? Or how many times did I have to tend one when you were takin' care of another one. And Emma's better at it than me. She does all the tastin'. Sean says…"

"Sean! You mean he knows about this?"

"Well, yeah. He helped us get started, but he doesn't know about the bourbon…"

"Bourbon? We never made bourbon. I know you didn't learn that from me."

"No, that was just an experiment. Emma read about usin' charred oak chips to add flavor while we aged the whiskey. I kinda charred the oak chips in a skillet so we weren't sure how good it might be, but Homer said…"

"Homer! Good God, Woman! Does he know about this too?"

"Well, yeah. He's the one who found the still."

"He found…Mattie, stop talkin'. Don't tell me any more about this. I already know way more than I want to know. Is Homer gonna arrest you?"

"Oh no, Homer's just fine as long as we keep on makin' bourbon."

Duncan got up, swallowed four aspirin and went straight to bed. If he lived to be a thousand, he would never figure Mattie out. But no matter. Monday morning he planned to buy her and Emma a proper oak barrel to make bourbon. It was the least he could do. The very idea of making bourbon with chips fried up in a skillet made his stomach turn.

Mattie finished the last of Duncan's pie, drank another cup of coffee, washed the dishes and went to bed too.

***

While Mattie was confessing to the "sin" she committed by making shine and keeping it a secret, Emma was listening to a different kind of confession. Like the preacher said, there are sins of co-mission and there are sins of o-mission.

"This is all my fault," Sean said. "It all comes back to what I didn't do. I coulda prevented this. I would have hated to do it, but I coulda worked a lot harder at makin' money all this time. Duncan tried to tell me about real estate, but I was afraid we'd get rich. Emma, why didn't you *tell* me leftovers were a good thing?"

"*Tell* you? Sean Calhoun, nobody's ever been able to tell you anything. I don't know where you got the notion that havin' extra money was bad. I just figured it was a streak of crazy that ran through your family and wasn't no use tryin' to fight it. Anyway, it's too late now. What we need is an old fashioned miracle."

***

The next morning Finn fired up his new Chevy, called Dog and they headed for the open road. Dog was fine as long as they weren't at the track. For Finn, being behind the wheel was the one place he could think clearly. He didn't like seeing Skye so upset, but trying to come up with a step-by-step solution to her problem made his head hurt. Instinctively he knew that what he needed was an idea. True to form, it didn't have to be a great idea, just something he could act on.

But because it was Skye, he decided he owed it to his twin to at least try to analyze the situation the best he could. He knew he was a good driver, but no matter how good he was, he knew he didn't really have much chance of winning the Darlington race. And there weren't enough other races coming up to help any.

The truth was, he couldn't think of anything else he was particularly good at. He was a likable fella and a pretty good storyteller, but there was no money in that. He didn't pay attention and remember book facts like Gus. He could take care of his car, but he was no master mechanic like Skye. He liked to have a good time, but that was mostly a way to spend money, not make it.

As Finn pondered on these things, he came up behind a Ford cruising along about 60 and passed him in a cloud of dust. That's when an idea hit him… well, tapped him on the shoulder at least. He had won the Chevy on a bet. When he played cards, he won. When he put money on a race, he won. When he acted on a dare, he won. He was never afraid to take a chance and he was good at gambling. So maybe…

Rather than worry his brain trying to *think* up a plan, Finn decided to just let his mind idle and trust his luck to come up with an idea. Maybe he *would* have a great idea, you never know. Anything could happen.

***

Down in Florida, the story was about to take a completely unexpected turn. Johnny "Madman" Mantz found himself in

Daytona, about the last place in the world he had planned to be. He had just run the six-day Mexican Road Race. Perhaps "run" was the wrong word. At the end, he could see the finish line, but he was out of tires and had to drive on rims at the end. He finished so far back in the pack he barely made enough money to pay for the trip from his home in California. He was an open-wheel, AAA-Indy racer and the only reason he entered the endurance race was for a chance to win the $6,000 purse.

But as fate would have it, he never made it back to California. During the week of the race, Mantz met Bill France and the rest of the Dawsonville boys. None of them managed to finish the race. They were all feeling right sorry for themselves and looking for some way to make up for their loses. That's when France mentioned the upcoming race at Darlington and the record $25,000 purse.

It didn't take much effort on France's part to convince Mantz to come home with him. France was always looking for a good promotional gimmick. As he saw it, having a well-known Indy racer associated with Darlington and the first 500-mile race in the South would be good for ticket sales.

And so it was that an open-wheel racer from Hollywood ended up in Daytona wondering why he was getting ready to drive in a *stock car race* at Darlington, wherever the hell that was.

CHAPTER THIRTY-FIVE

Nobody in Dawsonville had ever heard of Harold Brassington. In fact, not many people outside of Darlington, South Carolina knew his name. But that was about to change. In 1948 he witnessed the Indianapolis 500. It was the most wonderful thing he had ever seen. But it wasn't the cars or the drivers or the noise or the crowds that caught his imagination, it was the bricks: millions and millions of red bricks that lined the surface of the track.

At that moment, Harold Brassington had what could only be described as a biblical epiphany. He heard angels singing and a voice which said, "You will build the first paved track in the South. You will build it one and one quarter miles long. It will be the longest track in the South. You will cover it with black asphalt. You will call it Darlington International Raceway. No, change that. You will call her the Lady in Black." Harold Brassington accepted his divine mission. As he returned to South Carolina, he kept all these things and pondered them in his heart.

But he didn't ponder long. Within a year he had purchased 70 acres just off U.S. Highway 151 in Darlington from his neighbor Sherman Ramsey. The first hint that this project was going to be a test of faith came in the form of a plague of minnows.

Ramsey was delighted to sell the land, as long as the track didn't disturb his prized minnow pond. It was too late for

Brassington to start looking for another suitable piece of property, so he agreed and modified the traditional oval into a pear-shape. They sealed the deal with a handshake.

The next trial was a storm of engineers. They informed Brassington that since the turns were now different shapes, they would have to be banked differently and that meant more time and more money. Harold stayed true to his mission and agreed.

Although it hadn't been part of his original epiphany, Brassington was sure the first event had to be a 500-mile race, just like Indy. In order to pull that off, he needed the support of a sanctioning body. The Central States Racing Association signed on and named the race, "The Southern 500." It would be run on Labor Day and it would be strictly stock, American cars built after 1946 and bought off the dealers' floor, no modifications.

But Brassington's faith was still to be tested. Six months later, the CSRA had sold half the tickets, but only five drivers had entered. To put it mildly, Brassington was screwed. He prayed for a miracle and salvation appeared in the form of Bill France.

To tell the truth, France didn't think unmodified stock cars could stand up to the punishment of a 500-mile race. However, God works in mysterious ways. When France found out his arch-rival Sam Nunis was planning a 500-mile race for Labor Day at *Lakewood,* he changed his tune and agreed to sponsor the Darlington race. Ultimately the Lakewood race was canceled for lack of drivers. With the blessing of NASCAR, Brassington thought his worries were over. Think again, there were more tribulations to come.

At first Brassington didn't have enough entries, now he had too many. Eighty cars, to be exact. That would require two weeks of time trials and that meant the track had to be finished two weeks *before* Labor Day.

Like every building project since the pyramids, the Darlington Raceway was taking twice as long and costing twice as much as he had expected. But there was no turning back. Brassington had bragged to everyone that Darlington was going to be the first paved track in the South, so he'd just have to find the money somehow.

The one problem Brassington could not solve was time. His whole schedule had been based on opening the track on September 4, Labor Day Weekend. In a panic, he realized it was now the first of August and crews were still hard at work. To accommodate the time trials, the track had to be finished 14 days earlier than his original deadline.

Brassington vaguely remembered an Old Testament story about the Lord making time stand still. That was exactly the kind of miracle he needed. And sure enough, the Lord sent deliverance in the form of a human being looking pompous and wearing a suit and tie.

"Harold, my boy, how's it going? I know I joshed about this idea from the get-go, but damn if I don't think this race is gonna put Darlington on the map."

"That's what I'd hoped, Mr. Mayor, but I don't think we're gonna make it, not even workin' double shifts."

"The hell you say! Put on another shift, Boy. If you can't afford the extra expense, I'll send the county road crew over. We got the men and 24 hours a day. Let's use 'em!"

And so it was, that Brassington's faith had been rewarded. The track finally came together, the time trials proceeded and 75 cars were qualified. Labor Day dawned sunny and hot and the mayor and all the race officials came early in the morning to have a look at the track.

"Gentlemen, let me introduce you to The Lady in Black," Brassington said proudly. The track was midnight dark and shiny as a mirror. But as someone once said, "Pride goeth before a fall."

The mayor looked dubious. "It sure is pretty, but the damn thing looks slick to me." He knelt down and ran his hand over the surface. "I'm not sure I could walk on that, let alone drive on it."

Brassington was beginning to feel a real kinship with Job and his Biblical trials—but without the patience. One of the officials touched the warm surface and smiled, "Just needs some sand to give it traction." The truck rolled out and spread sand over the surface of the track. Once that was done, everyone stood back in admiration. The track was finished, the time trials were over, there was a sell-out crowd and they had four hours before the starting time of 11:00 a.m.

What could possibly go wrong?

CHAPTER THIRTY-SIX

With the exception of funerals, family reunions and tent revivals, the South had little or nothing in the way of public entertainment. That is, until dirt-track races came along. They usually ran at about church time on Sunday morning and they had enough power and glory to make those who felt guilty about skipping church feel comfortable. The first Southern 500 promised to be a gigantic family gathering and a historic come-to-Jesus meeting.

By Labor Day weekend, drivers, mechanics, promoters and fans arrived in droves. Unfortunately there was only one motel in Darlington so most folks ended up camping out in Army surplus tents.

Gus contacted Linc. "You gotta get up here. There's never been a race like this in the South before, you don't wanna miss this. Besides we could really use you on the pit crew."

As it turned out, Linc had a brother living near Darlington and Linc volunteered his services too. Gus gladly accepted the offer of another pair of hands. Everybody was scrambling to get their ducks in a row.

This was NASCAR's chance to get national attention and Bill France was trying to be everywhere at once. He made sure reporters were lined up to talk to Johnny Mantz and mentioned his Indy experience. Friday morning France went looking for Mantz and learned he had hitched a ride to nearby Myrtle Beach. He couldn't believe Mantz had left without permission.

Finn saw an opportunity to do a favor for Big Bill, so he volunteered to go get Mantz. He picked up Dog and they hit the road. Finding Mantz was easy. Finn started by checking bars along the beach. On his third try he found him, sitting in a booth nursing a huge hangover. Mantz looked at Finn through bloodshot eyes and all he saw was a crazy redhead trying to stuff him into a car.

The direct approach wasn't working, so Finn tried coffee. Two guys at the next table were in an arm-wrestling contest. So while Mantz sobered up a bit, Finn decided kill some time and take on the winner. Bad decision. The man not only beat Finn, he practically threw his shoulder out of joint. By that time, Mantz was on his feet and Finn coaxed him into the Atlantic to finish sobering him up. Then they headed back to Darlington. Dog gave up his usual place and fell asleep in the back seat.

Mantz was now wide awake and talkative. "You know what can win this race? A goddamn Plymouth, that's what. I've driven at Indy and I know how to drive on a paved track. This race is all going to come down to gas and rubber. You remember that. Gas and rubber." Then he passed out. When they rolled into Darlington, Mantz woke up. "Hey, Buddy, you know where I buy tires?"

"There's a Firestone dealer a couple of blocks over. You want me to drop you at your car?"

"Don't own one, but thanks."

Finn dropped Mantz off at France's office and Dog reclaimed his place in the front seat. For the next couple of hours, Finn drove aimlessly around town. He had a vague idea Mantz had said something important, but he couldn't quite put his finger on it. At one point he reached over to pet dog and a blinding pain ran up his right arm. At that moment, two things happened. Finn realized he could hardly move his arm, which meant he couldn't drive in the race. Gus was going to kill him.

And the second thing was he suddenly knew what Mantz had been babbling about. Finn nearly laughed out loud. It didn't matter that he couldn't drive, he could still save the day. Finally, he had a plan.

Finn's arm and shoulder were really beginning to hurt so he went to find Dixie, a young lady who worked in the local diner. He had met her earlier in the week and when she invited him to come home with her, he accepted. He was hoping to catch her on her lunch break and get a little ice and sympathy. But before he could do that, he had one very important stop to make.

***

Late that afternoon, just before the bank closed, Emma stopped in to make a withdrawal. It was Friday and she realized they were headed for a holiday weekend and no one would cash an out-of-state check. As nicely as possible, the young female teller explained there was no money left in the account.

"That's impossible," Emma said. She showed the teller her bankbook, "You see right here, there should be over $2,000."

"Yes, Ma'am. You *did* have that much, but now all you have is $7.65. Do you want to take that out in cash?"

"No! I do not! I want to know what happened to my money. Can I speak to your manager, please?"

The manager informed her that a Patrick Seamus Calhoun had emptied the account earlier in the day. He showed the proper identification. Everything was in order. Emma thanked him politely and left the bank, seething. She was ready to have Finn arrested or committed to the nearest lunatic asylum just as soon as she could get her hands on him.

When he showed up at the café, Dixie insisted Finn go to the local emergency room. They gave him a shot and put his arm in a sling. Finn didn't go home Friday night. He stayed with Dixie, which pleased Dog. He had liked her immediately because she let him sit in the booth with Finn. She even brought him some bacon and she didn't mind having him as a house guest.

Nobody saw Finn and Dog until they showed up Saturday night along with the rest of the Georgia gang, Red Vogt, Roy Hall, Red Byron, the Flocks and Raymond Parks, eating Carolina bar-b-que, drinking beer—or in Byron's case, Coca-Cola—smoking and talking. Curtis Turner and Lee Petty were also there along with most of the usual suspects.

The general consensus after the time trials was that the new track was a beast to be fought to the death. So rather than grouse about that, they argued about cars. Red Byron insisted his 1950 Caddy could take them all. This was met by raucous catcalls from everybody in the room.

"Caddy's way too heavy, Red. You're gonna run out of gas before you've gone ten laps." Lee Petty said.

"Not with this new one. It's lighter and it's got more power. Beat everything on the track."

"I'm tellin' you, it's just too big. My Plymouth can take that Caddy any day."

The Plymouth crowd backed Petty up. "There's no way a Plymouth can beat a Cadillac," Byron shouted over the noise. The beer flowed and the argument continued.

"Hey, Finn, ain't you gonna stick up for Ford? It's not like you to keep your mouth shut."

"Well, my brother-in-law's drivin' a Ford and my sister Skye is more than partial to them, but—he pointed to his wounded arm for all to see—since I can't drive tomorrow I didn't think I oughta get involved." He hesitated, "But if I did, I'd have to go with Lee. I think Plymouth's got this one."

More catcalls. "Now let me get this straight," Bob Flock chimed in. "Are you backing Lee, or are you dumb enough to back any Plymouth out there?"

"I don't know. I just got a feelin' that a Plymouth's gonna take this race."

That got the whole crowd involved. "A feelin'? Did you hear that boys? He's got a feelin'," Tim Flock laughed.

Someone in the back of the room spoke up. "Listen, I heard that guy from California, Morse... "

"Mantz, his name is Mantz. "

Tim was having a good time. "Well, I heard he's gonna drive that second-hand Plymouth France has been using to pick up stuff around town. You willin' to put money on *that* one?"

Finn smiled on the inside, but on the outside he managed to seem bewildered. He looked around as if he were waiting for someone to rescue him.

"Come on, Calhoun. It's time to put up or shut up."

Reluctantly Finn said, "Well, OK. Yeah, I'm gonna stick with my hunch. I still say that Plymouth can win."

"That second-hand gofer car?"

Finn nodded. More laughter and jeers. Finn stood his ground.

Red Byron was the first one to lay his money down. "I hate to take your cash, Finn, but this is just too easy. Here's $300 that says *no* Plymouth can beat a Cadillac. You wanna cover that?"

Finn awkwardly reached into his left pocket and came up with just enough to cover the bet.

Byron said, "All I want to know is who's gonna hold the money?"

Tim saw Homer Webster sitting at the bar. "How about Homer? He's a fed, but he's from Dawsonville and he's mostly honest. At least he's always played fair and square with us."

Homer agreed to get involved. Dog put his paws up on the bar to oversee the proceedings. Homer made a note of Byron's bet and saw Finn count out the bills to cover it.

Then Lee Petty stepped up. "I like Plymouths, but that car is not only second-hand, it's a 6-cylinder. It's got no chance. Can you cover another $200?"

Tim and Bob were still laughing as each brother laid down $100. Finn fished money out of several more pockets and managed to cover the current bets. After that, Homer couldn't take bets fast enough. The last man in line held out two tens.

"I'm down to my last sawbuck," Finn said.

"I'll take it," the man said and paid up.

Homer put the money in an envelope, sealed it and gave it to the bartender to put in his safe. The bar couldn't sell liquor after midnight, so the party broke up. Finn and Dog walked over to the café to meet Dixie. They were both smiling.

CHAPTER THIRTY-SEVEN

Emma spent the rest of Friday looking for Finn with no luck. Since she didn't want to discuss family problems in front of all the relatives, it was Saturday morning before she could get her immediate family together. She instructed Sean to sit tight and went to find Skye and Gus.

"Where's your brother?" she demanded.

"I don't know. With some girl I reckon."

"I wanna see you two in our bedroom and get Duncan and Mattie too," she said and stormed down the hall. When the family was all there, Emma closed the door. "Our money's gone," she announced, her Irish temper boiling. "Finn has cleaned out every red cent. Then he didn't come home last night and I wanna know what he's up to!"

"What do you mean the money's gone?" Gus asked.

"Gone. Wiped out. And the bank said Finn took it."

"If Finn took it, then he must be in some kind of trouble," Skye said.

"Oh, he's in trouble all right! You bet your boots on that." Emma had started out angry, worked her way through concern and now she was back to angry.

"Aunt Emma, you don't really think Finn stole the money, do you?" Gus asked. "He's done some crazy things, but he's no thief."

Gus didn't seem to be taking the whole thing seriously enough and that just made Emma madder. "I want all of you out there looking for him and when you find him, bring him to me!"

Following orders seems like the best thing to do at the moment, so they left to begin the search. Mattie said she would stay home to take care of Baby Mac, but actually she was keeping an eye on Emma. In the state she was in, there was no telling what she might do if Finn came sashaying in without warning.

Skye was worried about her brother. Gus was starting to worry about the money. Sean and Duncan were more confused than worried. Just to be on the safe side, they stopped by the local sheriff's office to inquire about car accidents. None had been reported, so that saved them a trip to the emergency room.

It was a little early to check the local bars, but Skye and Gus decided to make the rounds anyway. They talked to the cleaning crews or whoever was getting ready to open up. No luck. Next they went by the track and saw a small crowd just standing around. It was already getting hot and was due to reach 90 degrees for the second day in a row.

Finn was nowhere in sight. Someone said a bunch of the drivers had headed down to Myrtle Beach, so they drove over to take a look. No luck. It was as if Finn had completely disappeared. At the end of the day, they had no choice but to report back to Emma empty-handed. Duncan and Sean hadn't had any luck either.

The blue laws in Darlington meant nothing was open on Sunday morning but churches. There was not much chance of finding Finn there, but Sean and Duncan drove around and checked out the men talking and smoking outside.

Gus and Skye headed back to the track. As they were leaving, they ran into Red Byron. He and Gus shook hands,

Byron tipped his hat to Skye. "Have you seen Finn and Dog lately?" Gus asked.

Byron shook his head and chuckled. "Not since last night. That brother-in-law of yours is a card. He put on quite a show at the bar."

Skye and Gus exchanged worried looks. "What bar? What show?"

"First of all, he showed up with his shoulder bandaged and his arm in a sling. Then we got into a "discussion" about whether a Plymouth could beat a Cadillac. But the topper was when he bet everybody in the place that a Plymouth was going to win the race tomorrow. Really crazy part was he bet on that California guy who's driving France's go-fer car. You know, that second-hand Plymouth that's been sitting in front of his office."

Gus was confused. At first it sounded like Finn had been in an accident. But if he was clowning around at a bar, he couldn't be badly hurt. *But,* if what Byron had said were true and Finn had risked their money betting on some goddamn long shot that he knew he couldn't win, then Gus was going to be the one to hurt him. What the hell was he up to? "How much did he bet?" he demanded through clinched teeth.

Byron hesitated. Gus's usually easy manner was gone. His body was tense, his hands were balled into fists and he was breathing hard. "How much?" Gus demanded again.

"I couldn't say for sure, but he covered every bet until he ran out of money."

Gus whirled around, got back in his car and slammed the door. Skye managed to thank Byron and then she joined Gus. She was dumbfounded. Gus was livid. Skye had never seen him so angry. "He knows how much we need money right now. Why would he do something so goddamn stupid!?"

Skye knew better than to tell Gus to calm down. Instead she said, "Finn has come up with some harebrained schemes, but like you said, he's not a thief. He's reckless, but he's not stupid. He must have some reason…"

"Well, I hope it's worth dyin' for because I'm gonna kill him."

Unaware of the storm brewing or that he was being hunted by the whole family, Finn and Dixie slept late. A couple of aspirin and a slug of shine eased the pain, so they decided to head to Williamson Park for a picnic. If he had tried, Finn couldn't have found a better place to disappear.

The searchers met back at the end of the day. Sean and Duncan told Emma and Mattie they had heard rumors about Finn's monkeyshines at the bar the night before. Some said he bet Byron $5,000 he could beat him in the race. Others said it was $20,000. Still others said he bet all comers a Plymouth was going to win. The only thing they all agreed on was Finn made some kind of crazy bet about the outcome of the race.

When Gus and Skye came in, they confirmed the fact that Finn had taken the money and made a stupid bet he couldn't possibly hope to win. That shocked them into silence. There was nothing else to say.

CHAPTER THIRTY-EIGHT

As predicted, Labor Day started out bright and hot. Gus was so mad he couldn't think straight. He hadn't spoken two words since the night before. He and Skye headed out early to meet Junky, Linc and the rest of the pit crew. "Gus, I'm gonna drive Finn's car to the track. You never know he might show up yet. If Lloyd Seay could drive one-handed, then maybe Finn can too."

"Fine," Gus said and got in his car.

The rest of the family did their best to avoid one another. Mattie might have caught the gottados, but on the whole, she was not a worrier. In the beginning, she'd gone with everyone else to watch the races down by the river. Ready, set, go as fast as you could from start to finish and whoever got there first won. Just like when she was a kid. It was a little bit noisy, but it was fun and nobody got hurt. Then they started racing all bunched up on a track. Madness.

The first race she went to, there was a four-car pile-up. Since all the cars were black and looked pretty much alike, she couldn't keep track of where Gus or Finn were. The five minutes it took for the drivers to crawl out of the wreckage, were the longest minutes of her life. Since then she had looked for excuses to avoid the races whenever she could. When Baby Mac came along, she had the perfect reason to stay at home. She happily volunteered to stay with the baby.

Eventually Sean, Emma and Duncan left for the track. No one had the nerve to mention Finn's name. Emma stormed up the bleachers looking for their seats. Suddenly she stopped. There sat Finn with his left arm around Dog and his right arm in a sling. They were both smiling like a couple of Cheshire cats.

Before Emma could say a word, Finn bounded over to her and kissed her on the cheek. "Ma, I've solved all our problems. We're gonna go home with our pockets full of money." He stood back expecting to be showered with praise. Dog waited too.

Emma pulled away from him. "Patrick Seamus Calhoun, I'd like to slap that grin right off your face. How in the world could you do this to your family?" Dog crawled under his seat to get away from her angry voice.

Finn opened his mouth, but he was drowned out by the announcer who introduced Governor Strom Thurmond, the Grand Marshal, and his wife who cut the ribbon and opened the track. Thousands of fans cheered, 75 drivers revved their engines, the green flag dropped and the cars thundered down the straightaway and toward the first turn.

Emma wasn't about to let it go. Her voice cut through the racket. "Finn?!?"

"Remember that old story about the tortoise and the hare? Slow and steady wins the race? Well, that's all I'm gonna tell you or it'll spoil the surprise." With that, Finn sat down. Dog stayed out of the way. Finn settled in to watch the race with the unshakable faith of a true believer. Emma was speechless. Everyone else kept their distance.

Sean and Duncan turned their attention to the race. They knew that Finn had bet on a Plymouth, the trouble was there were nine of them in the race. Eventually Cotton Owens and his Plymouth took the lead. "That's gotta be it, number71,"

Duncan said and Sean agreed. They were happy for the next 23 laps.

No one was paying any attention to Johnny Mantz and the second-hand Plymouth, running about 75 miles an hour on the inside track. The other drivers flew past him, but he just kept going. Finn smiled.

Unbeknownst to the folks sweltering in the stands, the trials and tribulation of Darlington Raceway, which would have tested the patience of Job, were not over yet. It had started with the plague of minnows and it was about to deliver a scourge of a different kind.

Heat waves were rising from the asphalt that had been baking in the South Carolina sun. The application of sand to create traction had turned the surface into industrial strength sandpaper. Rubber tire treads wore through in a hurry and then the inner tubes started to explode. The first blow-out sounded like a gun shot. Pretty soon tires were popping everywhere. The noise was like the shooting range at the annual county fair.

When the tires blew, drivers lost control and pile-ups followed. Some drivers managed to pull their cars into pit row, and with all the comings and goings, it looked more like a free-for-all than a race. No one had come prepared for this disaster. When normal tire supplies ran out, pit bosses sent crewmembers into the infield to look for tires. Sometimes they bought them from anyone willing to sell, sometimes they just jacked the cars up and took the tires. With $10,500 on the line they weren't too particular.

Red Byron went through 24 tires. The situation was so critical, that even team owner Raymond Parks got involved. His white shirt and tie were easy to spot as he worked alongside the crew to help change Byron's tires in the pit. Gus used up the two extra sets of tires Junky had brought along.

Then he stripped the tires off Finn's car and finally took those of Link's car and his brother's as well.

With tire changes and the number of times drivers had to stop for gas, Sean and Duncan lost track of the Plymouths. They looked at Finn. He had a crooked smile on his face.

Sean knew that look. Clearly something was up. He followed Finn's line of sight, but all he could see was a little black Plymouth cruising along on the inside track. The other cars were passing him like he was standing still. But about every 20 miles the other cars pulled in for new tires. That Plymouth never stopped. Sean poked Duncan in the side. "Keep your eyes on number 98 and tell me what you see." Duncan watched for a lap or two. "Slowest car on the track. Got to be running in last place."

"No," Sean said slowly as he figured out what he was really looking at. "He's at least one whole lap *ahead* of everybody else. Maybe more. He might have made a pit stop for gas, but not more than once. And he's drivin' a Plymouth." They watched for a couple more laps and sure enough, Mantz and his Plymouth were saving tires and gas by running slow and steady on the inside track.

The two men looked at each other and the light began to dawn. If Finn bet on *that* Plymouth, then maybe…Sean couldn't resist. He leaned over to Emma, "Honey, I think you oughta watch number 98 and remember slow and steady wins the race." Emma just glared at him, but she did start to watch number 98.

On lap 50, the shocked announcer confirmed that Johnny "Madman" Mantz in number 98 was indeed in the lead. He also informed an astonished audience that Mantz was driving a six-cylinder, second-hand, go-for car. The audience shifted their focus to the little Plymouth and slowly started to count laps. Six, seven, eight, nine…

Mantz won the race nine laps—11 miles—ahead of the other racers. In the six-hour race he made only three pit stops for gas and he drove on only *one set* of Firestone truck tires. When the final announcement came over the public address system, Emma took Finn by the shoulders and spun him around so she could look him right in the eye. "You bet on *that* Plymouth?"

Finn nodded, "Every cent of it."

She threw her arms around him and started jumping up and down. "You did it, hot damn, you doubled our money."

Mantz collected $10,500 for first, Red Byron won $3,500 for second and Gus McLagan collected $2,000 for third place. Gus had just driven the best race in his life, probably because he had been too mad to think about what he was doing.

When Gus caught up with the family in the stands, he was covered in sweat and dirt and looked exhausted, but he was smiling, until he spotted Finn.

Skye saw the look in his eyes and grabbed him just in time. "Don't kill him, he bet on Mantz."

That stopped Gus dead in his tracks. "Mantz?"

"Mantz and the second-hand Plymouth."

Gus started to laugh. He threw his arms around Finn. "Oh my God, you bet on Mantz!" Then just as suddenly his face fell. "Oh my God, you bet on Mantz…"

"What's the problem?" Finn asked.

"We're not out of the woods yet. Byron is making a huge fuss. He's tellin' everyone there's no way a Plymouth could beat a Cadillac unless it's been modified. He and his mechanic Red Vogt are demandin' an official inspection. At first France refused, but I just heard he's gonna have Crisler do it."

All the color drained out of Finn's face.

"What's wrong?" Emma asked.

"Crisler is NASCAR's number one inspector. We told you about him, remember? He's the guy who stripped Glenn Dunnaway of his win in the Strictly Stock race over in Charlotte about this time last year. If they take away Mantz's win, I lose the bet. I lose all our money."

"But Gus won't lose his money, will he?" Duncan asked.

Sean was busy scribbling numbers on the back of an envelope. "OK, I'm tryin' to figure this out. If Mantz loses, we lose the $2,000 Finn bet. But if Mantz loses and Bryon gets pushed up to first place, that means Gus would get pushed up to second. If that happens then Gus will win $3,500 instead of $2,000. So do we pray for Mantz to win or not?"

CHAPTER THIRTY-NINE

Since Mantz was from California, he didn't realize what a hornet's nest he had stepped into. Bill France had made a special effort to have reporters on hand to interview Mantz and to cover the race in general. Now they were sniffing around for a bigger story. Al Crisler was the mechanic France depended on to rigidly enforce the rules. Crisler and Hubert Westmoreland had a history. Westmoreland was the owner of the car Glenn Dunnaway was driving when Crisler took away his victory at Charlotte the year before.

In this case, the second-hand Plymouth Mantz drove also belonged to Hubert Westmoreland and *Bill France*. That was why he had initially been against the post-race inspection, but then France realized that wouldn't look good, so he reluctantly changed his mind and the inspection was scheduled for later in the day.

Before they left the track, Gus and Finn made sure Linc and his brother got new tires to replace they ones destroyed by The Lady in Black. By the end of the day, the Firestone dealer sold out his entire stock.

After the race, Mantz's Plymouth was hauled to a nearby garage and the inspection began about eight o'clock that evening. Emma went home to Mattie and Baby Mac, but the rest of the family went to watch the proceedings. Sean, Duncan, Gus, Skye, Finn and Dog found a good vantage spot and sat down to watch. Gus spotted Red Byron in the crowd of onlookers. His mechanic, Red Vogt, was pacing up and down giving orders to anybody who would listen, "I want every nut, bolt, pin and piston looked at. I want to know how this second-hand, six-cylinder piece of crap beat…everybody!"

The Great Dismemberment had been fun and exciting, but this was different. There was no sense of wonder, just a grim determination to pull everything apart. They removed the motor and the transmission and broke each of those down to the smallest components. Parts started to pile up all around the Plymouth. Dog inspected each one. Although he was tempted, he resisted the urge to pee on any of them.

The inspection dragged on through the night and into the next day. The carcass of the Plymouth was being picked clean. By 8:00 a.m., the only thing that was left was a shell with parts scattered all over the floor. Twice they had gotten the local Plymouth dealer out of bed to come down and verify that some part or another was actually standard equipment. Sean and Duncan kept going out for coffee, trying to stay awake.

It had taken almost 12 hours and everyone was exhausted. Crisler shook his head, looked at the wreckage and finally announced his verdict. "It's stock."

Finn wanted to shout Hallelujah, but he realized a good many of the men standing around had bet against the Plymouth. It was only when it was all over that he realized what might have happened if he had lost. Not only would all their money be gone, but he wasn't sure the family would have ever forgiven him. That nearly brought him to his knees.

Red Byron had missed out on the biggest cash prize so far in the history of racing. But worse than that, his faith in General Motors had been seriously shaken. He walked away muttering, "No way a Plymouth can beat a Cadillac. No way."

Apparently there was no scandal, so there was no story and the reporters headed for home. Skye lingered looking carefully at what was left of the Plymouth. Suddenly she smiled. Finn was looking a little shaky, so she walked over and linked arms with him. As they left, she leaned over to him and whispered, "Tires?"

"Tires!" Finn smiled weakly and whispered back.

They finally let Gus in on the secret. By then, Finn was feeling better. "I knew it all along. Mantz said it was all about gas and rubber and he was right. But I gotta tell you I was scared to death they were gonna inspect the tires and figure out they were truck tires not standard issue. Turns out it wouldn't have made any difference because there's nothin' in the rule book about tires. I'll bet Big Bill changes *that* before the next race."

He looked around for Dog. "Well, we're off to pick up our winnings. The next time you see us we'll all be rich! Come on, Dog."

They ate breakfast at the café and later that morning met up with Homer. Together the three of them walked over to the bar to collect Finn's money, which he stuffed in a grocery bag. Then he bought drinks all around and got a bowl of beer for Dog. It was a bad habit he had picked up somewhere along the way. Finn suspected he'd been hanging out with the boys at the garage.

Finally the crowd settled down and Finn regaled them with his version of "The Second-Hand Plymouth That Beat the Brand New Cadillac." He left out the part about the tires.

***

Later that day, Finn said good-bye to Dixie and promised to see her again soon. Then the family packed up and headed home to Dawsonville. Finn was all for driving right over to the garage, giving Junky the money and telling him they were buying him out. Emma pointed out that they weren't in any position to *tell* Junky anything. They needed to do some smart horse trading where everyone got what they wanted and gave up as little as possible. They needed a plan.

The main problem was they weren't exactly sure how much the buyer had offered Junky. "Come on, Ma, we've got $6,000. Junky's like family. He'd probably *give* the business to Skye if she asked him real nice," Finn said.

"It's not Junky we have to worry about," Skye pointed out. "It's his wife, Leeann. If the guys are right and she thinks they're getting $10,000 for the garage, you can bet she's got plans for every cent of it."

The longer they talked about it, the more complicated the plan became. Finally Mattie spoke up. "Y'all are makin' this harder than it needs to be. Just go in there, lay your cards on the table and see what Junky has to say."

It was risky, but since they didn't have a better idea, they all agreed. Finn thought of himself as the chief investor. Gus would speak as the new team builder. Skye, of course, was their chief mechanic. Sean and Duncan represented both the racing team and the interest of the showroom and the used car lot. Dog considered himself the glue that held the whole thing together.

When they walked in, Dog was the first to realize all his friends were gone. There was nobody there but Junky. As soon as the delegation came through the door, Junky knew why they had come. He cut right to the chase. He confirmed that the buyer had offered $10,000 and even though he didn't have the money yet, Leeann had pretty much spent it all. "Skye, I'd sell you this whole place for a dime if I could, but my hands are tied."

No one moved. Maybe if nobody said anything, they could pretend they hadn't heard Junky's words. The price wasn't a million dollars, but it might as well have been. The tone of

Junky's voice left no doubt there was no reason to haggle over the price.

They left with as much dignity as possible. After two major wins at the track, everybody was sure their winnings would have given them plenty of room to negotiate. Nobody expected to get turned down flat.

When they got home, it was pretty obvious to Mattie and Emma that things had not gone well. If $6,000 wasn't the answer, then they had no idea what was. Nobody had even a bad alternate suggestion.

Emma looked at all their long faces. "If y'all aren't careful, you're gonna drown in a pool of mope. Come on, there's gotta be something we can do."

Mattie waited for someone to speak up, but no one did. Clearly they weren't seeing what was right in front of their faces. She didn't like getting in the middle of this kind of thing, but somebody had to do something.

"You know, maybe there *is* a way to make this work after all." That got everyone's attention. "The buyer has offered Junky $10,000 for the property and the building, right?" Everyone nodded. "Fine. Let him have the building and the land it sits on. We don't want that. What we need is what's *inside* the building. The machines, the tools and the inventory. Junky sure isn't gonna pack all that stuff up and move it to Florida. We'd be doin' him a favor to buy it."

Emma saw the possibilities in that idea right away. "Yeah, that's right. I bet he'd sell us all that stuff for less than $6,000."

"We could put everything in the big open space in back of the old furniture store. You know, the warehouse," Duncan said. "There's nothing back there now and we could still use the front of the store to show off the new cars. Since Junky owns that building, we could offer to rent the space and put the garage and the showroom all under one roof."

"Once we get set up, we could hire everybody back...or even hire them right now to help us move." Skye was getting excited about the idea.

Gus smiled. "I always told you you'd have your own garage one day. We could call it Skye Motors. Who knows, maybe someday you could actually start *building* race cars. Anything can happen."

They worked on the plan for the rest of the day, and presented it to Junky the following morning. Everything was going fine until Gus brought up the idea of renting the back of the storeroom.

"I don't wanna rent you space..." they couldn't believe their ears, "but I'll give you a 100-year lease for, let's say... a dollar a year. How does that sound?"

It sounded wonderful. The deal was set, everyone shook hands—paperwork would come later—plans were made to move the equipment, rehire the staff and set a date for the grand opening. They decided to start clearing out the storage room as soon as possible. Everyone was in high spirits.

Everyone, that is, except Dog. He considered the garage his second home and no one had told him anything about a move. Consequently on moving day he felt it was his duty to do whatever was necessary to protect his territory. "I don't like barking and snarling at folks, but if that's what it takes, that's what I have to do."

The movers called Finn to come over and have a talk with Dog. Finn sat down with him and explained that they were going to take everything inside the garage over to the new place. "We'll take the back-seat cushion Eli set up for you and find a good spot in the new garage."

Dog wasn't convinced until he and Finn went to check it out. When they arrived, Dog made a full inspection of the new location, sniffing out all the corners. He was still uncertain until he saw Eli and Lewis and they came over to pet him. "OK, we can stay," he said.

On opening day, drivers, owners, mechanics, new friends and old friends from Dawsonville and around the county came to celebrate. The crowd watched as the new sign "Skye Motors" was hoisted into place. Of course moonshine was part of the celebration. Dog made the rounds saying hello to everyone. Doc was there and as a final tribute, Mr. Gordon set off the siren at the Pool Room.

Red Byron and Red Vogt were still smarting from getting beat by a Plymouth, but they came to offer congratulations along with Raymond Parks and Lee Petty.

As the afternoon wore on, the conversation naturally turned to NASCAR. Byron announced that he planned to finish out the 1950 season, then he was going to part company with NASCAR in order to spend more time with his family— he and his wife were expecting a baby soon—and to get out from under France's control.

He and Gus shook hands. "I'm plannin' to do about the same thing myself," Gus said. "I'm gonna follow Mr. Parks' advice and concentrate on startin' a racing team, so this'll be my last year to race."

"Lee, what are you gonna do?" Byron asked. "France has stripped you of points more than once. You stayin' in?"

"Well, my boy Richard's 13 now and he's itchin' to start racing. I'm gonna hold him off as long as I can, but that's like tryin' to hold back the tide. Anyway, I reckon I'll stay in for a couple more years."

Skye picked up Baby Mac and walked over to join Gus, Finn and Dog. "I reckon we're stayin' in too," she said. It was all coming together just like they dreamed about when they were kids. She smiled and looked around, "As far as I'm concerned, I think this might be just...

THE BEGINNING!"

Acknowledgments

My most sincere thanks to Gordon Pirkle, the founder of the Georgia Racing Hall of Fame and the owner of the Dawsonville Pool Room. He was the first person I interviewed and he kept me on track throughout the whole process.

My second contact was the Dawsonville Moonshine Distillery and Cheryl Wood and Jeff Chastain. They both had information to share and stories to tell. The tour through their facility was my introduction to the world of moonshining.

Closer to home, I met the staff of ASW Distillery in Atlanta. Jim Chasteen and Charlie Thompson are licensed bootleggers! Justin Manglitz, the head distiller actually read a few early chapters. Chad Ralston rounds out their staff. They have provided help and encouragement to keep my spirits up.

Heather Forrest kindly gave me permission to use her poetic retelling of Child ballad number 220 (*The Dancing Lass of Anglesey*) published in *Wisdom Tales from Around the World,* August House 1996.

Owner Matt Booth and the staff at Videodrome helped me find video movies and documentaries on moonshining that do not exist anywhere else. Awesome!

My beta readers are the backbone of all my novels. Special thanks to Elva Acosta, Jan Allen, Kathy Barring, Judy Burge, Fontaine Draper, Julia Lee, Pat Lindholm, Cynthia Pearson, Babs Pennington, John Smith and Dawn Strickland.

Thanks to Frank McComb for his proofreading and his added knowledge about WWII based on his years as a history teacher.

I found a treasure living next door, Bao, who became the model for Dog, both in the story and on the cover. His family is Katheryn Grover and Wilson Oswald.

And although his name appears last, my husband, Jim Freeman is my first reader, my super fact-checker, my timeline monitor and my rock. He talked me off the ledge numerous times during the writing of this book.

About the Author

Grace Hawthorne is an award-winning author. She began her career working for a newspaper and has written everything from ad copy for septic tanks, to the libretto for an opera, corporate histories, and lyrics for Sesame Street.

She continued to hone her skills working as a professional storyteller, performing in clubs, at corporate functions, and at local and regional festivals. She has three storytelling CDs, *Waterproof Stories, More Waterproof Stories* and *The Gift, a tribute to 9/11.*

She is also an amateur photographer. She uses pictures to tell stories and words to paint pictures.

She was born in New Jersey, grew up in Louisiana, lived in Europe and New York City. Now she and her husband Jim live in Atlanta, Georgia.

Other books by Grace Hawthorne

SHORTER'S WAY

CHAPTER ONE

Willie Shorter's office smelled like shit. Manure to be polite, horse manure to be specific. The odor drifted up from the deserted Morganton Livery Stable downstairs but Willie hardly noticed any more. The afternoon heat however, was inescapable. The black oscillating fan simply moved the heavy air around the room and Willie found it hard to stay awake. He pushed himself out of his rump-sprung chair, headed out the door and down the back stairs in search of a breeze.

"Villie! Come, come!" Sol Goldman urgently summoned him.

Willie walked across the street to Gold's Mercantile where Sol stood beside a black man wearing faded overalls.

"This is Mr. Cunningham. He's a good customer, but he's got himself some big trouble." Sol looked at Cunningham and jerked his thumb toward Willie. "Tell him."

Experience had taught Nelse Cunningham to avoid dealing with white men whenever he could, but Mr. Goldman had always treated him with respect, so he couldn't very well refuse.

"Well Sir, Mr. Bull Rutledge, he hired me...."

"Harman Rutledge's son?"

"Yes Sir. You know him?"

"I know *of* him," Willie said.

Sol looked disgusted. "Bad man, he vould kick a dog just to hear him yowl. Go on, tell Villie what he done."

"Well Sir, he said he'd pay me $5 to clean out a couple'a acres back'a his house and I done it. Then he said I'd busted up part of his fence. Now he's not gonna pay me. 'Sides that, he's gonna take my mule to pay for the fence. How I'm gonna farm without that mule?"

"You are lawyer, Protector of Poor, Villie, so you help him, yeah?"

"Sure, I'll help."

Nelse shook his head. "I 'ppreciate your help Mr. Goldman, but I ain't got no money to buy a lawyer."

Willie smiled. "Don't worry about that, I'll think of something."

From the time he first opened his law office, Willie's main thought was his political future. In gold letters he introduced himself to the world, "Willie Shorter, Attorney at Law. Protector of the Poor."

How could he possibly say no? Willie had known men like Bull Rutledge and Nelse Cunningham all his life. And God knows he knew about being poor. He'd been born out of wedlock and by the time he was three, his 18-year-old mother, gave him to a widowed neighbor, climbed aboard a Greyhound bus and disappeared.

Aubrey Shorter was left with a skinny, silent child. Aubrey had a knack for saving lost, injured animals and Willie certainly looked the part. He carried the boy into the kitchen and pulled a chair up to the big wooden table. He padded the seat with a couple of Sears Roebuck catalogues and sat Willie on top. The boy watched as Aubrey mashed up some cornbread in pot likker and offered it to him. "Go ahead try it, Boy," Aubrey said gently. "You'll like it."

That was the beginning. Aubrey not only gave Willie his first taste of real food, he also gave him comfort, a home and a last name.

WATERPROOF JUSTICE

CHAPTER ONE
(Waterproof, Louisiana 1946)

The pale winter sun came through the glass in the top of the front door and wrote "Waterproof Sheriff's Office" in shadows on the floor. Nate Houston braced his hands on the arms of his chair and carefully shifted his position. Then slowly he opened his desk drawer and looked down at the bottle inside. He hesitated several minutes pretending he had a choice. Finally he took the heavy, brown bottle out and set it on the edge of his desk.

So this is what I've come to, not my proudest moment.

The pain persisted, working its way up from a dull ache to a knife edge. Not to worry, he knew how to take care of that, at least for a while. He hated to admit that he needed the doses more often now than when he first began using, but he still had the situation under control. He opened the bottle and poured out a generous amount. The fumes burned his nose, but that was a small price to pay for the soothing warmth to come.

Horse liniment.

The only thing that tamed the pain in his knee. A little souvenir from Germany. A fragment so tiny the doctors missed it, but big enough to get his attention on a daily basis. He massaged the liniment into his knee and relaxed as the heat began to drive out the pain. Nate put the top back on the liniment and stashed it in his desk.

When he first got home, he thought taking the job as sheriff was a good idea. But he soon found out that having seen war and death up close, it was hard to take a Saturday night bar fight seriously. It was harder yet to deal with what "normal" folks considered threats of life and death. As if on cue, the phone rang.

"Sheriff, come quick! Bud Garvey's got Luther up a tree and he's threatening to kill him." Nate recognized Lucy Castle's voice although it was pitched several octaves higher than usual.

"Does Bud have a gun?"

"No Sir, but he's got a baseball bat. I'm tellin' you it's a matter of life and death, Sheriff. You've gotta get over here right now."

Nate shook his head. He didn't see how Bud Garvey on the ground with a baseball bat posed any immediate danger to Luther up a tree. Oh well, welcome to law enforcement in Waterproof.

He grabbed his cane and headed for the door. The patrol car was a pre-war Chevy that smelled of cigarette smoke, Burma Shave, and Old Spice. It was a little past its prime but well suited for patrols through the rolling hills of West Feliciana Parish. A stranger—if ever there was one hanging around—would have had no reason to suspect he was looking at law enforcement. There were no markings on the car, not because of stealth, but because Nate had never found anybody to paint it.

Similarly, he refused to wear a uniform ever again. Instead, he wore a khaki shirt and pants, and an ancient Panama hat with a sweat-stained hatband. His one concession was the small sheriff's badge pinned to his left shirt pocket, which was totally unnecessary because everyone knew him.

He'd lived in Waterproof most of his life. His father had worked a small farm on the edge of town and his mother had worked at Parchment Products, which canned Grade A Louisiana yams—not to be confused with ordinary sweet potatoes. The culls of the yams were ground up, roasted, and mixed with cottonseed meal to make animal feed. Waterproof always smelled like a sweet potato pie that had overflowed and burned on the bottom of the oven.

CROSSING THE MOSS LINE

CHAPTER ONE

"We'll take the whole lot, the whole shipload."

The broker studied the two young men standing in front of him and shook his head. "Foolishness, total foolishness," he thought to himself. "The whole boatload?" But then, who was he to turn down money...and a lot of it too. Cash on the barrelhead, up front. That's the way he liked doing business.

The 300-ton Windward rode at anchor in the small harbor at Bunce Island. The trading site was in the Sierra Leone River about 20 miles upriver from Freetown. It was a small island in the country's largest natural harbor, which made it an ideal base for the large ocean-going ships of European traders.

Due to the conditions aboard and the length of the voyage, he knew the buyers would lose at least ten percent of the cargo in the crossing and that was probably on the low side. However, once the papers were signed and he had his money, he'd be on his way. Not his responsibility any more.

Caleb Harding and Patrick Donegan exchanged worried glances and tried to maintain an air of confidence. They knew they were on shaky ground; they just hoped it wasn't too obvious. Normally they would have dealt with a business agent in Savannah, but to save some money, they decided to handle the transaction themselves.

They pooled every cent they had, negotiated what they thought was a good price at $500 a head, and set very specific guidelines about exactly what they wanted. They also promised the captain a bonus if he delivered the cargo in good condition. If everything turned out as they hoped, they were on their way to owning the richest rice plantation in Georgia. If not... well, one way or the other, it was too late to turn back now. They followed the agent into his office to conclude their business.

The crew aboard the Windward paid no attention to them. They had enough to do with loading supplies and getting the ship ready for the long voyage ahead. In addition to spare sails, ropes, nails, pitch, tar, coal and oil, they loaded food supplies including ship's biscuits.

Jonesy, the new cabin boy, was as curious as he was green. "Here you go, try one of these," a craggy old sailor said and tossed him what looked like a cookie. Jonesy tried to take a bite and nearly broke all his teeth.

"Ahh come on, what's this?" he asked.

"Hardtack, me boy. Sealed up tight, it'll last for months at sea and there'll come a time you'll be glad to get it. Best soak it in your tea to soften it up a bit before you try to eat it, but don't forget to bang it on the table a couple of times first."

"Why would I do that?"

"To knock out the beetles and the weevils and any other nasty little beasties who've made a home for themselves in your biscuit." Jonesy looked a little sick and the crew laughed.

The seamen continued to load on the salt pork, dried fish and various grains. Finally Jonesy stopped and looked toward the hold. "How do you stand the noise?"

"Just ignore it. It'll quiet down. The first week or two's the worst. After that, things get quiet, sometimes too quiet."

Jonesy tried, but he didn't think he would ever be able to ignore the cries and wails coming from the hold. They made the hair on the back of his neck stand up. No language that he could understand, just mournful, eerie sounds.

"That's the way it started way back there in 1802," Granny Johnson said.

CPSIA information can be obtained
at www.ICGtesting.com
Printed in the USA
FSHW02n2035170618
49216FS